Knots

Myles McDonough

Copyright © 2023 by Myles McDonough

All rights reserved.

No part of this publication may be reproduced, distributed, or transmitted in any form or by any means, including photocopying, recording, or other electronic or mechanical methods, without the prior written permission of the publisher, except as permitted by U.S. copyright law. For permission requests, contact myles@mylesmcdonough.com.

The story, all names, characters, and incidents portrayed in this production are fictitious. No identification with actual persons (living or deceased), places, buildings, and products is intended or should be inferred.

Book Cover by Rafal Kucharczuk

First edition 2023

Contents

Get the Prequel to Knots	VII
Epigraph	VIII
Amendment XXIX	IX
1. Sean / Boston, MA / 2030	1
2. Jack / Boston, MA / 2030	5
3. "An Answer to the Problem" / Posted to r/SexualEconomy by cnghm89 / 2020	8
4. Sean / Boston, MA / 2030	12
5. Sean / Boston, MA / 2030	16
6. WIRED / "Top 5 Most Downloaded Apps of 2024"	20
7. Carl / Harwich, MA / 2003	21
8. Sean / Boston, MA / 2030	24
9. TIME Magazine / "The Lion and the Lamb: How the JI Movement Sparked an Unlikely Friendship" / 2023	26
10. Letter from Marie Rosenthal to Ellen Willis / February 10, 1997	29
11. Sean / Boston, MA / 2030	31
12. Sean / Boston, MA / 2030	36

13.	Al / Bracketville, TX / 2000	39
14.	Sean / Boston, MA / 2030	44
15.	The Wall Street Journal / "'Why Would I Need Lipstick?': The Economic Impact of the 29th Amendment" / 2026	57
16.	Pepper / United States Air Force Academy / 2025	59
17.	Sean / Boston, MA / 2019	64
18.	Marie / Boston, MA–Chicago, IL / 2024	66
19.	Carl / Boston, MA / 2024	70
20.	Verity / Atlanta, GA / 2020	75
21.	Jack / Boston, MA / 2012	78
22.	Pepper / Edwards Air Force Base, Kern County, CA–Cambridge, MA / 2027	83
23.	Law and Order: IAU / "Taking Out the Trash"	89
24.	Carl / Boston, MA / 2026	92
25.	Marie / Fort Dodge, IA / 2026	96
26.	Sean / Boston, MA / 2030	100
27.	"An Answer to the Problem" / Posted to r/SexualEconomy by cnghm89 / 2020	102
28.	Verity / Boston, MA / 2020	106
29.	Carl / Boston, MA / 2030	112
30.	Marie / Washington, D.C. / 2005	116
31.	Carl / Boston, MA / 2005	120
32.	Sean / Boston, MA / 2024	125
33.	Pepper / Cambridge, MA / 2028	128

34.	Lolita, Anita, & 'Ritas / "Ep. 267: Amendment A-schmendment: Casa Loca Habanero Tequila with Margaritaville Margarita Mix"	131
35.	Letter from Marie Rosenthal to Ellen Willis / July 24, 2005	133
36.	Al / Boston, MA / 2030	135
37.	Carl / Wellesley, MA / 2027	138
38.	Sean / Boston, MA / 2030	141
39.	Marie / Washington, D.C. / 2007	145
40.	Sean / Boston, MA / 2008	148
41.	Sean / Boston, MA / 2030	155
42.	Carl / Boston, MA / 2030	162
43.	Al / Boston, MA / 2006	166
44.	Jack / Boston, MA / 2023	174
45.	Pepper / Cambridge, MA–Boston, MA / 2028	177
46.	Jack / Boston, MA / 2030	182
47.	Marie / Washington, D.C. / 2010	186
48.	Sean / Boston, MA / 2030	188
49.	Marie / Boston, MA–Chicago, IL / 2011	193
50.	Verity / Boston, MA / 2023	204
51.	Jack / Boston, MA / 2030	206
52.	Carl / Boston, MA / 2030	210
53.	Verity / Boston, MA / 2024	217
54.	Sean / Boston, MA / 2030	219
55.	Verity / Boston, MA / 2030	223

56.	Letter from Marie Rosenthal to Ellen Willis / Boston, MA / 2030	224
57.	Pepper / Boston, MA / 2030	228
58.	Sean / Boston, MA / 2030	231
59.	"An Answer to the Problem" / Posted to r/SexualEconomy by cnghm89 / 2020	234
60.	Sean / Boston, MA / 2030	240
61.	Al / Boston, MA / 2030	242
62.	Sean / Boston, MA / 2030	243
63.	Verity / Boston, MA / 2030	251
64.	Al / Boston, MA / 2030	253
One Year Later		257
65.	Verity / Québec, QC / 2031	259
66.	Rosa / Nashville, TN / 2031	263
Get the Prequel to Knots		265

Get Your Free Prequel Today

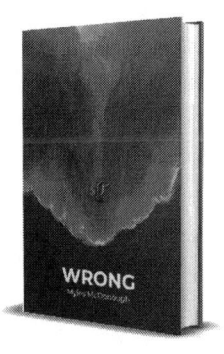

Mark Cunningham can't stop obsessing over Sam Healey. The pretty undergraduate lights up his classes with her intelligent questions. She reminds him why he became a philosopher in the first place.

The more Mark talks to Sam, the more alive he feels—and the closer he moves to a decision that could destroy his career. With the semester drawing to a close, Mark must make an impossible choice.

But acting out of love couldn't be wrong...right?

Setting up the dystopian world of *Knots*, this gripping prequel short story introduces the man whose work inspired the 29th Amendment to the Constitution—which guarantees every U.S. citizen one monogamous romantic and sexual partner.

Download your copy of "Wrong" today to find out how Mark Cunningham came to empathize with incels everywhere—and how this lonely philosopher felt about his own work in the end....

Get your free copy at
BookFunnel.MylesMcDonough.com

An entire sub-race race was born, different—despite certain kinship ties—from the libertines of the past. From the end of the eighteenth century to our own, they circulated through the pores of society; they were always hounded, but not always by laws; were often locked up, but not always in prisons; were sick perhaps, but scandalous, dangerous victims, prey to a strange evil that also bore the name of vice and sometimes crime.

Michel Foucault, *The History of Sexuality, Vol. 1*

Amendment XXIX

Passed by Congress September 12, 2023. Ratified February 8, 2024.

Section 1. Those lifestyles and practices which tend to inhibit the fair and equal distribution of erotic capital, or to impede the efficient release of sexual tension, including but not limited to non-monogamy, "kink," fetishism, and asexuality, are hereby prohibited in the United States and all territory subject to the jurisdiction thereof.

Section 2. Pursuant to Section 1, all citizens of the United States of at least 18 years of age shall be matched with a single sexual and romantic partner of reasonable compatibility for the purposes of health, mutual satisfaction, and public safety.

Section 3. The Congress and the several States shall have concurrent power to enforce this article by appropriate legislation.

Sean / Boston, MA / 2030

The young woman, whose name we don't know yet, has her arms pinned behind her back. They are held in place with a length of rope that winds in a tight, complicated pattern around her body. A switch-backing ladder of rope binds her legs together from waist to ankle; still more rope connects her ankles, torso, and hair to an iron ring, which is attached to a sturdy wooden beam eight feet off the ground.

She hangs in the air, back arched, and smiles.

Verity Smith, 31, wipes her forehead—she's done a lot of lifting—and gestures to some finer point of ropework. The man standing next to her takes notes.

Grinning, Smith digs her fingers under the woman's ribs—Black skin brushing White. The woman shrieks and tries to wriggle away, her body spinning in space. The man catches her and gives her a kiss, which she leans into as much as she can. Then he kisses Smith; and Smith the woman; and so on, back and forth between the three of them.

"Daghmn," says detective Carl Nguyen, around a mouthful of chicken parm sub. From the passenger side, he has to crane his neck to see out our windshield and into the second-story apartment. He frowns, swallows.

It's textbook intimacy misallocation. Not to mention consensual restraint and battery, incitement to indulge perversion, etc. I aim my camera, focus, and start taking photos. Smith and the man bring the woman down from her suspension. Slowly, they undo the ropes that hold her together. The camera picks up the red marks on her arms, chest, and thighs. The lights in the apartment go out.

Carl fumbles his sandwich, swears, and tries to clean a glob of marinara sauce off his tie.

Carl insists on stopping at the Walgreens on our way back to the station. His anniversary is on Friday. He and Levi have been together four years now. Not too surprising—they're optimal partners. They matched 96%.

"Oh yeah," he says, grabbing a card off the rack. "This is the one."

He hands it to me while he hunts for an envelope.

On the front is an illustration of a group of nuns. In the foreground, one of the women fumes, crossing her arms and tapping her foot. She is staring at a second nun, who sits on the church steps smoking a cigarette, her back turned to the first. The smoker wears heavy mascara, black lipstick, and black nail polish. Her tunic has been cut into an approximation of a crop top, revealing a fishnet undershirt. On her wimple is stitched the anarchy capital 'A,' enclosed with a circle. The caption reads: *Mother Superior had often lectured Sister Mary about her sinful habit.*

I know Levi. The card is perfect for him. In the car, Carl reads the caption again, and chuckles.

"*Sinful habit*," he says. "I tell ya."

A couple crosses Columbus Ave in front of us. Arms wrapped around each other's waists, they move slowly, in that bouncing gait that pairs have. They smile—talking, not watching where they go. His foot catches on the curb; with effort, she grabs him, and pulls him up. They laugh, and kiss.

The light turns green.

There's an ad in the bus shelter near Club Café. A man and woman stare into each other's eyes. The woman is frumpy. Her sweater is a bit dull, and not especially cute. Her sneakers are dirty—nothing terrible, but normal wear and tear for a pair of white shoes. Not brand-new. Her hair is a little thinner than it could be. He is mostly joints and fingernails. But their bodies aren't the point.

It's the look they're giving each other—the wide eyes, the way their mouths hang open just a bit—that grabs your attention. It's the surprise. The inability to believe their good luck. The photo captures the first three seconds of the rest of their happy lives together, and reminds you how much you crave what they have. It's an ad for a feeling.

Find the One, reads the tagline. The PRTNR logo floats in the space between the pair, suggesting potential.

There's a space on the curb tonight, and I take it. Carl grabs the camera bag and the rest of his sandwich from the floor, and we walk the half block back to headquarters.

A lanky, redheaded man stands by the station door in a tailored suit. Trying to text and walk at the same time, Carl bumps into him, nearly dropping the bag of Little Steve's leftovers.

"Sorry, bud," he says.

"You're fine," says the man.

He pushes his hair off his thin face—a big pile of long, red curls. His cheekbones are covered in freckles. His eyes are green.

The door swings shut behind me.

A printed copy of Cunningham's "An Answer to the Problem"—the unofficial bible of the Intimacy Allocation Unit—sits on my desk, close to the edge. The outer edge is scaly with multicolored post-it flags, and the margins are full of my notes. I imprinted a coffee ring on the cover, once, for realism. It's good for my reputation to have the book in plain sight.

I drop into the work. I move pictures from card to hard drive; sort, label, arrange; save and track copies of copies of copies. I file the relevant evidence in the folder "Smith, et al." For old times' sake, I click open the folder labelled "Debs."

A copy of Simon Debs' lease. Photographs from the apartment: an iron tripod with a ring below the apex; a garment rack draped in rope; a dress on the floor. We told the media that the dress was Simon's. The *Herald* had a field day with that—they all did. Even the *Globe*.

We didn't tell anyone the dress was too small for him, that we suspected a partner lucky enough to be away from the apartment during the raid. We hadn't ironed out the process yet, back then. We didn't mention that the dress smelled faintly of body oil. Citrus. Bergamot, and orange.

Carl stops by my desk on his way out the door. He puts up his hands, and throws a fake punch at my head. I slip it, and tap a loose fist into his gut.

"Still down for Thursday?" he says.

"You know it," I say.

An hour after he's gone, I shut down my computer and head out myself. The redheaded man is still standing outside. We make eye contact as I walk past him on the way to my car.

"'Night, detective," he says.

Jack / Boston, MA / 2030

The procurement team from the toothpaste company is butthurt about the proposed cost of custom photography, and the CMO of the men's-shaving-subscription-box startup doesn't think the latest round of creative is "burly" enough. Meanwhile, the copywriter on the soup account is having his bi-annual attack of artistic conscience, this time fixated on the phrase "tomatoey goodness," which he is refusing to incorporate into the new labels despite the client's clear direction.

I attend to them all with my most sympathetic face. I nod and frown at their complaints until they puke out the underlying traumas all over my desk, where I clean them up so business can proceed.

The toothpaste guys are afraid of budget cuts this quarter; I get a grumbly creative director to agree to stock photography, just for this campaign. The CMO's match is leaving him for a woman who runs a makeup-subscription-box service; he realizes that leaning on the design is an unproductive manifestation of his desire to lash out at anything feminine in his life at the moment, and volunteers to back off. The copywriter can't get a single agent to look at his novel; I tell him I'd love to read it, and he makes the changes. The client approves the new labels by three.

And while all of this is going on, as I solve one problem after the next, I think about the man in the police station, who has hidden himself away in a pack of wolves.

It is crazy to stand here, on their turf. I should not be on this stretch of sidewalk, by these doors, pretending I have some reason to be hanging around.

But I have to know.

No one bothers a man in a good suit. I poke at my phone while officers and attorneys walk in and out of the building, all assuming that I have some reason to be there because my clothes fit well. Human spillover from Methadone Mile helps the disguise. Toothless, sunburned men and women shuffle by with the rubber soles of their untied shoes distorted at horrible angles by foot-dragging, making me look like a Renaissance prince in my loafers. I hand out bills till I can honestly say *I'm out of cash*.

He arrives with his partner just after ten. The picture Marie showed us was an ID photo—dead-ahead, blank stare, deliberately framed to put as much emphasis on physical features as possible, and bleed out any underlying sense of character.

That lack of personality carries over into real life.

He's of average height, with a pig's haircut, cropped close to a skull made up of intersecting planes. He smiles at something his partner says, and it's as if he's inside his own head, directing the operation: first the crinkle at the corner of the brown eyes; then the slight lift of the sides of the mouth; lastly, a part in the lips, revealing a row of teeth with a hint of sharpness. He notices me for the first time when his partner, weighted down with a bag of takeout, bumps against me on his way to the door. He rotates his head just enough to look at me and takes in everything, from my hair down to my shoes. I have no idea what he sees. The two of them go inside.

I should leave. Instead, I hang around on a bench till the city quiets down as much as it's going to. A shirtless man with dirty dreadlocks hanging down to his waist limps past me, pushing a rattling grocery cart full of empty soda cans.

Hours later, the cop walks back out again.

Because I'm feeling bold, and stupid, I tell him goodnight. He turns away, and heads toward the parking lot, giving no sign that he heard me.

"An Answer to the Problem" / Posted to r/SexualEconomy by cnghm89 / 2020

On the afternoon of May 23, 2014, a young man in Isla Vista, California killed his three roommates with a knife. A few hours later, he visited a Starbucks and got a cup of coffee. Then he went on a shooting spree, killing three more people and wounding fourteen others before committing suicide in the front seat of his car.

Seventeen months later, at Umpqua Community College near Roseburg, Oregon, another young man shot and killed eight people, and wounded eight more, before shooting himself in the head.

Thirteen months after that, it happened again at a high school in Aztec, New Mexico.

2018 was a banner year, with a mass vehicular homicide in Toronto bookended by shootings in Parkland and Tallahassee. And so on.

Each of these killers has been linked to the still-growing "incel" movement—a mostly online community of "involuntary celibates" who come together to express feelings of pain and rage around their inability to secure sexual partners. Some of them wrote manifestos about it. The discourse around these mass killings has had little to say about these documents, other than to condemn them as the delusional writings of mentally ill persons, or else as nothing more than evidence of wider systemic problems springing from our culture's toxic expression of masculinity.

Fair enough. But our collective revulsion—or at least the performance of distaste, put on to cover up morbid curiosity—has cut us off from the texts which might contain the information we need to stop the violence. In brief: These men, these boys, say that a lack of sexual contact drove them to murder. What would happen if we took them at their word?

What makes sex worth killing for?

What role does sex have to play in ending the horror?

What I'm going to suggest in these pages is unpublishable ... but I guess that doesn't matter now.

In the manifesto he emailed out minutes before his shooting rampage, the Isla Vista killer explains his motivations, *as he sees them*: "All I ever wanted was to fit in and live a happy life amongst humanity, but I was cast out and rejected, forced to endure an existence of loneliness and insignificance, all because the females of the human species were incapable of seeing the value in me."

Much has already been said about the last part of this declaration: the blame the killer places at women's feet. I can add nothing to the discussion around this point; better writers than I have already pointed out the flawed logic. What this essay will explore is the feeling underlying the story that the incel tells himself; the root cause of the violence, extracted from a narrative that pits sexual haves against have-nots; the set of conditions under which faulty thinking can ripen into terror.

Let us put aside, for the moment, the question of whether or not the killer's interpretation of his situation was accurate. We'll come back to that later. For now, let's bypass the killer's explanation for his suffering—and focus instead on how he describes it.

In his own words, the young man feels "cast out and rejected." He is "lonel[y.]" He does not "fit in" because a force beyond his control has, somehow, segregated him from broader "humanity." There is a unit; the vast majority of people are a part of it; he is separated. We might say *cut off*.

It will help to clarify what the feeling is *not*: The killer-to-be, typing in his room, in the dark, does not feel smothered by his fellow humans. He is not crowded, not overwhelmed by other voices. There is only the one voice—his own—echoed, maybe, in online forums, but still his, cast out into the void and returned, unaltered, unchallenged, the same. Other people are not experienced as abrasive. In fact, they are barely experienced at all. They recede from his touch.

The boy felt not just by himself, but deliberately kept to one side of the whole. What, exactly, is the whole that he felt cut off from?

The Body Politic

The killer views his feeling of estrangement as unique. He does not project his experience of atomization onto the rest of us, imagining that we, too, might feel isolated and alone. On the contrary, he assumes he is the only one so affected—or, at most, a member of a small, oppressed minority. He feels he has been disconnected from a larger, cohesive *something*, composed of all the "happy" people intertwined with one another in a web of intimacy that starts with heterosexual intercourse and radiates outward to encompass membership in family—nation—species. What we might well call a *body*.

John of Salisbury, in his political manual *Policraticus*, argued that a commonwealth can be likened to a "body which is animated," in that it is composed of distinct parts in mutually beneficial relationship—from him and other medieval thinkers we get the term *body politic*. This framework allowed John to discuss statecraft in terms of the "health" of the state: The good health of the commonwealth depends on each of the parts working together toward a greater whole; the health of the state is reflected in the happiness of its subjects.

The parts of the body politic cannot function independently of the whole, just as an arm cannot live cut off from the torso. And the whole suffers greatly for the loss or malfunction of any of its parts. Thus, if individuals—such as the sovereign, or segments of society such as the military, banks, artisans, etc.—act purely in their own narrow self-interest—or are otherwise separated from the aims and workings of the broader community—the whole suffers in proportion. More bluntly, the removal of one segment of the community from the rest is not merely painful. It is *unhealthy*. Dangerous. Potentially lethal.

A cursory look at recent neurological findings seems to bear out some version of this theory. We now know, for instance, that human beings possess so-called "mirror neurons," cells that light up in response to the physical and emotional state of another and create a reflection of that state in our own subjective experience: Our gray matter echoes with the pain and pleasure of the humans around us. Moreover, it seems that recovery from trauma is not only improved by community involvement, but may ultimately *require* it: Our repair mechanisms don't work in isolation.

John's essential insight—that the entities we normally think of as *individual* humans can come together to form a larger conceptual body—is not limited to the realm of politics. From John's own Catholic tradition, we have the mass of the faithful that forms the *body of Christ*; individual Marines together make up the *Corps*; and so on.

The body religious; the body militant. Moving outward, we can imagine such a body coalescing around any of the phenomena that make up the shared experience of human beings. The body sexual, for instance [...]

Sean / Boston, MA / 2030

The man faces us, hands in the pockets of his brown, baggy pants. The toe of a wingtip peeks out from beneath each rumpled cuff. His full name is Special Agent Alan Bergman.

"But you can call me Al," he says with a Texan drawl. "Like the song."

His suit is brown. Noticeably brown. He looks like somebody's uncle. Bit of a paunch under his shirt, and the beginnings of major crow's feet at the corners of his eyes. In fact, he never stops smiling completely. Even when the lights go down, and most of the eyes in the room are on his PowerPoint presentation, a very slight curve pulls his lips up, like nothing in the world could bother him so badly that it would be reason enough to frown. The faint white line of a scar passes from the corner of an eye socket into his hair.

He rests his butt on the corner of the front table, by Schmidt and Baptiste.

"On April 29th at 1:34 a.m.," he says, "Marie Rosenthal arrived in Boston."

He clicks the stubby remote: a high-angle shot of a sedan on the Pike. Another click: the driver's face zooms to fill the screen. It's a woman in her sixties.

"It is now almost June," says Al, "and she hasn't been seen since.

"Rosenthal is one of the last holdouts. For years she's been one of a handful of people facilitating communication between target communities in cities across the country. Carrying messages that couldn't be trusted to email, helping known hoarders get across to Canada or Mexico, and so on. Even pulling in new recruits. She's one of the reasons misallocation continues to be a problem. One of the few left.

"Over the last couple of years, we've eliminated the cells in New York, LA, and Chicago that offered her safe houses and resources. The move to Boston is unexpected—she hasn't been here in years—which leads us to believe she might finally be stuck. In a dead end. Out of options.

"This is our chance. This is where we make our move."

He clicks to the final slide in the presentation—a white 'Thank You' against a black background—and hands the remote to Lieutenant Jones. Carl flicks the lights back on.

"Special Agent Bergman will be with us for at least the next few months, or whenever we get Rosenthal," she says. "Whichever comes first. While he's here, consider yourselves at his disposal. Keep up with your other cases, but know that this takes priority."

Al grins again, and it's wider than ever.

"Y'all are lucky," he says. "After this it all becomes routine: cheating husbands, frigid wives, the boring stuff. You do your jobs right, and this team gets to bring in the last of the legends."

Back at my desk, I review messages from the tip line. This was the mayor's idea, and it's our biggest pain in the ass. In today's pile alone, we have: an old man complaining about banging noises upstairs, which will no doubt turn out to be construction; a jealous husband reporting on his wife for getting coffee with an old high school friend; and, yet again, someone looking for tech support for the PRTNR app, which we do not provide.

I get up to go to the bathroom. The toilet on the far end of the row still has an "Out-of-Order" sign pasted on the stall door.

Bergman comes in after me. He nods, and pisses in the urinal two down from mine. We reach the sinks at the same time.

"I hate it when someone starts talking to me while I'm taking a leak," he says.

"Likewise."

"Sean, right?"

"Yep."

"Sean," he says. "I've been meaning to tell you—I'm glad you're a part of this."

"Yeah?"

"Hope you don't mind, but I had a look at your file before flying up, and I think you're uniquely qualified to help out on this case."

"That so," I say. I turn on the water, and pump a handful of soap.

"Nothing against the rest of the team, obviously—you're all great detectives. But they're matched. And you're not."

I rub my palms together under the water. I get in between my fingers and under the nails.

"What I mean is, sometimes it helps to have a different perspective. Lets you think in ways other people can't." He tosses his wet paper towel in the bin.

"Go places they can't go."

My hands have been clean for a while. I keep washing them.

"Mr. Bergman—"

"Please. Call me Al."

"Like the song."

"Like the song."

"Al. Are you asking for something?"

He's leaning on the edge of the sink. The man is a leaner.

"I need to find out what they're up to in your city. The poly people. The kinksters. I have a feeling you might know something about that."

No one's used the word *poly* in years. Usually it's *hoarders*. Or *pervs*.

"I ought to; I'm with the Intimacy Allocation Unit."

He chuckles at that.

"Fair enough. Maybe you don't want to talk about it. That's fine. All I know is that you've filed for an extension on your matching deadline every six months like clockwork since the Amendment got passed. You seem *determined* to stay single."

Baptiste rolls into the restroom. He grabs a Dixie cup, fills it with mouthwash from the pump-handle on the sink, and swishes the fluid around in his mouth. He gargles and spits a green puddle into the white sink. Then he notices us standing around, not saying anything.

"Sean," he says, nodding. "Al."

The pneumatic hinge on top of the door hisses, inching closed. Al waits for the wooden thud of door against frame before continuing.

"Look," says Al, "all I'm asking is: Keep your eyes open. Maybe say yes if any new opportunities come your way. And if you learn something interesting, let me know."

He slaps my upper arm, then starts to head back out to the bullpen. He pauses by the paper towels.

"If you do find anything, Sean, bring it to me. Just me."

The door shuts behind him. My hands drip into the sink.

Sean / Boston, MA / 2030

Another day off.

I roll up my futon mattress, fold the sheet and blanket, and stack them all in the corner of the room, on top of the wrestling mats that fit together like puzzle pieces. I nuke a bowl of white rice, crack an egg over it, and use my chopsticks to whisk it all together with soy sauce. I blow on the hot rice before popping it in my mouth.

The bamboo clinks against the glass. The bowl is empty. I wash it, and the chopsticks, and put them in the drying rack next to the sink. A flatbed carrying a load of lumber *thunks* into the pothole on the corner.

The library is four blocks away. I drop last week's books into the slot. Through the glass doors, toward the back of the building, is the shelf where they keep the reservations. It's a great system: There's a self-checkout kiosk right there. They process the orders online and deliver them right to the selected branch. No need to speak to, or look at, another person during the whole process.

I run around Jamaica Pond three times. During the first and second loops, a man in too-big Timberlands is doing an elaborate tai chi form on the small beach in the southeast corner. By the third time around, he's gone. Men in gym shorts and stained t-shirts set up fishing rods in shady spots along the path, pulling bait from the plastic shopping bags that serve as tackle boxes. Back in the apartment, I pinch my stomach and frown in the mirror.

During all this time, from the library to the Pond and back, nobody has waved at me or tried to say hello. And I haven't looked at anyone.

I shower with the curtain and door open. The sound of the water hitting the bottom of the tub echoes in interesting ways, and a ray of golden sunshine cuts straight across the apartment. It shoots through the spray coming down from the showerhead, making it sparkle like a rain of gems.

In the far corner of the main room, by the windows opposite the entrance to the kitchen, stands a small desk. My laptop sits on top of it.

In any given month, I make sure to route a normal amount of traffic through local servers: a bit of shopping; compilation videos of people falling down stairs; random encyclopedia pages. I save the VPN for special occasions.

The VPN connects my computer with a server in Brazil. When it's turned on, all of my web traffic appears to originate from an apartment in Sao Paulo. It's a cheap service—the sort of thing teenagers use to torrent low-res movies. A more expensive option could provide more security, but at the cost of unwanted attention.

It used to be easy to find anything you wanted: photos, videos, looping GIF images. There were illustrations—full-blown comics, even. So much of it was free, but you could set up monthly payments to help the artists out and keep the art going. Whole communities came together to support the work and the people they loved.

I never paid. Too traceable.

Foreign sites are the safest. Today I visit an Australian webpage I've grown fond of lately. They stage photoshoots in the Outback—pretty Aussies getting tied up and fucked on piles of red rocks, against a backdrop of gorgeous, alien vistas: sweeping dune fields, towering mesas, and a sky bigger than the inside of God's head. I finish as a young woman's head bobs up and down on a cock in a wide-angle shot that includes a huge stretch of salt flats. I delete everything, and shower again. The apartment is quiet.

It's the start of June, which means I can refile for an extension on my deadline. I pull the PRTNR app up on my phone, tap into Settings, and look for the button that lets me use my status as a law enforcement officer to delay matching.

It's not there. It's not anywhere.

The woman on the support line is cheerfully sympathetic.

"I'm sorry, sir, but that feature was removed with our most recent update. As of September first, all users will have to enter the general matching pool. Actually, we're making the official announcement in about an hour—looks like you beat us to it!"

I hang up. It got dark while we were talking. I go for a drive.

"'*But I will forewarn you,*'" says the man on the radio, "'*whom ye shall fear: Fear him, which after he hath killed hath power to cast into hell; yea, I say unto you, Fear him.*' Now, I think that's all pretty straightforward. Don't you, folks?"

I drive west, to a long stretch of highway with no streetlights.

"'*For there is nothing covered, that shall not be revealed; neither hid, that shall not be known.*'"

A can of Monster rattles around in the cup holder. The box of Cheez-Its I crammed in the door is still half full. White lane-divider lines materialize, one after the other, at the far end of my circle of light, then disappear beneath the hood of the car. Beyond that, blackness. I speed up, and the flickering tempo increases.

"'*Therefore whatsoever ye have spoken in darkness shall be heard in the light;*' says the Lord."

No other cars. Just me and the preacher. I could turn the radio off. But I don't.

"'... *and that which ye have spoken in the ear in closets shall be proclaimed upon the housetops...*'"

I reach around the steering wheel for the knob that controls the headlights. I step hard on the gas.

A quarter-inch turn—that's all it takes—and I'm flying in darkness. I flick the lights back on immediately, the muscles around my eyes twitching. Blood rushes through my temples. I take a breath, lick my lips, and do it again.

Lights off. Count to three. Back on.

"'*Be ye therefore ready also: for the Son of man cometh at an hour when ye think not.*'"

Off.

One, two, three, four, five, six, seven ...

WIRED / "Top 5 Most Downloaded Apps of 2024"

The PRTNR app is a bit of an outlier, given that it's the first compulsory download ever featured on our list. Still, the numbers don't lie: with more than 200 million active profiles, PRTNR is the first and only app in history to be used by every unmarried adult citizen in the United States. A surprising joint effort by Apple, Microsoft, Facebook, and Alphabet, the app began taking the country by storm back in early March, when a package of legislation passed in conjunction with the 29th Amendment made it illegal for anyone above the age of consent not to have it. With questionnaire answers backed by polygraph data—courtesy of an integration with touch-screen lie-detector app CherryTree—and access to data pulled from health records, rideshare applications, GPS services, and social networks, PRTNR claims to match users with an unprecedented degree of accuracy. Let's hope so—users who elect not to pair with their initial matches after a first date will be placed back into an ever-shrinking pool of candidates, a feature which PRTNR believes will incentivize users to "make it work" [...]

Carl / Harwich, MA / 2003

The first layer of sand is hot, dry. This part is more pushing than digging. Sand runs off the blue plastic head of the shovel as we clear out a circle big enough for both of us to stand in. I pull a packet of candy cigarettes from my waistband and offer it to Sean. He tucks one in the corner of his mouth. I do the same. He holds one cupped hand up in front of my face, blocking the wind with the other. He flicks his thumb against his forefinger. It makes a little raspy noise. I take a drag while he lights up. I exhale—Sean nods at the imaginary cloud of smoke. Then we get to work.

The next layer is the thickest. We find a rhythm; he digs in while I throw, and then we switch. The sand is cool and damp. Heavy.

The adults drink beer wrapped in koozies from the Raw Bar. The mermaid on the side—the one carrying a tray of oysters—is supposed to have her titties out. But Sean's mom got fed up with it one day and drew bras on all of them with a black Sharpie.

They talk about police stuff, and celebrity news, and eat homemade sandwiches with crunchy Cape Cod chips. Sean and I dig down past our ankles, our knees, our hips. Like always, the hole starts to look more like a cone, and we take a minute to widen the bottom and straighten out the sides.

The sand gets heavier the more we go down. Blister territory. I throw the clods way up over my shoulder to get them out of the hole. They *thud* on the ground—the sound travels through the sand.

A young father peers down, holding his kid's hands. Sean squints up at him, wrists limp over the butt of the shovel. We're ankle-deep in salty brown water that crawls with harmless translucent bugs.

"That's quite a hole you've got there," says the man.

"Yep," I say.

He coughs. He and his son walk away, toward the water's edge. They disappear quickly behind the wall of sand.

I go for a swim, but only to cool off and take a piss. When I get back, Sean's reinforced the north wall with a pair of boogie boards. I fill a bucket with the fine sand from the water hole and kneel on the floor with him to fill in a couple of gaps. We need to do some demolition work to make up for the new structure: Sean pulls two Bomb Bags out of his pocket. We pop the blister packs, shove the growing foil squares in the sand, and scramble out of the hole to take shelter behind a dune.

There are two little *pops*. The wall stays still. I throw a rock at it and the whole south side caves in. We spend twenty minutes clearing the debris.

Finally, there's that layer of pebbles that waits under the beach, at the bottom of every hole. Nothing else to do. Sean goes to grab the Capri Suns while I carve two small chairs into the side of the hole. I sit.

Up there the wind blows in big puffs; waves crawl up and go back; seagulls shout; girls scream at the cold water. None of the sounds get down here. Sean comes back and tosses me my pouch. We sit in the hole and listen to the quiet. Our parents will make us cave it in at the end of the day.

After a while, we get up and head for the water. The first bit is covered in dead seaweed, limp and rubbery like the used condom I saw at the Franklin Park Zoo earlier in the summer. It doesn't bother me much, but Sean hates it. He scrunches up his face and rushes in, trying to get past the slimy stuff as fast as he can.

There are lots of little things he can't deal with. He won't put on his sandals if his feet have any sand on them—he has to go down to the water's edge and rinse his feet off there, then walk slowly back up the beach. That way the bottoms of his shoes are the only thing that gets sand stuck to them. And he doesn't eat Cheetos, or Jax, because he hates the way the cheese powder sticks to his skin. One time a kid at school stuck his orange fingers all the way into his mouth to suck the powder off, and Sean almost threw up his sandwich.

Last year, I tried to rub a piece of seaweed on his face, just to mess with him. He hit me, and I hit him back, and we both cried a bit. Now I don't do that anymore.

We're in the water up to our waists, but the water's still not clean enough. Sean keeps pushing out, moving down the slope till we're in up to our necks on our tiptoes, and have to hop over the waves as they roll in. The water is cool. It washes the sunscreen off my skin—little drops of oil float on the surface.

Sean stares out past the buoy, at the open ocean. I look back. Our parents are waving their arms and shouting at us. Too windy to hear what they're saying, but they'll be pissed we went out so far. I jog-swim back to shore a few feet, but stop when Sean doesn't join me. He stands there, in the water, waves around his nose, staring out at the nothing like it's the prettiest thing he ever saw.

Sean / Boston, MA / 2030

Tonight I'm watching old clips—vintage stuff from the aughts and tens, filmed in San Francisco back in the day and saved from the crackdowns by luck and piracy. Enthusiasts in other parts of the world are happy to preserve the footage. There's a growing movement of foreign anthropologists interested in examining "the last days of American fetish porn." On-screen are a man and a woman—twenty years older now than they appear in the video. If they're still alive. If the courts got to them first.

It only happened a few times—people acting on their own—in the months just before the Amendment passed. But those were enough. There was a YouTuber down in Southie, who posted a video. In it she outlined a long list of counterarguments to the Cunningham paper. We found her face-down on the Castle Island beach, a seagull pecking at her back, where the word "HOARDER" had been carved in big block letters.

What I do is an improvement.

The performers are acting out a scene in a locker room—one of that studio's regular sets. The model has her legs tied in a full split to either end of a long wooden bench. The top is smacking the bottom in her face when a chatbot window pops up on the right side of the screen.

Did you ever see The Matrix??

I smile. It's a fun hook. Usually they send out a greeting, then follow it up with *Hello??* Or *Guess you don't want to fuck me . . .* I close the window and go back to watching my clip.

The window bloops back into existence.

Maybe that was before your time. Bad intro.

Persistent. Weird.

The woman on the bench is begging for permission to come. The man grants it, and her groan mixes with the ping of a new message:

I know what you're watching, Sean.

I stop moving. My hands are cold.

My name's Marie, the window says. *We should talk.*

There's a way to operate on autopilot, with all higher functions temporarily shut down. You're not even afraid—fear would be inefficient. There's only you and the thing that needs doing.

It's in this state of mind that I ignore the blinking cursor waiting below the latest message, nuke my browsing history, and cancel my VPN subscription.

TIME Magazine / "The Lion and the Lamb: How the JI Movement Sparked an Unlikely Friendship" / 2023

TIME: We should address the elephant in the room. In a viral video that circulated not too long ago, you two can famously be seen attempting to murder each other on the steps of the Lincoln Memorial.

Daniella Reeves, Ph.D.: Hey, now—not according to our settlement.

[All laugh]

TIME: And yet here you are, just a few years later: speaking together at conferences, giving interviews as a pair. You even co-authored a book. What changed?

Rev. Martin Holbecker: Well, obviously, if you'd asked me back then where I thought my ministry was going to take me, "sharing a platform with a famous women's studies professor" would've been the last thing on my list. And honestly, we still disagree about so much. Sometimes this one opens her mouth and I just want to . . . [mimes throttling Reeves].

Reeves: Don't even get us started on complementarianism.

Holbecker: [chuckles]

Reeves: That's the thing about Just Intimacy. It cuts across the usual dividing lines. We can arrive at the same destination from completely different starting points. We talk about this in the book. I take my cues from thinkers like [Andrea] Dworkin and [Catherine] McKinnon: I see patriarchal oppression at work in pornography, sadomasochism, and so on.

Holbecker: Whereas *I'm* not even convinced that [mimes air quotes] "patriarchal oppression" is nearly the problem Dani makes it out to be.

Reeves: [rolls eyes]

Holbecker: But I do know that sexuality is a gift from God, and that such deviant behaviors are an abuse of that gift. Sins, plain and simple. And so we wind up opposing the same things, for completely different reasons.

TIME: And those reasons lead both of you to conclude that BDSM is in some way "unjust," even between consenting partners.

Reeves: [shakes head] That's the problem, right there. Definitions. Nobody can "consent" to abuse.

Holbecker: [nods] And *that's* what BDSM and other kinds of "kink" are. Ab-use. From the Latin *abuti*. To use someone else, their body, their sexuality, incorrectly. Ultimately, the purpose of sex is to hold societies together. [Reeves] and I might not agree on the exact details of how those societies should be structured—I have a stricter definition of what counts as a "family," for instance—but there are certain things that so obviously run counter to that really basic, pair-bonding *telos*.

Reeves: There's a right way to love people. And ropes and chains will never fit into *my* definition of right relationship.

TIME: And how does JI's insistence on compulsory monogamy fit into all of this? How did you two come to support arranged partnerships?

Holbecker: I'd say it isn't ideal for either of us—

Reeves: But it's a practical solution—it checks off a lot of boxes. Marty comes at it from a standpoint of Christian justice. Polyamorists, people in the S/M scene, and so on are, in a certain sense, committing the sin of greed, or avarice. Hoarding too much for themselves—coveting what isn't rightfully theirs—while others go without, in a world where there's only so much affection to go around. As I understand it, JI is his way of lifting up the disadvantaged—people who would otherwise have a tough time getting intimacy in their lives because of looks, shyness, what have you. Sermon on the Mount stuff.

Holbecker: [grinning] Well, shucks. You listened.

Reeves: What? I pay attention when you talk. Sometimes.

Holbecker: But yeah, I'm an idealist. Just trying to follow the rules. Dani's a Marxist-materialist. For her it's all about who controls the means of production—how women labor to produce sex and intimacy—and how, in the current sexual economy, they don't get what they ought to in exchange for that labor. Safety. Respect. For her, JI is an honest-to-goodness revolution of the proletariat. Not my cup of joe—but again, it doesn't really matter what you call it. What matters is the result.

Reeves: And we can both get behind that.

Letter from Marie Rosenthal to Ellen Willis / February 10, 1997

Dear Professor Willis,

You always told us to focus on sensory details. Here are a few:

The woolen gloves I wear in the apartment make it impossible to code.

The mice who shit in my Cheerios recently made off with my chicken cutlet. An *entire* chicken cutlet. Did you know they're omnivores?

When you turn on the kitchen lights, the scattering roaches look like angry riot cops from an old-timey film. They wave their antennae like batons, off to beat up some six-legged Charlie Chaplin.

Nineteen-year-old boys smell like yeast.

A young man in my section is fond of eating mayonnaise-heavy tuna sandwiches during class. His lips are very chapped. The mayonnaise lives in the cracks.

I did a pratfall on the icy sidewalk yesterday, and I haven't thought about my thesis in weeks. How do you deal with students? The bullshit excuses for late homework? How do you not murder them when they ask questions covered on the first page of the syllabus?

You know I never read that Lee Miller piece you assigned to us, right? That I bluffed my way through the entire section meeting? I assumed you knew. But in case you didn't, here's my confession. Guess you'll have to report me and get my degree rescinded—then I'll have to come back to

New York and take your class again, and drink tea in your office while you explain how the world works. Haha.

I did read up on her eventually. She's fascinating. I want a print of the photo where she's in Hitler's bathtub.

How are you, Professor Willis? Who or what are you taking down this year? Please send me your latest article, or let me know the name of the publication so I can steal a copy from the COOP. I hope it's nothing glossy—the rest of the magazine will double as toilet paper, which I also can't afford.

Yours, as Much as Anyone's,
Marie

Sean / Boston, MA / 2030

Carl got me to come out to the bar tonight with Levi. He failed to mention the Bruins were playing.

We're surrounded on all sides by well-matched couples: pairs of humans with a shared passion for discount appetizers and watery lager. Their presence here has a concentrating effect. Barbecue sauce smells tangier. Cheddar cheese, oozing through grinning teeth, appears oilier. Mouths everywhere, opening and closing, exhaling garlic knot aroma over utensils and glasses, squeezing fried jalapeno poppers till they burst, liquefying those mysterious, boneless chicken wings . . .

By the end of the second period, Levi's put away three G&Ts.

"Now," says Levi, "I *know* you said you're not looking to match right away, and that's totally understandable. But seeing as the deadline is coming up, just as something to consider—"

"Levi, come on—" says Carl.

"—when he's ready, I was going to say! Not right this second."

He has his photo app open on his phone. He scrolls through pictures till he finds a screenshot of someone's PRTNR profile. He passes the phone over to me.

"Her name's Brighdie," he says. "She works in my office; she's *so* sweet."

In her About section, Levi's friend Brighdie has written a small treatise identifying her favorite seasons of *The Bachelor*, and explaining why each stands out.

That show has been off the air for years—ever since the Amendment passed. Which would make Brighdie an amateur historian. Of *The Bachelor*.

"If you want to match," says Levi, "I've gotta friend over at the IAB. Could move a few numbers around, if you know what I mean." He wiggles his eyebrows.

"You are dating a cop," says Carl.

"I'm just *kidding*," says Levi. He turns his head so Carl can't see his lips, and mouths to me: *No I'm not*.

"Be right back," says Carl, sliding off his stool. "Leave Sean alone."

Levi kisses him on top of his head, and Carl goes weaving off through the mass of paired-off hockey fans toward the bathrooms. Levi leans his chin on his hand, watching him go with a sloppy smile on his face. Tonight, he's wearing Carl's lucky Marchand jersey over his usual Oxford shirt. The yellow and black sleeves cover his fingers to the second knuckle.

He's too tipsy to notice that I'm not paying attention to the game. To ask why I'm just staring, barely blinking, down at our table.

How did she find me? It shouldn't be possible. I was careful. I always used the VPN. I always cleared my cache, history, everything. No downloads. No trace. And yet she knew where I was, and what I was doing. She sent me a message.

What does she want with me?

Levi sees something on the other side of the room, and jumps up like a prairie dog popping out of a burrow.

"Isn't that your friend Rob?" he says.

"Oh, no," I say. "Levi, you don't have to—"

But it's too late. Levi, red in the face, is waving those big baggy sleeves up over his head like an inflatable tube man, and Rob Lanahan has spotted us, and is headed this way.

Rob treats his mustache like a pet. Wax, conditioner, careful trimmings, the works. It flexes when he grins, like a big hairy caterpillar creeping along the underside of a branch. He arrives, in all his Rob-ness, musses Levi's hair, and notices Brighdie's profile on the open phone.

"You turn straight on us, slick?"

"Har, har," says Levi, swinging the toe of his shoe gently into Rob's leg. Rob flinches like it hurt a lot more than it possibly could have.

"We're trying to set up Boston's most eligible, least willing bachelor."

"Still single, Sean?" says Rob, with a smile like a Bowie knife.

"Just focusing on work," I say.

"You need to learn how to relax," says Rob. He has another look at Brighdie.

"She's a looker, Sean. You could do a lot worse."

Carl returns to the table with another round, balancing two beers and a glass of water between his fingers. Levi sees the water and starts to pout, but Carl fixes him with the dead-eye till he takes the pint glass with both hands, grumbling. Carl offers to get Rob another Heineken, but Rob waves him off.

"Can't stay," he says. "Got a job later tonight."

Levi tips back his glass for a big sip of water, and sloshes half of it on the collar of the jersey.

"Why's anyone need a *contractor* in the middle of the night?" he says. "It's stupid."

"Well, Levi," says Rob, "some things just can't wait."

He turns to me and Carl, and winks.

During commercial breaks, sanctioned couples lick buffalo sauce and blue cheese dressing from each other's faces. They pet each other's hair and laugh with other paired-up couples in groups of six to eight. They play footsie under the tables. Rob watches them with something like pride.

Rob's number isn't saved on any of our phones, but we all know it. He's never set foot in headquarters—he's not a cop, and it wouldn't be appropriate for him to be seen there. Instead, we meet him in places like this, during odd hours.

He owns some land, out in Wellesley, that he's outfitted with an obstacle course and shooting range. There, he hangs out with a core knot of middle-aged men—also not cops—and the college boys who treat their every word like gospel. Mostly White. They spend weekends at Rob's, running tactical maneuvers in the backyard. He hosts big barbecues out there every summer.

I dislike Rob. I don't know how the other cops feel about him. But regardless of how I feel, he, and guys like him, are necessary. Part of the ecosystem.

Even after the little protests died out—after people got used to PRTNR, and started enjoying the new approach—even then, nobody liked to see uniformed officers carting away such normal-looking people. People who didn't look like *perverts*, or *hoarders*, so much as neighbors. People who wore suits and cardigans. Seeing people like that get arrested in broad daylight made the rest of the public uncomfortable. Felt too close. So we stopped making a show of it. We outsourced.

When we have a name, a location, and a description, we call Rob. He takes care of the rest.

Rob's beer is down to its last swig. He raises the bottle and waits for us to clink our glasses on it.

"*Sláinte*," he says.

"*Go dtuitfeadh an tigh ort*," I say.

The three of them look at me, drinks hanging in the air.

"May the road rise up to meet you, Rob."

I down my beer. Levi pivots his head and looks at me, pursing his lips the way he does at pictures of puppies.

"You are such a *good guy*," he says, pinching my cheek in his free hand. On massive flat-screen TVs around the bar, the Bruins' center takes a shot.

"We'll find you somebod—OH, FUCK YEAH!!!"

The bar screams. The puck's gone in the net.

Carl wraps Levi in a bear hug from behind. Levi squeezes his forearms, and leans back into his chest. Rob grins.

Sean / Boston, MA / 2030

From our spot on Comm Ave, we can see through a gap in the trees straight into Smith's apartment. She's supposed to be meeting that couple here, at their usual time. But her lights have been off all night. Carl's saying something. I ignore him, keep my eyes fixed on the window, and review what happened the other night.

It's impossible. I covered every step. I was meticulous. There were no tracks to follow. No way to tie my activities back to a single computer in Boston. And definitely no way to know who was using that computer at the exact moment the message came through.

But someone calling herself "Marie" did know. And the message was addressed to me. It follows that I'm being watched by someone who's put even more effort into finding me than I've put into not being found. As for what they want—

"... Sean? Hey, Sea—"

"Fucking, what, Carl?!"

"Jee-sis ... I asked what you want to eat. I'm going to Little Steve's."

"Oh. Sorry. Turkey club."

He forms the 'OK' sign with his thumb and forefinger before slowly lowering his ring and pinky fingers. When he feels I've gotten the point, he opens the car door, gets out, and slams it shut behind him.

"Seriously, I'm sorry," I say. "I'm ... frustrated."

The windows are open, so I can hear him muttering as he stalks off:

"... surprised you have room for more, after biting my head off..."

Carl turns the corner onto Mass Ave and disappears. He'll be better after we eat. He gets cranky when he's hungry. Maybe we both do.

I get out of the car and lean back till my hips pop. Then I bend forward, pulling at the stiff, jerky-like muscles in my neck. Blood rushes to my head when I stand back up.

A thin figure is crossing the Back Bay Mall, walking straight toward me.

It's the man who was standing in front of the police station. With the red hair. No jacket today, and his fitted white shirt is open at the collar. He's rolled up his sleeves, in a way that's somehow both spiffy and casual. He looks like a cologne ad.

He rests on the hood of our unmarked car.

"They're gone," he says. "I told them you were watching."

It isn't often my mouth falls open. "How—?"

The man tips his chin toward the inside of the car. The floor around the passenger seat—Carl's seat—is layered an inch deep in compacted Little Steve's takeout bags. From the restaurant around the corner from this apartment. They're identical to the bag Carl held in his hand when he bumped into this man the other night.

"I could arrest you," I say.

"Don't remind me." It's a warm day, but he's hugging himself. "Coming here wasn't my idea."

"Whose was it?"

"Someone you've been looking for. Someone very interested in a vice cop who looks at bondage porn in his spare time." He picks his nails. "Think hard, detective."

I stand there like an idiot, hands hanging by my sides. I don't know what to say.

The man considers me again, and frowns. He shakes his head. "Forget it."

Shouldering past me, he stalks off down Comm Ave, eastward, toward the Common. I keep still. My heart thuds. I wait.

In a moment, he stops. No hand on his shoulder. No cuffs on his wrists. He returns, and looks right past me. He leans in: "Do you want to meet her?" he says.

"I don't know."

"The garage under the Regal," he says. "Thursday, 8:00 p.m. Bring some rope."

Thursday: boxing night with Carl.

"I have a thing—"

Which is honestly the reason I give to him. A scheduling conflict.

"Fine," he says. "Don't come."

That's it. He's already walking away.

"Which entrance?" I say. "Which level?"

"Any of them," he says. "We'll find you."

Al / Bracketville, TX / 2000

The town is dirt roads—literal dirt roads, plus a Methodist Church and what's called the "Heritage Museum." The only street lamps in town are posted at the right-angled intersections. We roll between patches of light and darkness.

I yawn, and lean my head more comfortably on the passenger-side window. The rest of the SRT is loaded up on caffeine pills and taurine. Not me. Negotiation and jitters don't mix. Not that they need the help now, at three in the morning. Four sleepy drug dealers against twelve wired ATF agents in riot gear isn't exactly a contest. I'm a formality tonight. . . .

The van hits a pothole, and my head smacks against the glass. We're here.

Guns out, the team hustles to the safe house at a crouch, like they're storming Normandy. They breach the flimsy wooden door and disappear inside.

I rub my eyes and tap my cheeks with my fingertips. Is it even worth thinking about sleep? By the time we get back to Del Rio, wrap things up, and return to the Holiday Inn, the sun will be coming up. And I don't think we even get hot breakfast. Just continental: toast from a plastic case and yogurt floating in a bowl of icy water. And then it's right back to Dallas.

Room by room, flashlight beams illuminate the safe house from the inside. Shouts in English and Spanish. No gunshots. Inside of two minutes, tactical drags four shirtless, tattooed guys out onto the driveway. They struggle against the zip ties and spit on the team's boots until they're shoved, face-down, in the dirt.

I stretch. My shirt is rumpled and sweaty under the bulletproof vest, and my underpants are bunched up from the ride over. Picking at my crotch to air them out, I walk around the back of the house to find somewhere to take a leak. A Joshua tree grows next to an old truck, up on cinder blocks. I consider both, and pick the tree.

The night is quiet, except for crickets and distant cursing in two languages. The tree I'm pissing on bends a little in a cool breeze. The sky is half white with stars.

I zip up, and something clatters on the ground behind me.

A boy squats behind the rusted-out truck. He's a few years younger than the guys inside, maybe sixteen. Sweaty. A shitty mustache graces his pointy face. He grabs the dropped pistol off the ground and clutches it like a teddy bear.

He has forever to shoot. When he doesn't, I step forward and hold out my hand.

"*Damela*," I say. "Give me the gun. It's okay."

He's about to. He doesn't want this to escalate any more than I do. My team is composed of frustrated, tired, middle-aged men, more or less high out of their gourds and decked out with as much military surplus weaponry as we could get our hands on. A lot could happen out here in the desert. And there's nobody around to record it with a phone.

It can go so well, if he does nothing stupid. He's still a minor. We can say he was coerced—maybe it's even true. Maybe the possession charges get reduced, or even dropped under the circumstances. A whole bright future opens up for this kid. If he can let go of that gun.

And I want that for him. He has no way of knowing it, but I want that even more than I want to get out of this dead, dusty town with my brain still in my skull. Though that'd be nice, too. I want so badly for him to make the correct decision. If I can bend his mind in the right direction, in this moment, I give him the freedom of years outside of prison, and lift the weight of murder from his soul. I create a life.

But one of the men out front shouts loud enough to remind us what we're doing here. The boy swallows, frowns, and the chance is gone.

The numbers are adding up in his head—a series of calculations that pit opportunity cost against social capital. And the result doesn't look good for me. By pulling that trigger, he wins the respect of those guys on the front lawn, plus whoever they share the story with. That sets him up for a degree of safety in prison, if not comfort. And if he gets out, in ten years or forty—assuming the state doesn't strap him down to a table and pump him full of potassium chloride—he'll have a job waiting for him, killing people. Just like he's about to kill me.

A kid that young, with a dead cop to his name. He'd be a god.

My heart cracks open because now it's too late for him. In his head, he's already aimed the gun, and fired, and accepted the consequences—or, at least, his limited understanding of what the consequences might be. He doesn't understand how long a day can be when it comes after one that was exactly the same—and before another that will be just like it. He can't imagine what a brain will do to itself when it has nothing to look at but four concrete walls, nothing to listen to but a heartbeat. And I don't have time to tell him. Because it's a matter of instances now. Moments, in sequence, like slides in an old-fashioned projector. His life ended the moment he saw opportunity in this situation. But mine can still be saved.

A sharp-edged brick lies on the ground between us. Slowly, I open my hands, and reach for it.

"¡Ay—!" says the boy. He points the gun at my head.

I'm lucky. Very lucky. The boy is young. Not hard, though he thinks he wants to be. The reflex to blow away anything that comes within his sphere of influence hasn't been beaten into him yet. An older man would've fired, instinctively, without saying a word. Some part of the boy still thinks he can warn his way to safety, like a rattlesnake shaking at an incoming boot. It's thanks to that hesitation that I can put a finger to my lips, grab the brick, and back up.

Pressing the edge into my eye socket, I gouge it across my temple.

I remember the first time I fell off my bicycle as a kid and didn't cry. We lived on a dead-end street, which I'd ride up and down on my two-wheeler for hours, by myself, speeding up sometimes and taking my time at others.

That afternoon was nothing special. Just a lazy turn at the end of the loop closest to my house. It should be an insignificant moment, wiped from my memory like the many thousands of times I did the exact same thing without a problem. But on that day there was a patch of sand in the road, and my back tire found it as I leaned into the turn, depending on the rubber to keep its grip on the road and hold me upright. The support was plucked out from beneath me like a Jenga block, and for a second lines became crisper, and colors turned deeper, while I hung in the air, somewhere between recognizing I wasn't riding anymore and admitting I was falling.

But then I did fall, and the momentum carried me sideways. Between them, the bike and the sandy asphalt chewed the skin off the outside of my leg.

I sucked in air to yell, and scrunched my face up in anticipation of tears. But then it occurred to me—and I remember how distinct and clear the idea was—that there really wasn't any point. The cut was made, and my blood was in the sand. I knew by then that no adult could undo something that had already been done, and that as badly as some part of me wanted their company when these sort of things happened, they were usually a lot of trouble for a little comfort: I'd scream, and they'd fuss, and patch me up, but I'd never feel really fixed as promised.

So I decided not to cry. I held the sound in my throat, like a balloon on a string, and pushed myself up from my side to my butt.

I never knew skin could look like that. Pink and wet, glinting where it wasn't covered by sticky sand. Like a dropped pork chop. I let the bike crash on the front lawn, then quietly walked through the house and into the bathroom. I took off my shoes, put my leg up on the toilet bowl to catch the drips, and patted at the raw place with wet paper towels till my mom saw it and shrieked.

That was worse than the brick, which I'm done with. I throw it into the neighbor's scraggly bushes, and blink at the boy through the blood.

His wide eyes are fixed on my head. I snap my fingers till he pays attention.

"*En el aire*," I say, pointing up. "I'll tell them you shot at me."

It takes him a few seconds. But he figures it out. He nods. He shoots into the sky. I guide him to the ground, and roll us around in the dust till the others show up and drag him away.

It's a good deal—nobody can call him a chickenshit for not trying anything, but he doesn't have to face down a full murder charge. When we're in earshot of the others, I make a big, loud fuss about what a fight he put up, and how close I'd come to kicking it.

"Crazy motherfucker," I say, holding my hand over my entire eye. The guys from the safe house don't know I still have it. Might as well go big.

The boy's buddies stare at me, then at him. Their mouths hang open.

Sean / Boston, MA / 2030

I look at light fixtures, bathroom faucets, and mulch before I finally take a breath and walk down the aisle with the rope. The Heavy's "How You Like Me Now?" pipes in through overhead speakers.

A wall of options, hung up on pegs or wrapped around giant plastic spools—in case I wanted to choose my own length. As if I know what the right length would be. Nylon, cotton, manila—something called polypropylene—braided or twisted, ranging in thickness from delicate twine to hauling rope a full inch wide. The sort of thing you'd pull hand over hand to hoist a grand piano. An occasional splash of neon breaks up the brown and white ropes designed for securing things to trucks.

Who's bringing hot pink rope to a job site?

The nylon is slippery—surprisingly so. I read somewhere that it's made from oil. I remember pictures, videos: legs tied together, or apart; wrists bound one to the other; waists cinched tight.

Outside of the evidence locker, illegal internet surfing, and my own imagination, I have no concept of what the right kind of rope is supposed to look like. Or feel like. And there's no one I can ask.

There's a rattling down the aisle. An old woman paws through a basket of superglues, squinting at the labels one by one. She smiles at me.

"Going on an adventure?" she asks.

"Hahhh," I say. I grab a shrink-wrapped package at random, and hurry back to the front of the store.

The twenty-something running the cash register drums his fingers in time to "Short Change Hero." He hums the chorus, and holds up every item handed to him at arm's length. Then he levels the price-checker, shuts one eye, and sights down the top of it. He pulls the trigger on a pack of D batteries.

"Prrkow," he says.

I get to the front of the line, and he takes the rope from my hand.

"It's for clothes," I say. "To hang them up. Outside."

The boy grins. "Yeah, this'll do it," he says.

"I don't like the machines," I say.

He looks at me. In the back of the store, a paint mixer whirls round and round.

"Too noisy," I say. "Air is better."

Slowly, he nods. "Cool, man," he says.

I pay for the rope and leave.

Outside, I examine what I've bought: cotton, white, three-eighths inch. Fifty feet, bundled tightly and sealed in plastic.

According to the label, it actually is a clothesline.

Seven o'clock. I can still ignore the invitation.

Five after seven. Still time to take the rope out of the duffel bag, toss it over the fence into the neighbors' dumpster, and go to bed.

Less than an hour. It's a good night for a walk. I like walking. Footsteps make noise on the paved walkways that skirt the Jamaicaway. Even now, the cameras haven't spread that far from the roads. It's still a wilderness in there. More crickets than car horns.

I once took a walk through the woods by the Orthodox university on the north side of the Pond. There was a group of students sitting in a circle, chanting Greek scriptures in a clearing filled with candles—little ones, glowing in the hollow trunks where they'd been placed next to prayer cards and rosary beads. I stood on the edge of the light and watched as they lifted icons and bowed their heads.

Eight minutes after seven. Still time to be safe. It doesn't have to be complicated. I had contact with a member of the Boston rope cell. It's a very simple thing to report that back to Al right away, before anything else happens. Get it on the record, exactly as it transpired. Add another fact to the growing case file, until we have the information we need to move forward with confidence against the woman who claims to have very dangerous information about who I am, and what I like, and what I've done to get some limited access to it.

There's a system. I stick to it, and I don't get stupid, and it works. I don't disappear.

Still time to follow standard procedure. To be blameless. Still time to go to work tomorrow the same guy who left.

Nine minutes after seven.

Ten.

Twelve.

I grab the bag and jog out the door. I return just long enough to text Carl:

Sorry bud, gotta do something for Bergman, can't come to the gym tonight.

I leave my phone, with its GPS tracker, on my desk.

I wish I weren't so sweaty.

Every few minutes, bodies stream out through the sliding doors, talking about after-movie drinks. They dump half-full popcorn buckets and candy boxes into the trash.

The young couple from Verity Smith's apartment holds hands by the self-pay machines. Both have bags slung over their shoulders. There's the line of people filing out of the theater stalls, and then it's just the three of us and the glass doors.

"Hi," I say.

Their hands clench. They pull a little closer together.

"Hey," says the woman.

"I'm Sean," I say. "Are you here for the . . . the thing?"

Their eyes narrow. I'm being scrutinized. It's going poorly.

This is stupid. This is so stupid. I shouldn't be here. I don't belong here. They don't even know who I am yet, and already they hate me. And that's not going to improve when they find out what I do for a living.

I scrape my foot on the ground, and the sliding doors fly open with a *Star Trek* whoosh. I turn around and stare into empty space.

The bang of tires rolling over a grate makes us all jump. A pair of headlights rounds the far corner, and a gray Subaru Outback pulls into the garage. It follows the painted arrows on the floor up one lane and down the other, looping around to stop in front of me. Tint covers the rear windows.

The back door pops—a leather-booted foot pushes it all the way open. The redheaded man grabs the roof, and pulls himself up and out. He stands there, hands in the back pockets of his jeans.

"Well," he says.

The couple takes another look at me, then slides into the car. The man who invited me nods at the open door.

In basic self-defense classes, retired cops teach anxious housewives to go along with a mugger's demands—up until the moment he tells you to get into a vehicle. That's when you're supposed to unleash your inner ape and start clawing his eyes out, biting his ears off, ramming your knee into his testicles as hard and as fast and as many times as you can. Give them anything they want—cash, credit cards, even sex if it comes down to that—but never, ever allow yourself to be put into a car. It's the ones who want to move you away from the scene of the crime who have bad shit on their minds.

Ducking my head, I tuck myself into the seat.

The boy from the apartment sits to my left, staring at the headrest in front of him. The girl clambers into the rear and buckles herself into the backward-facing jump seat. The redhead sits on my right and pulls the door shut.

A tiny, pale face, black hair buzzed on one side, appears over the shoulder of the driver's seat.

"So this is the pig, huh?"

Verity Smith sits in the passenger seat. Her afro brushes the top of the car.

"Turn around, Pepper," she says.

Pepper squints, appraising me. She pouts.

"Thought you'd be fatter," she says. Then she slumps back and clips on her seat belt.

The redheaded man rips open a roll of duct tape.

"Close your eyes," he says. I do it, and he fits a piece of tape over my face, molding it to the bridge of my nose, the underside of my brow. No light gets in.

Tires squeak as we roll out of the garage.

There's a turn, and then we stop at a set of lights. More turns, and more stops. Eventually we pick up speed and drift over to the left, to the ticking sound of Pepper's turn signal.

At the other end of this car ride are people like me—people who like the things I like. People who know how to hide. From the app. From me. Blind, voluntarily trapped in a stranger's car, and heading who-knows-where, I'm on my way to meet my fellow freaks.

Hopefully they don't shoot me in the back of the head.

There's a beep as someone turns on the radio. Country music erupts out of speakers in the doors and ceiling. Then there's another beep, and the twang of steel guitar strings is cut off, replaced with the steady hum of tires.

"Aw, come on," says Pepper.

"Absolutely not," says Verity.

"Boo."

We slow down around a large curve, then ride another stretch of highway for a while before taking what feels like an exit. We turn, and turn, and turn. Long straightaways punctuated by regular stops. An hour or more, rumbling along in the dark.

We park. Pepper cuts the engine. We could be down the Cape by now.

"Are you sure about this?" she says.

The man and I answer at the same time:

"No," from him.

"Yes," from me.

Pepper giggles.

"Eager."

A pair of hands holds my head steady, while someone places a pair of glasses over the duct tape. My hosts guide me out of the car, and down a length of sidewalk. Lots of voices, and music. The heat of bodies. We're near a strip of bars, or nightclubs.

We walk around a corner, into an area where the sound from the street is much quieter. A door squeaks on its hinges. We walk through it.

The skin around my eyes is elastic: The stuck portion pulls away from my face before peeling off the tape and gliding back around my skull. The redheaded man is careful with it. Slow.

My pupils adjust to the light.

Tasteful modern furniture is shoved up against the walls of the room. Where it would normally rest, a layer of rush mats covers the floor. A metal tripod with a ring hanging down from its apex occupies one corner. There are a couple of leather jackets, thrown over armrests and the backs of chairs, and boots lined up at the door—but also a pair of khakis, a Hawaiian shirt, and a sensible blouse. They lie neatly on top of duffel bags much older than mine. One is unzipped. It's bursting with rope.

Besides the gang I rode in with, there's a couple in their early forties—a big man, with a thick beard and a wide belly, and a blonde woman I assume is his wife. They and the others are clustered together by the sofa, staring at me.

The husband puffs up his chest, presses his lips together, and steps forward between me and the group. He holds out a hand—a gold watch nestles in the fur which grows thick on his arm, rising from the backs of his fingers and covering his elbow before trailing off into the sleeve of a pink polo.

"Sorry about the blindfold," he says.

More hair, curly and hard-looking, peeks out through the collar. He's the color of baked sweet potato skin—except around the eyes, where the outline of a pair of wraparound sunglasses stands out from the brown. Two pink ovals, connected by a line over the bridge of his nose. His palms are rough, and when we shake, his bulk doesn't move much. He's dense.

"I'm Kevin. That's my wife, Daphne," he says, pointing to the woman behind him. She waves.

"This is our place. And that's my partner, Ilana, and Daphne's going out with her match, Luke—"

Luke and Ilana—the young couple from the theater—glare at Kevin.

"Oh," he says. "Right."

A woman in a gray linen dress enters from what must be the kitchen, sipping from a mason jar full of ice water.

"Maybe we can save the introductions," she says.

Marie Rosenthal stands in the doorway, leaning on the frame and taking in the scene with the corners of her lips curled upward, like a cat's. She crosses the room toward us and stops in front of the man who invited me here. Then she smiles, places the jar on the nearest end table, and hugs him tightly.

"It's good to see you, Jack," she says. She stands back, squeezes his arms, stops just short of asking him whether he's been eating enough. She hugs Smith—a head taller than her—and Pepper—a head shorter—before grabbing Luke and Ilana all at once, one in each arm. When that's done, she turns and faces me.

"There's some space near the back," she says.

The chatter picks up as I follow Marie, stepping over bags and folded clothes. Somebody turns up the music—lo-fi beats—and people start unpacking. Zippers are pulled open. Rope comes out of bags. The group breaks off into pairs, and Jack takes off his shirt. So does Kevin. Like a grizzly bear tossing away a picnic blanket.

Marie sits cross-legged on a yoga mat by the floor-to-ceiling windows. She pats another mat with her free hand. The curtains are drawn, and I don't try to peek around them. Instead I sit, hugging my knees to stay upright.

"Should I have taken my shoes off?" I say.

"You're fine," she says.

I clear my throat. Marie takes another sip of water. She's one of those people who actually sighs a little after, like she's in a soda commercial.

"You can look," she says. "We don't bite—not without permission."

It's hard to turn my head.

They shouldn't exist. They've always been virtual, never material. But here they are, right in front of me. Stretching, sweating; on the ground and going up in the air; guiding the rope through their hands or accepting it. Those doing the tying stand off to one side of their partners, analyzing their work; or else they hold these people close, wrapping them in their arms before painting the rope slowly over their bodies. There's a strong sense of doubt that this could actually be happening. That any of it is real.

The one brick-and-mortar sex shop I ever went into, back in college, had a section toward the back where they kept the kink stuff. The whole place was dark and crowded, with a film over everything, like the oil on the skin of a nose. Sebum. The lady behind the counter was old and wrinkled, wearing a t-shirt and slacks that hung off her like sheets from a drying rack. I held her appearance against her, which was cruel of me, and stupid to boot—was I expecting a model in leather shorts and a waist-cinching corset? Yes. Yes I was, because before that the fantasy never had to interact with the actual world. It was all images.

On a shelf next to the fuzzy handcuffs was a ball gag—a poorly made nylon strap threaded through a red rubber ball that was probably toxic to human health. But it was a physical object. It had been manufactured somewhere in China, and packaged up, and shipped overseas to this upsetting, dirty showroom where I could gawk at the fact of its very existence, while the shopkeeper drummed her big purple nails on the glass counter where they kept the weed bowls. Impossible to look directly at something like that—the box was one magnet, and my eyes were another, and we had the same polarity. Even when I finally got a fix on the thing, it didn't look real. It had all the substance of a JPEG until I picked it up, and felt its weight, and bought it with cash from the ATM across the street.

When the Amendment passed, I ground the ball up in a food processor, and scattered the bits in different vacant lots around the city.

On the other side of the room, the man named Jack closes his eyes and tucks his head to his knees, stretching out his back. Next to him, Verity combs through a bag, pulling out various bundles and laying them on the floor. She catches me looking at them, and her nostrils flare.

"She really liked that apartment," says Marie. "It's tough finding a place with hard points."

Verity turns her back on me and begins—a bit roughly—to tie Jack's wrists together.

Looking at them all is like looking into the sun. My eyes keep sliding off to one side.

"You came," says Marie.

"You invited me," I say.

Her head tips to the side. For the umpteenth time tonight, I'm being analyzed. This time by the woman I'm supposed to be hunting down for Al. There are so many things I should do: memorize the layout of the room; look for clues as to where in New England we are; listen in on the other conversations in the room to pick up on any scrap of information that could help us out in the near future: names and addresses, preferences and fears. Anything that will lead to more arrests.

But then, the big one is right here. Marie Rosenthal—the person we've been tasked with finding—is sitting across from me, taking in the activity like a mom on the edge of a playground. And in the face of this woman, who's evaded capture for years while crisscrossing the country—ducking highway patrols, moving refugees, and promoting an unconstitutional lifestyle—I find I can't do much of anything, except wait for her to tell me what comes next.

"Well," she says. "Are you just going to watch?"

"Oh," I say. "I don't..."

Pepper yawns. She uncurls herself from the arm of the couch.

"Hey, narc," she says, "need someone to tie with?"

"Technically, narcotics is a different unit—"

But she isn't listening. She tosses her shirt in a corner—along with her jeans and socks—and plops herself down in front of us.

"Do you know a single column?"

"Uh..."

Marie pulls a tightly coiled hank of rope from her bag, slides a finger through a loop, and snaps her wrist. The rope unspools from itself, pouring out of her hand like blackstrap molasses from a jug.

"You brought rope, right?" she says.

My zipper is the loudest thing in the room. My bundle of clothesline sits alone at the bottom of the empty bag.

"Christ on a stick..." says Pepper.

The shrink wrap won't come off. The stupid plastic is heat-molded around my shitty rope and my fingernails are too short to get enough traction to break the seal. The sweat on my hands makes it worse, and these two people I've just met are sitting there staring at me, while I pick at the thing like a pigeon going after bread crumbs.

I bite a hole in it. Finally the bundle breaks open in my hands and falls to the floor like a pile of sticks.

Marie picks up the clump and straightens it out—with her eyes closed. She draws the rope through her hands, an inch at a time. At certain points, her eyebrows pop up. Then she rolls a section of rope in her fingers till she's satisfied before moving on, like a violinist twisting a peg to tune a string. Eventually the stiff rope is as neat as it's going to get. Marie holds the halfway point in one hand, and cuts there with a pair of safety shears. She wiggles them in front of my face.

"Never, ever," she says, "tie without something you can use to safely cut the rope. That means an implement that won't break skin. Ordinary scissors ain't it. And for God's sake, don't even try to use a knife."

One half of the rope she keeps for herself. The other is for me.

"Grab the ends," she says, "and tie an overhand knot in each. It'll make them easier to find."

She shows me how to find the bight—the midway point—and how to pull the doubled-over rope through my hands.

"A column is anything you wrap rope around," she says. "A wrist, a leg, a torso. Even a fence post."

She sends the bight three times around Pepper's right wrist—a column. In her hands, the rope moves like a snake climbing up a branch.

"Send the bight under the wraps, then make an overhand knot with it and the running ends—these things." She waggles the rest of the rope, leading down to the knots.

Marie twitches, and suddenly there's a knot, securing a cuff around Pepper's wrist. Between the knot and Marie's closed fist, the running lines are taut.

"Remember to keep the tension," she says. "It helps the tie, and it makes a better experience for you and your bottom."

She undoes the cuff, and passes me the rope.

"You try."

I find the bight. I lay down the wraps. I pass the bight through, and form the loop. I pull. My work slides off Pepper's wrist and unravels to the floor. Marie smiles.

"Find the bight again," she says.

After a few reps, my lumpy cuff stays put. Eventually my wraps roughly line up with one another. I've learned a single-column tie.

It takes me a second to register what I'm feeling—or, rather, what I'm not feeling. The tension in my jaw is gone. My shoulders hang loose. My stomach is soft, and at some point my eye must have stopped twitching.

It's *real*. This thing that I've obsessed about for two decades actually happens, and I'm here with the people who practice it. Maybe the last ones. If I'm crazy—for liking this, for wanting this—at least I'm not alone.

The word comes to me. I'm happy. I catch most of the smile before it reaches my face.

Pepper lets me try the same tie on her ankle and thigh before she has to go to the bathroom. Verity has forgotten me completely—she and Jack are in their own world. He spins upside-down, hanging from a rope that grips his calf and thigh. She catches him, and with another line attaches his chest to the ring above. She pulls; he twists, and groans like he's on a massage table. This makes her smile.

"Wild," says Marie.

"Yeah," I say.

And eventually the evening winds down. Rope goes back into bags. Hugs are exchanged. Not with me.

I'm blindfolded led downstairs, and folded into the backseat of the Subaru. We twist and turn for an hour through the quieter streets of Massachusetts after midnight. Eventually I'm dropped off at the back entrance to the movie theater.

I watch my hosts drive away, then walk home along the Emerald Necklace, scattering frogs and rabbits that hide in the grass.

The Wall Street Journal / "'Why Would I Need Lipstick?': The Economic Impact of the 29th Amendment" / 2026

But perhaps most astounding has been the devastation wrought on the domestic luxury market. See if you can spot a pattern:

- 27% of the high-end women's fashion brands in business in late 2023 have declared bankruptcy since the Amendment's passing. Moreover, cosmetics sales are down across the board—even Sephora was infamously forced to shutter nearly half of its retail locations simply to keep afloat.

- Demand for gold watches and cologne has allegedly evaporated, while sellers of yachts and imported Italian sports cars are in serious trouble.

- Companies specializing in tooth whitening, liposuction, and hair replacement/removal, as well as plastic surgeons offering breast enhancement/reduction find it increasingly difficult to keep the lights on.

With no need to impress, Americans seem less willing to spend big bucks on appearances.

On the other hand, certain sectors of the economy have seen a positive boom. A surge in demand for athleisure has spawned a revolution in the design of sweatshirts, lounge pants, and wool socks—if it's *hygge*, you can expect to see Americans stomping each other's teeth out over it this coming Black Friday. Subscriptions to video streaming services also continue to rise, even in the face of significant price hikes [. . .]

Pepper / United States Air Force Academy / 2025

I've read the book cover to cover, though I've never actually checked it out of the library. An overview of the structure and function of the shogunate in medieval and early modern Japan, with the usual emphasis on military topics. One chapter, dedicated to the rise of centralized policing during the Edo period, has a section exploring the methods used to capture and punish criminals. It's crazy how many non-lethal options the officers had for grabbing suspects and keeping them still. Three of them—a group of pole weapons called the *torimono sandōgu*—were little more than oddly shaped metal heads fixed on long wooden poles, designed to snag on the elaborate clothes of the day, or trip people up and pin them down, all from a safe distance.

There's also a brief paragraph—with accompanying illustrations—describing a technique called *hojōjutsu*.

For whatever reason, metal restraints didn't really catch on in Japan for much of its history. Instead, police units restrained subjects with a particular thin sort of rope, carried in a bundle in the sleeve until ready for use. Generally, the various forms didn't end with a knot. Instead, a retainer would keep pressure on the rope by pulling at the running end as the prisoner was led to trial. This, combined with the deliberate placement of the ropes over painful and potentially dangerous pressure points like the throat and upper arms, was enough to discourage escape attempts.

The section features a few woodblock prints from the period, and a handful of more recent diagrams and illustrations, each showing a different completed form. In the old prints, men and women in rope are led through the streets or forced to kneel in front of panels of magistrates. The looks on their faces range from defiance to despair. The ties themselves are beautiful.

Weird thing to say about a method of torture, but it's the truth. The ropes form symmetrical patterns on the prisoners' bodies: diamonds, triangles, and hexagons that intersect with the angles of their bent elbows and shoulders. It's all so blatantly non-useful. No matter how skilled a practitioner was, it'd take precious minutes to tie someone up in such a pretty way. Faced with one of the most dangerous situations out there—bringing in a potentially violent criminal—they decided to focus on aesthetics. They put people on display, publicly, like pieces of art. Then there's the rope itself. Thin, and made of tough fibers. It would have bitten into any exposed skin. . . .

There's a knock on the shelf at the far end of the aisle. Like it's a door. Tom Mahelona leans with his elbow on one of the black metal shelves.

"Whatcha readin'?"

I've been given to understand that Tom counts as "handsome." His face is symmetrical, his eyes bright. A cadet's uniform sits well on his body. Someone else might call him charming. Right now he's standing in front of the calculus section.

"A book," I say, reaching around him to grab another.

He laughs. Like the fact that I'm trying to disengage is funny.

"So, uh, listen . . ." he says.

As if I have an option. His shoulders are as wide as the aisle, and he's blocking the way back to my carrel.

"The Ring Dance is coming up, and I was wondering . . . if you're not going with anyone else—"

"I'm not," I say.

He perks up like a plant in fresh rainwater—like I run through him, giving him a reason to stand up straight.

"Great!" he says. "I mean, cool."

Cool. A third-year cadet in the United States Air Force—an officer-in-training—and he says *cool*. I thought people who made it this far would be serious. But there's no escaping dullness.

He waves his hands in the air between the two of us.

"Does that mean you'd want to—"

"I'm not going with anyone," I say.

"I'm sorry?" he says. I think I accidentally cut the power to his brain.

"It's ridiculous," I say. "I came here to learn how to fly hypersonic killing machines. To become a warrior. And now I'm supposed to wear a dress? Take a bunch of selfies?"

Tom scratches his head.

"Most people just think it's fun," he says.

"I'm not most people," I say. "I'm staying till they bring out the food. Then I'm loading up a plate and heading back to my room to study. Excuse me." I squeeze past him, books between us.

"Hey, hold on," says Tom. He grabs my upper arm in his big hand.

I don't respond well to people suddenly touching me.

The whole thing takes two seconds. It isn't planned—there's no time to think—but I feel my skin get cold, and then I'm moving.

All of a sudden, Tom's on the ground, clutching his dick through his pants.

"Oh my God! Tom, I'm so sorry, I don't—"

He sucks in a big, ragged breath. "*Cunt,*" he says, through a clenched jaw.

He writhes on his side, curled around himself and hissing through his teeth. I pick up my books and walk out of the library.

Back in my room, I dump everything on the bed and sit at my desk. My laptop is still open to the page I was trying to get away from. It's the PRTNR registration form. The one that'll be used to pair me up with someone when I get back to civilian life. The one that's due at midnight. It's all filled out: Social Security number; dietary restrictions (none); favorite films and TV shows. Every box but one.

The dropdown menu for "Orientation" lists *Heterosexual*, *Bisexual*, and *Homosexual* as options. There is no *Other*, no fill-in-the blank. No way to list myself as asexual.

Be optimistic. There's still Test Pilot School. Or maybe I'll get deployed. Maybe they'll shuttle me off to a base somewhere in the Middle East, where I can run bombing missions and wait till this whole thing blows over. Or I could just delete everything on the form. Let the deadline pass. See what happens.

That'd be a laugh. Some horny incel on Capitol Hill, grinding his teeth because he's short one set of survey questions. Why, the very thought of my unregistered, under-utilized pussy wandering freely about in the world without some limp dick crammed up inside it—the poor boy would lose his mind.

I'm clearing off my bed when I notice it—the book on feudal Japan. The one I'm not supposed to check out because it has content that, with the recent passage of the Amendment and the laws that have tagged along with it, has become highly suspicious. I must have grabbed it with everything else.

Panic. There's got to be a way to get it back before anyone notices—but no. It got scanned at the front desk with everything else. It's on my record now that I checked out this book, with those pictures in it. Forever.

I'm being silly. It isn't likely anyone's ever going to know. Nobody should care. And even if they did, it's one mistake in an otherwise spotless checkout history. I have plausible deniability. The book has tons of other useful information in it. I could have checked it out for any of that. Feudal cavalry tactics, Tokugawa-era political structure, it's all in there. Methods of execution for dissidents . . .

It's paranoid to think like this. It's one paragraph in a 400-page book, which is one book out of hundreds that I've checked out, not to mention whatever I add to that count next year. They'd have to know already that I'm thinking bad thoughts, and then sift through all the years of evidence to *find* the material, and then make the connection between me and it. There's so little reason for any of that to happen. It'd be crazy.

But then, it's hard to say nowadays that any one thing is too crazy to happen. Craziness, in and of itself, is no longer a reason to dismiss an idea out of hand. The Amendment got passed. The world changed. People went to trial and were convicted on flimsier evidence than this. Others just disappeared. And now the school network has irreversibly logged a connection between me and a book containing suspicious material. And there's not a thing I can do about it.

I pick an orientation at random and click *Submit*. Then I lie back, crack the book open to the pictures I can't stop thinking about, and study.

Sean / Boston, MA / 2019

We sit in rows. Black cap; black shirt; black pants with a blue stripe down the side; black gun in a black holster; white gloves. BU red all around us—stadium seating, mostly empty.

The call—*Attention*—brings us to our feet. The Commissioner—a thin man with expressionless eyes—reads us through the oath of office. We raise our right hands.

We solemnly swear to support and defend the Constitutions of the United States of America and the Commonwealth of Massachusetts. We agree to obey all department rules and regulations with integrity and to the best of our ability; to faithfully and impartially discharge and perform all the duties incumbent upon us as police officers of the Commonwealth. We form our right hands into fists and snap them to our thighs.

We're finally in. We're finally safe.

In these clothes, we are no longer former school bullies and victims; perverts of every stripe; cheaters, nags, dumpers and dumped; abused altar boys; dropouts, workaholics, alcoholics, prudes; distant or controlling parents; dull party guests; lardasses or beanpoles or dykes or fags. We are no longer merely human.

We are not our anger; our anger belongs to us. What we do, we do in service. Whoever we cuff, whoever we shoot, whoever we track down and take away in the night—we defend the body of the Commonwealth.

We are justified. We are sanctified. We wear the shield.

Marie / Boston, MA–Chicago, IL / 2024

When Simon goes missing, I send Susan a text to check in on them.

Three days later, when they haven't replied, I send another.

The next week I write to an email address I vaguely remember them mentioning, once, at the end of a panel on the intersection of kink and witchcraft. I'm in the living room, picking piles off the couch, when the phone buzzes on the kitchen counter. I trip over my boots and pick it up.

It's a push notification. The pizza I ordered is downstairs.

I call them. I call them again. I put the phone down, walk to the M Street beach, and throw a discarded brick in the water. I rush home and up the steps and dial again.

I'm on the floor, breathing in and out on a four-count, when I get the reply I've been waiting for.

Please stop, they text. *I can't talk to you anymore. I'm sorry*.

My heart stops pounding. They still have their phone. They're okay, for now. Assuming that's actually them texting me back, they're okay.

I take a bite of the pizza, then throw the rest in the garbage.

In Chicago, Ray agrees to put me up at his place for a few days, in spite of everything that's going on. He doesn't say so, but he's taking a risk. I'm grateful.

The living room overlooks Millennium Park. Down below, school groups in matching polo shirts walk around the Bean, and tourists take pictures of their upturned faces reflected in its surface. A red kielbasa sizzles in a black cast iron pan, while Ray sips white wine and dices onions. Benny Goodman plays over speakers hidden somewhere in the ceiling. I run my finger around the edge of my glass.

"Have you heard anything from Susan?" I say from the couch.

Ray pauses, unscrews the bottle, and tops himself off. He takes a gulp that brings the level of wine right back to where it was a moment ago.

"No," he says, picking up the knife. "They're not talking to anybody. No one's seen them in days."

He gets back into his rhythm. The blade knocks softly against the wooden cutting board. Far below, Lake Michigan washes up over the embankment.

In the Museum of Contemporary Art, a sculpture made entirely of interwoven strands of yarn stretches up from the ground floor through the middle of a spiral staircase, to a hook embedded in the distant ceiling. I wonder if I know the artist.

A scenic footpath crosses over the Chicago River by way of a metal bridge. On the other side of the big steel struts, cars whizz by over clanking metal grates. A dividing line cuts across the middle of the bridge; the whole thing can snap in half like a chocolate bar to allow boats in and out. I place my hand over a fist-sized rivet, and think about industry, bootleggers, and slaughterhouses.

On Navy Pier, I watch the Ferris wheel go around, and eat a hot dog with a pickle in it. A pair of security guards walks by, en route to the arcade. I lower the visor of the White Sox hat I bought from a man with a pushcart full of tchotchkes.

Susan lives in Wicker Park. They never told me that. I found out for myself.

At night, Ray and I tie because that's what we would have done under normal circumstances. We think, magically, that the rope will restore the normalcy. It doesn't. Ray takes me through a suspension sequence he and his partner have been working on—a complicated series of positions, held one after the other while the blood rushes to my head. Upside down, surrounded by his boxy, modernist furniture, I stare out the window at a pair of lit-up skyscrapers.

I run into Susan before I mean to. Their place is on the corner of Leavitt and Pierce, but they're walking out of a coffee shop on Milwaukee Ave when they see me waiting at a red light.

They've changed so much in the time we've known each other. Their brown hair has grown out, in a more manageable cut. They're a parent now, to the most adorable six-year-old boy I've ever met. They're making mortgage payments. But they still rock that same leather jacket.

I'm expecting surprise, almost certainly. Maybe fear and sadness, too, around everything that's happened. I'm ready for anything . . . except the anger that pulls their beautiful face into a scowl.

And now I recognize what I've done here. Susan is more than a person I've tied with a handful of times over the years. They have a life and existence independent of me, which they likely value very much. And my being here has put those things at risk. After they told me they didn't want to be contacted. They made their answer clear, and I ignored it. Because I thought I knew better.

When the light turns green, I hang left to go back to Ray's and grab my bag.

Carl / Boston, MA / 2024

"I'm transferring to the Intimacy Allocation Unit," says Sean.

Without even looking at me, he says it. Then he squirts mustard on his hot dog and takes a bite, like it's no big deal.

"What, perv patrol?"

He catches a falling string of sauerkraut and puts it back on top of the pile in his hand.

"Yeah," he says.

"Here ya go, buddy," says the hot dog guy. It's to get my attention, though—no smile, and he's holding my Italian sausage out in one hand. He isn't really my buddy.

I pay the man and catch up with Sean, who's already walking toward the courthouse. It was nice in the shade between the Park Street T entrances. Now we're out in the sun. A wrinkly, toothless addict yells at her boyfriend, who's looking at anything but her with an ugly, flat face. The bums sitting on the wall—the old ones with their telescoping canes, and the young ones with tattoos and sweat suits—laugh at them as she hobbles around, sweeping the air with her skinny arms and trailing a dirty pink blanket from her shoulders. One flip-flop is gone, and she bobs up and down in front of the guy, who is starting to frown. She sounds like she's about to cry.

Sean scoots around them, taking another bite.

"This is bullshit, you know that," I say.

"I don't think so," he says.

"The IAU is for weirdos!"

A German tourist, blocking the intersection, catches me in the eye with the corner of his big, folded out map. He and his wife try to apologize—*Ich bitte Sie!*—while I wave them off and smack the button for the Walk signal.

"Since when do you care who's fucking who?"

He tosses a last bite of hot dog in the garbage, then stops for a second, looking through the fence at the graveyard. He stands there, arms crossed behind his back, with a folder full of documents in one hand.

Always looks like he's posing for a portrait. Like he thinks the whole world is watching him, all the time. We're not. We've got other things to do. Can't be devoting all of our attention to one selfish pissant—especially when you never know what he's thinking of pulling next.

Things are finally where we wanted them to be. We're detectives. Not partners, sure, but after years of school, and the Academy, and working our separate beats, we're on the same unit, working cases together. Like we always wanted. Like we planned. And now, when it's all finally good, he wants to screw it up.

I should feel betrayed. But I'm annoyed. Like I've been waiting for this to happen.

In the graveyard, a squirrel sits on one of the headstones, tearing into a leftover chicken wing.

"Whom," he says.

"What?"

"Who's fucking whom. The second one's an object."

I could push him into traffic. One clean shove, and all of my problems would be over. They'd never convict me.

My eye's already stinging when a big gust of wind blows a cloud of winter sand down Boylston Street and into my face. A grain of rock salt flies straight into the eye that got a free LASIK treatment from the tourist and his map. Water wells up in the corners, spilling onto my cheek. I'm supposed to take the stand in an hour. I'm gonna look like an asshole.

"I've been reading up on the theory behind the Amendment," he says. "That guy Cunningham, and the rest. I've decided it's important work. It'll help people."

"You already do important work," I say, jogging up the steps next to the escalators that have never worked. "Real work. You already help people. I don't understand this."

"Well, Carl," he says, passing through the metal detector, "maybe you don't need to understand everything."

Should've written a memo, if that's all he has to say.

The courtroom is mostly empty. Connolly, the guy we're here to testify against, sits next to his attorney—that asshole Donovan. The handcuffs are like tinfoil around the defendant's wrists. He's a boulder in a suit. When we open the door, he turns his head like a tank turret to look at us. His face becomes even more scrunched up than it already was. Sean ignores the man. I salute him with two fingers at my temple. We take seats on the prosecutor's side, toward the back.

The wooden bench hurts my ass. The guy in front of me has a mole on his neck the size and shape of a chewed piece of gum. How does he stand it? Just a quick snip with a pair of scissors, he'd feel so much better.... Sean is called up to testify.

He talks like a robot: Yes, we were at the Dunkin' Donuts in question on Thursday the 25th. Yes, Mr. Connolly was there. We observed Mr. Connolly arguing with the cashier over the staleness of a low-fat blueberry muffin. After several minutes, we observed Mr. Connolly climb over the countertop and hold the young man's ear under the milk steamer and crank the nozzle....

It doesn't make sense. Sean's a homicide detective. That's his *dream*. We've been planning this since we were little kids. He's never cared what people do with their own lives. When I came out to him, in senior year, all he said was *So?* So clearly that kind of thing isn't a big deal to him. And now, all of a sudden, he wants to—

The judge coughs loudly in my direction. He, Sean, and everyone else are staring at me. The prosecutor speaks quietly.

"I call Detective Nguyen to the stand," she says.

I sit down in the box and take the oath. The prosecutor asks her questions, and I confirm Sean's account of what happened. Then Donovan begins his cross-examination.

"And you claim, Mr. Nguyen, that you see the man in question in this courtroom today?"

"Yes," I say. Squinting, I point to Connolly. "He's right over there."

Donovan grins.

"You sure about that, Carl?"

He turns to the jury, and winks. It gets a weak laugh. Prick.

Sean always takes the seat next to the aisle. After the sentencing, before he has a chance to get up, I shove past him to get the hell out of here.

"Wait," he says.

He's turned around, one arm hooked over the back of the bench, looking at me.

"I'm sorry I snapped," he says. "Look . . . there are lots of open slots. People aren't exactly gunning for this job."

"No kidding."

"What I mean is . . . well, you could come, too. We could partner up. If you want."

I leave without answering, pick up my gun, and head for the subway.

On the Orange Line platform at Downtown Crossing, a Black guy in black and purple leather plays Prince's "Batdance." The train screams its way into the station, and I watch my reflection in the flashing grimy windows. The crowd boards. We clatter away into the tunnel.

The IAU. An entire police unit dedicated to making sure losers get laid. This is what your tax dollars are funding, folks: forcing single people into the dank bedrooms of our city's mouth-breathers at gunpoint. Never mind that people are getting away with murder across the nation as conviction rates drop. *This* is what our brave officers of the law ought to be doing with their limited time. Nothing says "protect and serve" like throwing people in jail for fucking the wrong way.

And Sean wants in on it. It's not just some passing idea: he doesn't seem to get those. Whatever his faults, when Sean makes a decision, he follows through on it. Probably has the paperwork signed in triplicate already. So it's a done deal. Sean is going over to the kooks. Using his brainpower to track down Boston's swingers, adulterers, and pain junkies. It's absurd. And if I want to be his partner, I have to buy into it, too.

The next day, I stop by Janine's desk.

"I'd like to request a transfer," I say.

Verity / Atlanta, GA / 2020

"Like, *Boston* Boston?" says Aliyah.

She bounces up the stadium stairs like a goat climbing a mountainside, yoga pants and matching top dry and free of wrinkles. I haul myself up behind her, dripping sweat on the concrete. My thighs chafe.

"It's where... the jobs are," I say, sucking muggy air through my mouth. "Not much... biotech... in Atlanta."

We finish the set and take a water break near the bottom. Aliyah sits cross-legged on the bench, back straight, head up. I peel my t-shirt off my stomach. It immediately sticks to my lower back.

"In my U.S. history class in high school, Boston had the first couple of chapters pretty much to itself," says Aliyah. "The Pilgrims, and the Revolution, and everything. Then nothing till the seventies, when they took that picture of the White guy trying to stab a Black guy with an American flag."

"It was an anti-busing protest," I say. "White folks weren't happy with the state putting Black kids in their neighborhood schools, and sending their own kids to Black neighborhoods."

Aliyah takes a deep breath, and squeezes her knees with her hands. Color drains from her fingertips where they press into black fabric. I realize that statements of fact aren't helping.

"But that was a long time ago," I say.

On the field below us, the football team does football stuff. Kids in plastic armor sprint and shuffle along the white chalk lines in time with a coach's whistle. An enormous boy with a heavy, swinging gut launches himself at one of those padded metal racks, slams into it, and shoves it down the field with tiny, fluttering steps of his white-cleated feet. Frowning men with stopwatches and clipboards stand off to the side, tracking everything.

Aliyah's eyes are pointed down at the bench in front of her. She picks at her shoelaces with her perfect fingernails.

"If it's a money thing, you could stay with me," she says. "I don't mind. Or if not me, I'm sure someone in the polycule would—"

"It's not a money thing," I say.

I've got my breath back, and the words come out sharp. She's hurt. It hurts to say. I didn't want to talk about me leaving tonight. I'd hoped we wouldn't. I just wanted to spend some of this last bit of normal time I have left with her. Before I pack up all my stuff and ship it north. Before I sign the lease on a new place. A few more simple moments while our interactions can still just be about enjoying each other's company, before those last couple weeks when every word and look will become part of an extended goodbye, whether we like it or not.

I hate goodbyes.

I should have known Aliyah would get ours started as soon as she found out. That she wouldn't understand the importance of pretending, just for a little while, that everything was normal. Of course not—she's so direct. Always poking at the difficult things, starting conversations that are better left un-had. The community knows her as the "clear communicator." And now she's forcing me to tell it like it is. To break her heart and mine.

"This is just what's next for me," I say.

She sniffs, and pushes her fists into her eyes, one at a time. The tears come off on the back of her hand, and somehow her makeup is unsmudged. She puts on makeup to work out.

"I'm gonna miss you," she says.

I scoot closer to her, and she leans her head on my damp shoulder. Below us, the team packs it in for the night, pulling off helmets and tossing footballs into big mesh bags. With the sun going down, we have the bleachers to ourselves.

"I've been at this school for ten years, and in this city my whole life," I say. "Never once have I gone to a game."

"You trying to see one before you leave?" says Aliyah.

"I would literally rather die."

Lifting her head, Aliyah stares at me with those big, shiny eyes . . . those irises like wet earth flecked with gold. Then she closes them and leans in toward my mouth.

I panic. Someone could see—they'll find out—they'll know . . . but it's just us and the mosquitoes here in the stands. Heart thudding from dumped adrenaline, I cup my hand around the back of her neck and press my lips to hers. In my free hand, I wrap up the tiny wrists I've cinched together so many times before, pulling her to me for a while.

Jack / Boston, MA / 2012

Dominic comes in my mouth, his big hands squeezing the sides of my head while his flat stomach clenches up. I think we're in Sandra's little sister's bedroom, and I don't want to spit into her wastebasket full of crumpled Hello Kitty notebook pages. Instead, I use the toilet in the half-bath down the hall, and rinse with a swig of Listerine. Not urgently or anything—just feels like the smart thing to do. A precaution.

When I get back, he's buttoning up his pants. He spends a second fixing his hair in the mirror before he notices me. He looks sweaty.

"Hey," he says, sliding past me out the door. "So, uh. Thanks."

Then he grins, and after a second gives me a double thumbs-up. He's down the stairs before I can say *You're welcome*. I give him a few minutes before heading back to the party.

For the rest of the night, he laughs a little too loudly whenever we're in the same room together, his eyes flicking over to check on me between shots. In the living room, somebody's turned the lights off and people are dancing, school blazers tossed on the couch. Alison has Teddy's tie wrapped around her forehead. She leans on my shoulder with a bottle of Malibu Strawberry in her hand.

"Where were you earlier?" she says.

Dominic sits in the armchair with Sandra on his lap. He teases her about her new haircut. She laughs really hard.

"Bathroom," I say.

On the way home, Alison pukes the rum and half a Domino's pizza into the gutter. I walk her around the neighborhood till she's sober enough to get into her parents' house without crashing through the screen door. Then I go home, hang up my uniform, and crawl into bed.

I lie there, not sleeping.

It isn't the fire that makes Hell scary. It's time. An eternity of it. A day, and another day, and another day. Forever. It's the fact that it's permanent—that I could do something wrong and die before confessing, and never be able to fix it.

If God is all-powerful, then He writes the cosmic dictionary. He defines what it means to be a "loving" God. He decides what is "good," and what constitutes a "sin." Because He wants to. And He can change His mind whenever He likes, with or without telling us—and it would or wouldn't be "wrong," depending on whether He'd made it so.

He can rewrite history in a moment. Maybe He just did. And He can hold you accountable for the sins newly added to your record, which were not there in a timeline that no longer exists and never did exist, if it pleases Him a while.

This isn't the catechism. This is me, making anxious, logical deductions. If God is all-powerful *and* all-loving, then "love" somehow also has to include Rwanda, and Hurricane Katrina, and being used by people you like.

He is the Master of physics, and everything else. And I can't *prove*, logically, that He isn't there. That He isn't mad at me. And that I won't suffer eternally, in Hell or by His side.

If I didn't like it, what the fuck would I do about it?

The sun comes up. My sheets are damp with sweat. I shower, throw on clothes, and walk the mile to St. Bernardine's by myself.

Mom stopped going to Mass after the *Globe* articles came out, and the girls took the opportunity to beg off Church for good. Dad kept up the Christmas and Easter visits for a bit, but now even he's at home Sunday mornings, eating oatmeal and watching *Meet the Press*. When I get back, we'll switch over to channel thirty-eight and watch *The Phantom Gourmet* together. We'll make plans to visit the restaurants that get a "Gourmet Greatness" or higher.

At the door, I dip my fingers in the holy water, and make the sign of the cross before walking in. It's still a few minutes before the service starts. People yawn and take off their jackets, stuffing them in the pew corners. I take a seat near the back, just off the middle aisle. Right in Jesus's line of sight. I do the full genuflection that always pissed Dad off because it took too long: knee on the ground, head bowed, taking time to touch the forehead, the heart, both shoulders. Somebody's kneeler crashes into the marble floor with a boom that echoes from the narthex to the sacristy. I lower mine gently and say an Our Father before sliding up onto the bench.

There's a wheezing in the aisle. A giant old man lumbers up toward the altar, stiff-legged like an elephant. Huge black orthopedic shoes and white compression socks squeeze a pair of feet swollen big as footballs. With hands like oak branches, he grips two standard-issue aluminum canes, the push-button extenders stretched out to their greatest possible length. He moves by picking up one limb at a time and pushing it forward—first a corduroyed leg, then an arm wrapped in a gargantuan sweater sleeve, and so on.

I'm reminded—I can't help it—of the Landstriders. Those stick-legged Jim Henson puppets from *The Dark Crystal*. With the organ warming up behind us, and his big body passing through the shafts of rainbow light that fall from the stained-glass windows, he's like a holy monster out of Revelation. One of the heavenly host, with a strange name ending in -im, or -el.

The hymn picks up, and the congregation stands. A woman with her roots showing offers the first reading—the collapse of the walls of Jericho. She stops before the part where Joshua orders the execution of every man, woman, and child in the city. The cantor—a balloon-shaped man being strangled by his own bow tie—raises a hand, and we join him in the responsorial psalm. The Gospel reading involves Jesus transferring a demon from a man to a herd of pigs, who go crazy under the influence of possession and drown themselves in a lake.

The homily is a haze of boring, comfortable words, pouring out of the tinny wall-mounted speakers like smoke from a censer. I ignore the speech, and stare at the tabernacle.

Father Joe takes the bread and wine from that gold cabinet. He blesses it. He and the deacons line up at the heads of the aisles, and together, we rise. The rows at the front shuffle their way toward the middle of the church, and walk up to the front, hands folded, to receive Communion.

It is bad to take Communion while there is a mortal sin on your soul. I'm supposed to sit here and wait, while the rest of the congregation goes through the motions of the sacrament. I'm meant to go to Reconciliation this afternoon and wait in line with the other sinners to tell the priest about all the dirty things I did since the last time we sat in the box together. *Forgive me, Father, for I have given head to a closeted linebacker.* I've done the ritual many times.

The row in front of mine stands and files out toward the front of the church. I get up, genuflect, and fall in line.

My palms are wet, and my knees shake. My lower back is burning.

This is holy ground, says the choir.

We're standing on holy ground. . . .

As a body, we surge forward, toward the Eucharist. Toward the man on the cross who is also a god, whose pain saves us. As part of that body, I take one step, and then another.

For the LORD is present,
And where He is is holy. . . .

The deacon holds up the Host. "The Body of Christ," he says.

"Amen," I say.

I make a little bed of my hands, and he places the wafer there. I breathe, open my mouth, and take the Body of Christ in the back of my throat.

I swallow.

Pepper / Edwards Air Force Base, Kern County, CA–Cambridge, MA / 2027

My flight commander delivers the letter to me personally. Hat in hand. We sit at my kitchen table while I read it, and my Cheerios get soggy.

"It isn't fair," she says, and for a half-second the woman flashes through a crack in the officer's face, surprising both of us.

"Pepper . . . I'm sorry—"

"It's fine," I say.

"What?"

"Really," I say. "I'll be fine. Thank you for letting me know."

At her prompting, we salute on my doorstep. Her in uniform. Me in my day-off jeans. Civilian clothes.

"For what it's worth," she says, "the app works pretty well. You'll get matched with someone nice."

I reread the letter once, then sit at the counter for the rest of the afternoon, stirring the inedible mush in my bowl. An honorable discharge. A bit of a pension, at my age. It's more than a lot of people get. And all I'm required to do in return is go home, and enter the matching pool. Let the app find me someone whose interests and temperament line up with mine, and make a life with him. And fuck him.

Micah is scheduled to go up today. He officially reports in as "sick." No one calls him on it. The rest of the squadron is standing out on the tarmac when I arrive to take his place for one last flight. They watch me take off.

This month's wildfire is a ring of orange on the green and brown patch of Angeles National Forest. A column of smoke rises up from the middle, leaning south with the wind. It mixes with the smog over the city, thickening it, turning it from ochre to dark brown. The San Fernando Valley looks like a bowl overflowing with beef broth.

I clear Long Beach, then bank right and fly out through the clear space between the islands. Sky above, and sea below. I'm surrounded by two shades of blue.

I apply back pressure and execute an aileron roll to the right, then again to the left. The two hemispheres flip around me. I slide up into the shoulder straps, then back down. Next is a barrel roll; flat scissors; wingover; yo-yo; pitchback. The AFB gets a readout of all the numbers. I report on the subjective things. Like the g-forces crushing my meat body into the seat.

I deal with them. I enjoy them. I'm lucky to be here to experience them.

The thing I'm flying is more robot than airplane. It flies better, sees farther, and shoots straighter than I ever could. It's better at math than I am. It could beat me in a game of chess. I have a sneaking suspicion it could fly itself if it wanted to. Which means I'm more valuable to the United States as a warm body than as a pilot.

The tightness in my chest rises up to my throat before I catch it. A single yelp escapes my mouth and is smothered by my mask.

No more. I swallow the rest of the feeling—fold myself around it—crush it down to the bottom of the can with all the other emotions. I stare at the dividing line of the horizon. Edwards gives me the clear for an Immelmann.

I pull back, and the ocean falls away beneath the rim of the canopy. My nose points straight out into space. With enough fuel, and the right kind of aircraft, I could just keep on going. Pierce the blue shell around the planet and rocket out, into the black. Into weightlessness...

I flip over and hang out for a minute in the topsy-turvy world where I'm free. Then I complete the maneuver and fly back to base.

I spend a few weeks in my Somerville apartment without furniture. My footsteps echo as I walk back and forth between the fridge and the blanket nest I've made in the living room.

One day, while I'm lying on the floor, tracing cracks in the baseboard, my phone lights up. I check the screen. I have a date.

When I get to the pizza place, my match is hunched over the candy crane machine, biting his lip in concentration. With small twitches of his wrist, Gary Benson moves the swinging metal claw one millimeter at a time. Taking advantage of the side windows, he leans around the corner to get a better view—his big, bearded head just barely fitting in the dusty space between the Ms. Pacman machine and the wall. Based on what he sees, Gary makes one last y-axis adjustment, makes the sign of the cross, and presses the red button in the middle of the joystick.

With the sound effect of a bomb falling out of the sky, the claw drops down, into the mountain of candy. The hooks nestle in among the colorful wrappers before clamping down, catching on something beneath the surface layer. The winch cranks; the wire tightens; and the claw rises back up toward the crane, a fun-size PayDay bar clenched in its grip.

"Damn," says Gary. His shoulders hunch as the candy *thunks* into the bin.

"Not what you were going for?" I say.

He jumps, and rubs the back of his neck.

"Yeah, I'm more of a chocolate guy," he says, grinning.

Gary is big. Not obese, but shaped like a barrel, or a bear. In a sweater and collared shirt, he is a plush purple mass. His short beard is well-kept. It looks soft.

We order a cheese pizza to split. While we're waiting, Gary offers me the PayDay bar.

"I'd rather eat mulch," I say.

He laughs, and I do, too. When the pizza arrives, we both reach for the marinated hot pepper in the middle of the pie. Gary hands it to me, and I cut it in half with a plastic knife.

"Your profile said you're in the Air Force," says Gary. He folds his slices in half and eats them one-handed.

"Was," I say.

"Why'd you leave?"

"I didn't," I say. "I mean, I didn't want to. Budget cuts. And, you know. The Amendment."

Gary puts his pizza down. His round face crumples. "That's awful," he says. "I'm sorry."

I wait for the *but* that's surely coming. The joke or cliché that'll bring the conversation back to a positive, surface-level discussion of our favorite movies and TV shows. It never comes. On the jukebox, Billy Joel sings about movin' up and movin' out, and Gary just sits there and allows my life to be the mess that it is right now.

There's one slice of pizza left on the pan. I pick it up, then put it back down.

"Do you want to go for a walk?" I say.

In the park down the street from the restaurant, we lie on the grass, and look at the handful of stars not drowned out by light pollution.

"I like to think of it as 'out,' instead of 'up,'" I say. "Like we're all walking sideways most of the time."

"You want a real trip?" says Gary. "Say that we're 'up,' and the sky is 'down.'"

I ponder it for a minute, and suddenly the universe reorients itself around the two of us. I'm on top of a world that has no bottom, about to tumble into the black. Instinctively I reach out to grab a handful of grass. I catch Gary's fingers instead. Thinking I did it on purpose, he shifts his big hand, wrapping it around mine. It's not the worst thing in the world.

It's a warm hand. It'd be sweaty if the weather were hot. But it's a cool night. Gary holds the pizza box with the leftover slice in his other hand as we walk. Cold by now, the pizza slides around the inside of the box and clunks against the cardboard whenever he gestures, which is often.

"Don't get me wrong, Kirk is fine," he says, "but Picard knows how to think. He doesn't just punch his way out when things go wrong. He has other options."

"I relate to Data," I say.

"How so?"

I shrug. "People are weird," I say. "They do things that don't make any sense. Most people aren't like Picard. They get angry or happy out of nowhere, and it makes them act crazy . . . I dunno. It's nice to watch someone like Data who also doesn't just 'get it.' To see him figure people out."

Gary nods like I offered him some sage bit of wisdom.

"You know I met Brent Spiner once?"

"What?!"

"Nicest guy in the world."

We walk down to Harvard, then back up again. When we get to my corner, it's past midnight.

"This was fun," says Gary.

"Yeah," I say, "it really was."

He offers me the pizza box. I take it, and he turns to cross the street. On the other side, he shouts back: "I'll text you!" He waves.

I wave back. Back at my place, I shove still-packed moving boxes to one side of the counter so I can put the pizza down. I scare up some tinfoil, and open the lid to grab the slice. It's nestled in the corner, next to the PayDay bar and a piece of mulch.

Law and Order: IAU / "Taking Out the Trash"

EXT. CITY STREET - DAY

Car horns BLARE and engines RUMBLE. Detectives Carmichael and Ibanez stand on the sidewalk while garbage man TONY ESPOSITO dumps metal cans full of trash into the waiting compactor of his truck. He wears a rumpled, stained coverall, sleeves rolled up to the elbow.

Carmichael pulls a notebook from his jacket pocket and clicks open a ballpoint pen.

>CARMICHAEL
>Have you noticed anything unusual about Mr. Bauerman in the last few months?

>ESPOSITO
>Hey, look, man, Nate can be a little weird, but he's a good guy, y'know? I don't wanna get him in trouble.

>IBANEZ
>Here's the deal, Tony--we think your buddy might be getting involved with some people who are gonna get him in really BIG trouble if we don't find him soon. Know what

I mean?

CARMICHAEL
Anything you can give us is only going to help him out.

ESPOSITO
Well . . . all right. We all went out to Sal's Place on New Year's, right? Like we always do. I saw Nate sort of grabbin' on our friend Carrey . . .

IBANEZ
(aside to Carmichael)
The wife's friend.

Esposito crouches to pick up the foot of a bed frame. Another GARBAGE MAN takes the head, and the two of them heave it into the compactor with a THUD.

ESPOSITO
Now, I don't get involved in anyone else's business, but they were getting, y'know, kind of hot and heavy, and I thought I should say something to him about it. But then Mitch comes in--that's Carrey's boyfriend--and he plants one on Nate, right there! And Carrey's just smiling the whole time like it's no big deal. At that point, I'm like: "I'm out."

IBANEZ
Looks like we know who we're talking to next.

CARMICHAEL
Do you know where we can find Mitch?

Esposito approaches the lever that controls the compactor.

ESPOSITO
Sure, he's the bouncer at Roundhouse, that new club downtown. I think he has a shift tonight. I can give you the address.

Esposito pulls down on the lever; the compactor WHINES and CRUSHES the bed frame.

FADE OUT.

Carl / Boston, MA / 2026

In my car, in front of the rearview mirror, I pull my face up and down. I make circles around my eyes. It all feels excellent and invigorating while I'm doing it. Then as soon as I let go, the fatigue rushes back. The neon sign on top of the bar shines down on this section of the parking lot, turning me pink.

Sean and I spent fourteen hours camped out in front of that house in West Roxbury, following a tip from a neighbor. Turns out the shipments of leather and rivets were for upholstery—the husband makes furniture on weekends, as a hobby.

A full day in a car that smelled like hash browns after our trip through the Dunkin' drive-through. Plus Sean getting all moody, the way he does when we're not following a verified lead or actively arresting someone. Said maybe ten words the whole day. And me, up till three-thirty the night before, doing paperwork.

I'm cop-tired. Firemen don't know this kind of exhausted. And definitely not the office critters, scarfing down burritos on the Common and tiptoeing around puddles in their loafers, all while complaining about the T. We *know* that the Red Line breaks down too often, and that there are too many stops on the Green Line. Who are you helping by pointing out the obvious? What's the point of talking if you're not actually going to *say* anything . . . ?

The EMTs might know what it's like. They smoke enough to make you think they're trying to burn something away. And they tell the sickest jokes. Dead babies and pitchforks and so on . . . how do you go on a date when you're this burnt out?

Does this even count as a date? Feels more like an interview for a job I don't really want. I got a helpful push notification this morning, reminding me that my assigned match and I had agreed to meet here at 8:30.

It's 8:25 now. I'm gonna have to go inside soon.

Everyone gets a few photo slots on their profile—they use your driver's license photo if you don't put in the effort to post something. Levi's photos are mostly of him at parties, his arms around other guys' shoulders, all of them holding colorful drinks in their hands and laughing at something hilarious off-camera. In one of the photos, he's got a flower woven into his hair. In another, it looks like he's wearing makeup.

I'm not sure what the app is thinking—I'm not really into femme guys, and I think I made that clear on the survey. I wouldn't call myself masc4masc or anything. I'm not a dick. But I like what I like, and Levi doesn't seem to be it. So much for advanced algorithms.

I want to go home, watch the Pats, and black out till my shift tomorrow, but the penalty for not even meeting a match is too steep. I don't want to end up paired with somebody else's reject.

The phone timer beeps. I haul my sweaty carcass out of the driver's seat, smooth out the polo shirt I keep in the trunk for emergencies, and walk inside.

Cigarette-hoarse townie voices shout from every corner of the bar, which is blue and black like the inside of the Aquarium—most of the light comes from a row of flat-screen TVs mounted around the perimeter. The hostess, a White woman in her forties with hair bigger than my head, has a bit of coke caught in the hair on her upper lip.

"Just meeting someone," I mouth over the noise, waving away her cheery offer of a menu. I scan the place for anyone close to my age.

He sits on a high stool at the other end of the room, elbows resting on the round table in front of him. Chin in the palms of his hands, he keeps his eyes fixed on one of the TVs over by the liquor shelf.

He's cute. I'll give him that. The outfit is less encouraging: a floral-print shirt, and what looks like a pair of capris, with white boat shoes, no socks. He's crossed his legs at the bare ankles, and hooked a foot over the metal rung so the other one dangles. Sure, they're nice ankles. But they have no business being out in public. I walk up to the table.

"Levi?" I say.

He looks up and smiles. And I forget to hold out my hand for a shake.

"Carl, right?" he says.

I sit, and he leans in toward my ear.

"Sorry about the noise," he says. "I didn't want to miss the game."

He tips his chin toward the screen he was looking at when I came in. The Patriots' wide receiver catches a high, arcing pass, and sprints toward the Dolphins' end zone. He runs straight into their cornerback and jackknifes around his massive shoulder. The poor kid's helmet flies off.

I look at Levi, then back at the TV. I slide my stool next to his, so we're shoulder to shoulder.

A waitress comes around to our table. I order a Budweiser. Levi asks for a Malbec, and settles for a Cabernet.

He holds what has to be the bar's only wine glass with his fingertips, sipping and grimacing at the action on the screen. Studebaker gets the handoff from Hardy and makes it all the way through the Dolphins' defensive line. Then he trips over his own shoelace and fumbles the ball. Edwards, Miami's new lineman, carries it forty yards.

"It isn't the same with Belichick gone," says Levi.

"You know, I was at the game where it happened."

"No way!"

"Full-blown cardiac arrest, and he didn't say a word. Just crossed his arms and frowned at everybody. The man died standing up."

"Fucking legend," says Levi.

We split a plate of pretzels. I'm reaching for the last one when Levi darts his hand under mine and snags it, along with the mustard. He shoves the whole thing in his mouth at once.

"Too flow," he says, cheeks full of dough. He sticks out his tongue, and I lean in like I'm going to eat the chewed-up pieces right out of his mouth. He backs off, laughing, almost choking.

Not even once does he bring up the weirdness of the situation—the matching system, and so on. How, in theory, we might be together for years, even though we've literally never met before tonight. He just sits next to me, and watches the game, and checks me out every so often. I catch him doing it. He turns away a little, then winks.

Ali pukes on his jersey and passes out from heatstroke. The game ends, and we pay our tab, splitting it down the middle. Outside, a light drizzle turns the sidewalks damp.

"I liked hanging out with you, Carl," says Levi, one thin hand up against the rain.

"Likewise," I say.

He's halfway to the bus stop before I shout out to him. "Levi! Do you want a ride home?"

Marie / Fort Dodge, IA / 2026

In the yellow and brown bathroom of a Love's Travel Stop north of Fort Dodge, I cut my hair with a pair of child's scissors. I wrap a few Ace bandages tight around my chest, bracing for back pain. Baggy jeans and a parka hide my waist. I tuck what's left of my hair under a baseball cap.

The man behind the counter is nose-deep in a *Deathlands* paperback. While his head's down, I cram buns and fat jalapeno-cheddar hot dogs into a foil sleeve. I slip out the front door without paying, the warm packet nestled into my stomach. Alone on the road, I eat methodically—six bites to each greasy link. I burn from my asshole to my nostrils.

On the drive through northern Iowa, I remember light and shadow mingling in the crevices of a blooming rust patch, on a lamppost by the cheap hotel in Austin; smoke drifting around neon signs in New York's last leather bar; wooden beams creaking in an abandoned warehouse, with spilled gasoline rippling on the surface of a puddle of rainwater. I remember someone slapping my face and whispering *I love you* . . . sweat beading on my upper lip . . . me saying back: *I love you more.*

I never learned Raiche's legal name. We had sex—awkwardly, once, at a con—and I have no idea what's written on his birth certificate. Which isn't to say that's his "real" name. "Raiche" is real enough. But there are no social media accounts under the name "Raiche." Not anymore. No emails, no whitepage listings. I never asked for a mailing address.

It's very likely that he's dead.

It could be worse—he might still be alive. In a room made of cinder blocks, somewhere, with somebody hitting him. Someone else in the corner, wearing pressed trousers, asking him why he's making such a fuss, considering he used to volunteer for this kind of treatment.

Maybe it's better. He could have been at a seminar in Germany or Japan. Gotten asylum. Or maybe he's still Stateside, but on his way out—hiding under a pile of coal, on a train heading north.

Maybe he's braver than that. Maybe he's a guide: a coyote, a conductor. Maybe he has a secret room full of blueprints and candid shots of key politicians, academics, and clergy. Maybe he's also in disguise, somewhere, wondering about me, and what I'm up to.

But he's probably dead.

Every so often, a section of gray sky will twist around on itself in a lazy little circle. Like God's got his finger in the clouds, and is trying to decide whether or not to make a tornado. Instead, the dome of the sky turns white, and snowflakes tumble down out of the air. They settle on the infinite rows of harvested corn stalks on either side of the highway, and on the black of the road.

The engine craps out an hour past nowhere. With the last of my momentum, I roll the car onto the shoulder. I rest my forehead on the steering wheel.

They don't tell you that driving hurts. That your back seizes up, and the vertebrae on your neck clamp down on each other, and when you finally do get out of the seat, you crackle like a bag of fresh potato chips. It'd be nice to give up. To lean the seat back and rest here, while the temperature drops and snowflakes land *phat, phat, phat* on the windshield. . . .

A rapping on the window clears a knuckle-sized hole in the buildup. The rest of the snow falls mostly in the car as I turn the window's hand-crank—never thought I'd see one of those again, but that's what you get when you hot-wire strangers' cars—and lower the window.

A state trooper looks down at me, hands on his knees.

"Hell of a night to get caught out here," he says, squinting against the wind. "Need a jump?"

My teeth show themselves.

"That'd be great," I say. "Thank you."

He crunches back to his cruiser, and I clean off the rearview mirror. He gathers up an armful of jumper cables from the trunk and shuts it with his elbow. On the way back, he pauses by my rear bumper. Balancing on one leg, he raises a boot and scrapes off the snow covering the license plate. He frowns. Straightening up, he returns to the window.

"Sir," he says, pointedly, "I'm gonna need to see a license and registration."

I stare at him, squeezing the wheel in my frozen fingers. He stares back. Then he hefts the cables into one arm and reaches for the radio clipped to his shoulder.

I grab the handle, throw my weight into it—hard—and catch him on his exposed temple with the cold metal edge of the door.

He crumples to the ground, arms and legs wrapped around the bundle of cables like a kid with a favorite blanket. He doesn't move.

Careful not to push any buttons, I unhook his radio and throw it into the corn. I do the same with his car keys and shoes. I walk ten paces into the corn before stopping, rethinking.

Snow already covers part of the man's face. His skin is turning frostbite-red in the wind.

Jalapeno cheddar sizzling in my chest, I heave the man an inch at a time back to the cruiser. My feet slip on the road as I shove him head-first into the back seat and shut the door behind him. His socks rest on the window. There are holes in the heels. I wait a second, just to confirm he's still breathing.

Then I turn, face the corn, and start running.

Sean / Boston, MA / 2030

Al's snub-nosed revolver dangles from a harness, hung over the back of an office chair. He sips a Diet Dr Pepper and tosses the last of our green Post-its at the wastebasket. It falls short, adding to the field of paper cabbages.

The carpet is full of pale, doughy crumbs from the pack of strawberry frosted Pop-Tarts we split. We sit for a minute, sucking jelly out of our teeth.

"Anything interesting happen lately?" says Al.

"I got invited. To a . . . party, I guess."

"Yeah?"

"I went. Verity Smith was there. And the kids from her apartment. And some others I've never seen."

Al is still leaning back. But he's not relaxed.

"And Rosenthal?"

The way he says it . . . there's a hunger there that he tries to hide. But I catch it. I think about the people I met the other night. About the warmth in the room, and the way Pepper grinned when I finally started to get the single-column tie. How she pulled on the cuff, and it stayed on. I think about how I tied someone up, for the first time in my life, and that it happened in a fancy condo. And how, so far, I'm still breathing.

"No sign of her," I say. "They drove me there . . . some kind of warehouse space. Could have been anywhere."

Al nods. There's a slight frown on his lips. "If you get another invite," he says, "go."

"An Answer to the Problem" / Posted to r/SexualEconomy by cnghm89 / 2020

"Sex Is Worth Dying For"

The incel believes, at some level, that he has been cut off from the body of humanity. Underlying this belief is the still more fundamental idea that a lack of sex, intimacy, and love *can* separate an individual from the whole in the first place.

In at least one sense, he's right.

In *The History of Sexuality, Vol. 1*, Michel Foucault identified the role that sex has played in our society since the deployment of sexuality began in earnest:

> The Faustian pact, whose temptation has been instilled in us by the deployment of sexuality, is now as follows: to exchange life in its entirety for sex itself, for the truth and the sovereignty of sex. **Sex is worth dying for** [...]
>
> By creating the imaginary element that is "sex," the deployment of sexuality established one of its most essential internal operating principles: the desire for sex—the desire to have it, to have access to it, to discover it, to liberate

it, to articulate it in discourse, to formulate it in truth. It constituted "sex" itself as something desirable.

In the context of our particular society, sex is everywhere. It permeates the social body, saturating the space between its individual members. The "element" of sex is the substrate in which contact with the Other, and immersion in the whole, becomes possible. To be without sex is to be without "truth," "liberat[ion]." Here, to go from day to day without access to sex is to lose the "life" we have already exchanged and get nothing in return. For us, sex is the connective tissue that holds the social body together. To lack it for any reason is to be cut off, atomized, alone.

"The logic of martyrdom"

A lack of sexual contact is not unique to the incel. History offers many examples of willing celibates in the monastics of the Middle Ages. Foucault himself devotes many pages to detailed descriptions of the devices and techniques used to prevent "precocious" expressions of sexuality in young people well into the twentieth century. And in our own time, self-identified asexuals baffle a cultural sensibility that views sex as both prime mover and ultimate *telos*: so much so that the writers of *House, M.D.* felt justified in penning a script in which an asexual man is "cured" of his affliction, much to the delight of his long-suffering wife.

But these examples must be looked at in context. The monks and nuns made their vows centuries before the widespread deployment of sexuality went into effect, in a time before the "imaginary element of sex" was made the be-all and end-all of human existence. The tweens stuck in Foucault's boarding schools were caught up in the middle of that deployment—unlike the monastics, their celibacy was imposed on them from without by surveillance, chastity belts, and cold water. Asexuals claim to feel little or none of Foucault's "desire for sex."

Unique among celibates, the incel *does* feel that desire, *is* subject to the deployment of sexuality, and feels as though his celibacy is forced on him by external pressures, even in the *absence of obvious technologies of oppression*. Unlike the schoolchild, the incel has no praefect to watch over and scold him.

However it happened, he finds himself lacking a resource he needs to survive: the "element" of sex, as fundamental to human existence (he's been taught) as water and air.

The incel intuits that his "self" cannot survive in isolation from the whole. And because sex is the glue that keeps our particular social body together, the lack of it presents the incel with a real existential crisis. Those unlucky enough to get pinned as the "owners' of that resource—the women who generate it, and the "alpha" men who hoard it for themselves—present a threat.

In his seminal 2003 essay "Necropolitics," Achille Mbembe provides insight into the phenomenon of suicide-bombing as a means of resistance in the face of oppression:

> In the logic of martyrdom, a new semiosis of killing emerges. [...] The besieged body becomes a piece of metal whose function is, through sacrifice, to bring eternal life into being. The body duplicates itself and, in death, literally and metaphorically escapes the state of siege and occupation.

A similar transformation occurs when the incel sets off on a shooting spree with the intention of dying, either by his own hand or a police officer's. His perceived "state of siege and occupation" is experienced in the body: heartache, frustrated lust, and loneliness all have their physical dimensions. By turning the source of his pain—the body—into a weapon, he accomplishes two goals. On the one hand, he regains his lost agency by striking back at what he would consider a class of oppressors, the privileged few who have boxed him out of social contact through their greed and pettiness. On the other hand, as a bonus, he destroys the troublesome mechanism that makes the experience of anguish possible in the first place—his body, his self [...]

Verity / Boston, MA / 2020

I push the button, and the centrifuge whirls on like a stubby helicopter, sorting out blood into its component parts. The others are shutting their laptops, putting on their coats, telling jokes. It's Friday—Laura said something about a bunch of them walking over to Central to check out that combination bar/arcade with the grilled cheeses. I go to the bathroom, pick a stall, and wait it out. I had to pee, anyway.

It's been quiet for a while when, without warning, the heavy wooden door squeaks open.

"Verity?" says Laura. "You in here?"

My fingers rest on the green, anti-germ coated handle. The faintest trickle of water creeps through the pipes and down the inside of the bowl. It's too awkward to say anything. But every second I don't say anything multiplies the awkwardness we'd both feel if she looked over at the stall now. Or now.

A sneaker turns on the tile. The door closes.

I wait a few minutes, then flush. Back in the lab, I turn off the centrifuge, and finish with the samples. I turn off the lights behind me as I leave the empty office and walk out into the cold.

Pitch black, and it's not even six-thirty yet. Wind blows a promised snowfall around the bridge between Kendall Square and MGH, whips the river below me into foamy waves, and tosses handfuls of icy chips off the handrails, the lampposts, into the blushing faces of people who didn't want to wait for the Red Line, which is broken again. I stop halfway across, and stand on one of the little half-circle balconies jutting out over the water. The wind goes under my collar and up my sleeves, touching skin, raising hair follicles, and sending blood rushing back to my middle.

In Atlanta, the sun beats down most of the year, and the wet air traps the heat like a lid on a pan, till the human biomass of the city melts and oozes freely through the doorways and out into the streets. No one's a separate person in Atlanta. Everyone drips into everyone else, feels everyone else's feelings.

Not here. Here a person can solidify, like an ice cube in her own little tray; spend half a year cocooned in a parka that shuts out the world; go through a work week without making eye contact.

I liked that, at first. But now I'm lonely. Not just for any contact—I'd be out at the bar with my coworkers if that would solve it. For months I've put off doing the thing that would solve it. Seeing the people I need to see. I wanted to be alone.

Downtown Boston is full of brick sidewalks. Crazy, crooked, ankle-snapping. Whole neighborhoods lined with bloody teeth. In the Park Street graveyard, beneath headstones capped with falling snow, the dust of old Puritans mixes with the soil, while across the way the windows of a Dunkin' fog up and drip. For a second the whole city is quiet, except for a cold wind trapped in the twisted streets.

I've passed the entrance to the School Street bar three times. I stall in the Walgreens, picking up bags of penny candy and putting them back down again while I wonder whether or not to walk back over to the door and step through it. I check in with my body, to see what it wants. As always, this is a mistake. My gut wants everything and nothing: a knot of people to dive into forever; a hut on a mountainside where I can wrap myself in a bearskin and never see another human again; the big bag of knock-off

Swedish Fish. The girl behind the cash register snaps her gum as I push through the revolving door, and wind up back on the street, facing the bar.

My phone buzzes: The Red Line is running again. I can turn around and be at Downtown Crossing in five minutes; back in Davis by nine; back home and in my pajamas by nine-thirty. A cozy evening, with no pretending. Without anyone to impress.

Instead, I pull open the bar door, take a nametag from the host, and walk over to a huddle of folks in leather jackets. My first Boston munch.

After the first munch, there's another in Cambridge, in a food court. And then a third across the river—also in a food court. There's one at a bar near North Station, and another in Salem. I go to all of them.

Am I the only one who worries that the waiters can hear us?

I hate the people who make it more obvious than it already is: the girl with the cat tail pinned to the back of her waistband; the woman in the floor-length leather trench coat, whose husband follows her with a bowed head; the guy wearing a t-shirt from a rope convention, on which is the silhouette of a bare-chested woman in a box tie. Because of them, people who are out of earshot and wouldn't otherwise notice our group turn to look at us. They whisper to each other. Sometimes they giggle. More often they just stare, and I panic inside. Just inside. When an obvious kinkster talks to me, I grit my teeth and smile. I shake their hand, and pretend nothing is wrong.

The Boston scene has no public face. Not like Chicago or Austin. There is no rope bombing; no studio; no "Shibari on the Common." There's no address to visit, and no phone number to call. I think I know why. Shame is in the air here, like salt off the Harbor. I'm not sure I've ever met more closed-off people. Even in New York they let their crazy hang out, if nothing else. Not so here. Boston keeps its feelings on the inside of a hard wall.

This suits me fine. In fact, I like it, and hate the scene's quirkier members all the more for being the rare cracks in a barrier I want to get behind.

It takes time. It's a matter of networking. When everything worth doing takes place in private homes, a certain amount of unspoken vetting is going to take place. So I load up my CharlieCard and ride the Red Line north and south, from Cambridge to Boston and back again. I take the Green Line out west, to the occasional event in Allston. I ruin the first pair of winter boots I've ever owned walking up and down train station staircases slick with brown slush. I listen to anybody who's speaking, and look friendly, and keep my mouth shut. I trade names and numbers. I get noticed.

In April, a sixty-five-degree day breaks winter's back. The jagged piles of dirty ice go round at the edges and melt into the sewers. The city turns green, and I'm invited to my first play party.

The cookies are those soft white circles covered in different frostings depending on the season, the ones that barely seem like they've been cooked. No nuts—I checked the label. No one said anything about food restrictions, but it's better to think ahead. I put them on the table between the sodas and the seven-layer dip.

Wooden beams crisscross the bottom floor of the loft. Under each hangs a set of straps, ready for a carabiner or ring. Real tatami mats cover the floor.

People mingle: White men with long hair; White women with short hair; two petite Asian women with much older White boyfriends. Me. Most of the people are familiar after my months of schmoozing. I reciprocate hugs when they are offered, ask how things are going. Not to find out, but to ask, and be heard asking. One of the new faces is the Marie I've heard so much about. This is her place.

The emotional temperature of the room is warm. These people are happy to see each other.

After snacks, an opening circle: name, pronouns, what we're looking for. A man at the far side of the room, with sleeve tattoos, looks at me twice.

He's meaner than he looks. With his rope, he twists me like a wet dishrag. My whole weight hangs from two uplines. My feet are higher than his head. My hair brushes the mat. I hold myself tightly.

Simon—his name is Simon—walks around me, trailing fingers. He unties something, pulls something else. His foot is on my hair—very much on purpose—and it yanks on my scalp as he hauls my torso up toward the beam. I don't make a sound.

He steps back, ties things off, and crouches down in front of my upside-down face. He holds the sides of my head in his hands.

"It's easier if you relax," he says, and winks.

"You top your way," I say, "and I'll bottom mine."

I muscle my way through the rest of the sequence, gritting my teeth through the transitions. I won't tell him so, but he's fun. A lot of fun.

Later, someone brings out a bottle of whiskey. I'm done tying for the night, so I pour some in a red cup and mix it with Sprite. One of the bottoms, still rope-drunk, opens a window and scrambles up the fire escape, laughing at their top who grumbles as he struggles over the sill. A handful of others follow, while Marie and the rest settle in around the kitchen counter to talk. Simon, crouching on the landing, catches my eye. He sticks his hand back in through the window, holding it out to me.

After an awkward minute, it turns into a wave: *Come on!* He stands and disappears up the clanging metal stairs.

I surprise myself by following him.

The lot of them stand around on a tarred roof, watching a sunset so pink it feels made up. They hug themselves and each other to keep off the chill. The grumpy top has caught the bottom and holds them by the collar of their pleather jacket. They snort and lean into his chest.

From the middle of the huddle, Simon flashes me the peace sign. I hang back.

Carl / Boston, MA / 2030

Two black leather armchairs sit next to the vending machine in the BPD gym lobby. A dusty houseplant wilts in a nearby pot.

It's ten minutes past six. Sean still hasn't showed up.

A young patrolman scowls as he hovers over the drinking fountain, adding whey, creatine, and what looks like raw coffee grounds to a protein shaker. Three gray-haired older guys pass through on their way to the sauna. The one with the biggest gut is laughing at his own joke.

"So then," he says, "the Asian guy says . . ."

He notices me sitting next to the plant. He coughs. He and his buddies duck through the doorway leading to the locker rooms. One returns to grab a packet of Cheetos.

Sean's not coming.

I don't slam my locker door. I'm not a kid. I get dressed, put on my wraps, and walk past the free weights to the corner where they keep the boxing stuff.

Sean's no good at the speed bag. He has no rhythm. He can throw a hard punch—harder than I can—because that's just mechanics. He can think his way into a perfect hook. But slipping, weaving, flowing with the guy you're fighting—that's where I get him.

Under the wooden circle, I take a second to breathe. "Down Under" plays over the gym speakers. I do what Sean doesn't know how to do. I feel it out. Light touches at first, arms raised. Just to get it moving. Then snappier, faster, in infinite little ovals. Me and the bag and the Men at Work fall into our groove. The hard leather bulb sounds like a steam engine pulling out of the station, slow at first, then getting faster—clack . . . clack . . . clack clack clack clackclackclack racketa-dacketa-racketa-dacketa . . .

After that it's the heavy bag. I hate the heavy bag. Big, slow, stupid. It's all about power shots. Raw physics—no poetry. It's Sean's specialty. He doesn't make the bag swing. When he plants his feet, and digs in, the bag jumps straight up in the air, like it's supposed to. Like it got scared.

I have to move all around. It's exhausting. I'm pissed.

He's supposed to be here so we can hold the bag steady for each other. So we can get in an actual workout, instead of me prancing around the stupid thing all by myself. He said he'd be here. He promised. And once again, he's off doing whatever the fuck it is he's gotten into since Al showed up. And I'm left by myself, looking like an idiot.

A sloppy hook sends the bag off. I throw a right cross as it swings back toward me, straight at the bottom—the hard part of the bag, where all the sand is packed in tight. The punch connects.

Something pinches in my wrist.

"Sssssshhheeeyyiiittt—!"

I kick the same spot on the bag, bruising the top of my foot. The timer goes off. I limp over to a bench, and sit down.

This is the third week in a row. He tells me nothing about where he is or what he's doing. He doesn't ask me to help.

The timer rings again. I take off my wraps and throw hooks till my knuckles leave red jelly smears on the canvas.

When I get back to the apartment, Levi's already started cooking. He holds out a bag of sugar. I shake my head.

"Sugar in red sauce is a sin," I say.

He rolls his eyes. "I actually *have* Italian grandparents," he says.

I kiss him on top of his head. "Then you should know better."

While he squishes together eggs, raw beef, and breadcrumbs in a big metal bowl, I remove the halved tomatoes from the broiler, and peel off their skins. In a large saucepan, I sauté chopped onion and fresh-pressed garlic. When the aromatics are browned, I add in the chopped pepper and the roasted tomatoes, put the lid on, and leave the whole thing to simmer. I open the oven door, and Levi slides a cookie sheet packed with meatballs into the waiting heat. We fuck on the ottoman while the pasta boils. Socks on.

Levi strains the pasta a minute early to keep it al dente, the way I like it. I puree the sauce with the immersion blender we got from Pier 21. Then Levi drops the browned meatballs into the pot, one at a time, with a pair of tongs. He leans his head into the steam and inhales. We stand in front of the stove together, watching the red surface bubble like lava. Then we pull down our pajama pants and rub out another quick one, Levi's hips pressed against the counter.

Full plates in hand, we move to the living room and plop down on the couch. He puts his feet in my lap. When I'm not twirling spaghetti, I play with his short brown hair.

Chopped is the ultimate couples' show. They make about three new episodes a day, so you never run out of stuff to watch. Levi and I try to guess what the chefs are going to make each round. I'm good at it because I've watched enough to realize that bread is bread, whatever form it comes in. Cookies are bread. If something is a starch, you can crumble it up and reshape it in whatever way you want.

My third grade teacher used to say: *You get what you get, and you don't get upset*. I hated that at the time. But now I get it. Smart people make do with what they have.

I have Levi. And that's good. He's smart, and gorgeous, in a willowy sort of way. The kind of pretty that makes straight men panic a little. And he's kind. It's been a long time since I was with someone who was just a good person.

That's not to mention all the things I get to do now that I'm half of a couple. I can go out to a restaurant or see a movie without people looking at me like I'm a walking disaster. And then there's the Groupons—wine tastings, rock-climbing classes, museum tours, cheese-making lessons . . .

I have someone to eat dinner with. To sit across the table from, and talk about how our days went, even if they were terrible. There's a bit less empty space on the couch, and in the bed. I'm free, of something. A worry I wasn't even fully aware of before the app picked Levi out for me. I don't have to hunt for love anymore.

On-screen, a short order cook from Arizona juggles creme fraiche and a handful of gravlax. I drift, catching every other word. I have a belly full of pasta, a nice apartment, and a beautiful boy on the other end of the couch who says he loves me. I was alone before. Now I have everything a man needs. Everything he could possibly want.

Everything.

Levi rubs my crotch with his foot. My stomach is so stuffed it hurts.

"No, babe, I can't—"

But it turns out I can. I haul myself over to Levi, pull his pants down, and wonder what Sean's doing with his day off.

Marie / Washington, D.C. / 2005

A call went out from Azerbaijan early this morning to a number with a Brooklyn area code. We picked up the words "guns," "border," and "shipment," which was enough to send up a flag and get me assigned to the case. I'm examining street cam footage that puts the owner of the phone number near Red Hook Terminal at 1:37 this afternoon, when an elbow appears over the side of my cubicle. A man in a brown suit is leaning into my workspace.

"They let you wear that?" he says with an easy smile. The hand unoccupied by a coffee mug points at my cargo pants and tank top.

"I'm good at my job," I say. "I wear what I want."

The grin falters, like it doesn't fail often. I can imagine.

"Alan Bergman," he says, sticking out his hand. "Just transferred over from the ATF."

"Marvin," I say, putting my headphones back on. "From Mars."

"Oh, yeah—'Where's the kaboom,' right?"

I keep typing. After a minute, Bergman pulls back his hand, raps it twice lightly on the division, and nods. He takes his coffee and walks away.

Can't believe he got the reference. What a nerd.

The next week, Bergman sits at a table in the breakroom, half-eaten box of Popeyes growing cold as he reviews a stack of files. When my bag of Cheez-Its lands in the bottom of the vending machine, he looks up.

"You weren't kidding," he says.

"About?" I say, chewing.

"Your job," he says, undeterred. He jiggles the file in his hand, like he's weighing it.

"You are really, really good at it."

"You sound surprised."

"Call it impressed," he says. "You've definitely earned those... what the hell are you wearing now?"

"They're called joggers," I say.

The grin is back.

"To clarify," he says, "*Marie Rosenthal* has earned the right to wear joggers in a professional setting. I don't know what the hell you think you're doing, Marvin."

I flick a Cheez-It at his face. It dings off the corner of his eye, where the thin white line of a scar extends back into his hairline. He grabs the broken orange pieces off the tile floor and pops them into his mouth.

They send him down to Peru in August, to oversee negotiations between representatives of two paramilitary groups we have officially disavowed in every way possible. It's early in the morning where he is.

They flew me in coach, *Marie,* he texts. *Like a pack animal, or an Irishman.*

Al, I text back, *you are the softest human being I ever met.*

I'll have you know I'm still alive after eating ceviche yesterday. That's raw fish. Anyway, we're going up into the mountains soon. You'd like it—supposed to be freezing.

On his first day back, Al tosses a brown paper package on my desk. Inside is one of those funny hats with the ear-flaps, made of alpaca wool. It's bright green, with a gold fringe on top.

At the office holiday party, we drink like people who've seen too much. The Cold Warriors from upstairs hang out in a knot by the printers, sucking down bourbon and laughing about Nicaragua, and Reagan, and the good old days. Somebody rigged a projector to a machine with a Super Nintendo emulator installed on it, and now a crowd of thirty presses in on a pair of programmers playing *Mario Kart* with their keyboards. Mike from accounting stays busy filling tiny plastic shot glasses with Evan Williams. Every time someone makes a successful hit with a green shell, we all have to drink. Al walks past everybody, smiling, shaking hands, but always steadily moving toward the exit. He's wearing his coat, and his briefcase is in his hand.

"Tapping out already?" I say.

"Yeah, I've got some reports I need to wrap up. Good seeing you, though."

"Wuss," I say to his back.

He turns around. "'Scuse me?"

"I'm just saying you're a little bitch is all." My mouth tastes like rum and coke. I speak directly into my Solo cup. "Soft."

Al stares at me, perched on the reception desk like a gargoyle. He laughs—a single, sharp breath out through the nose—shakes his head, and bites the corner of his lip. His white canine tooth digs into the pink flesh.

"Been on my case eight fuckin' months . . ." he says, tossing his suitcase at my feet and elbowing his way back through the crowd. When he returns, he's holding two shot glasses full of brown liquid. He downs one, and I reach for the other. He snatches it away from me, drinks it himself, and wipes his lip with the side of his thumb. A cheer goes up from the projector—another race won.

"Grab a keyboard, Marvin," he says. "I'm about to kick your ass."

And he does. He *laps* me in Bowser Castle, and then again on Koopa Beach. I'm seconds away from overtaking him when I fall off the edge of Rainbow Road, and whip the keyboard across the room at the projector screen, where it explodes in a burst of plastic keys. I have to lend Travis mine so everyone can keep playing. I promise to buy him a new one.

On the way to the coatrack, I smack my hip against the corner of a desk and stumble a few steps. Al catches my elbow.

"Can I walk you home?" he says.

"Sure," I say.

Al offers me his arm. I don't need the support. But I lean on it, anyway. When we get to my front door, he waits to make sure I've got it unlocked, then says goodnight and turns to leave.

"You don't have to go," I say.

He pauses on the steps.

"I mean," I say, "we don't want your precious little ears to freeze off."

"No," he says, "we don't want that."

I step back to let him in.

Carl / Boston, MA / 2005

For once, my stick is better than Sean's. He still has the one he's been using all summer—long and straight on the top, with a fat handle at the bottom. It looks exactly like a big pistol. He's been keeping it tucked in the waistband of his pants since we got out of school. He's very proud of it.

But this morning I found an even better one. Longer than my arm, with a curve at the end that tucks right into my armpit, just like a wooden stock. I spend all morning picking the twigs off it and peeling away the bark. Then I head over to Jake's front porch, where Sean is already hanging out. He frowns when he sees my new stick.

"You can't use that," he says.

"Why not?"

"Because cops don't use big guns. They only use handguns."

I feel stupid. I'm angry at the stick for being the wrong size. My old stick is back in the garage, next to the bikes. Now I have to run back, get the key from mom, open the door—

"Actually," says Jake, picking a booger off his glasses, "my uncle's a cop, and he says they use all kinds of guns to catch criminals. He showed me a shotgun one time. He keeps it on a rack between the seats."

Sean looks like he wants to shove Jake off the stairs, but Jake doesn't know it because he's cleaning his glasses on his shirt and he can't see his own hand without them. Sean glares at him for a minute, but Jake's too focused on getting the smear off one of the lenses. After a while, Sean gives up and rolls his eyes.

"Fine," he says. He stands up, and we fall into formation, heading around the house toward the back yard. Sean takes point. Jake and I bring up the rear.

I'm excited to show Sean how useful this new stick will be in the field; angry at him for being angry at me; worried that he doesn't like me any more, and won't want to be my friend; smug because we both know that my stick is even better than his today, and that'll give him something to think about.

The criminals sit on a picnic blanket in the middle of the yard, under the tree that drops slimy little apples all over the grass in the fall. They rot there and make Jake's family's house smell like sour candy for a month. We crouch against the side of the house, hidden from the criminals by the steam pouring out of the white plastic dryer vent. Through the basement window, Jake's mom sees me. She takes a break from balling up socks to wave hello. I wave back.

Sean holds up a fist. He sticks out two fingers—waits—then points forward. We jump out from behind the fog, lift the latch on the chain-link gate, and charge into the backyard, guns blazing.

Jake's sisters look up from the colorful plastic strands of gimp they're threading into box-stitch key chains. Dee, the youngest one, screams—she's young enough that she has a hard time telling the difference between real life and pretend sometimes. Veronica, the oldest, grabs her hand, and pulls her up to her feet.

"Get up!" she says. "We need to run!"

Dee starts to cry, but Veronica grins, tongue poking out a bit through the space where her most recent tooth fell out. The two of them take off into the woods behind the house. Sarah, the middle girl, groans. The gimp is in a big tangled pile all around her feet.

"Come *on*," she calls after her sisters. "Not again!"

But her partners in crime are already on the lam, disappearing through the bushes that line the family property. Guns drawn, we form a triangle around the picnic blanket.

"You're surrounded," says Sean. "Put your hands up."

"Bite me," says Sarah. She sorts out her project from the mess and picks up where she left off, weaving a rainbow of plastic strings over and under each other.

"Come on, Sarah," says Jake. "We caught you; don't be a bitch."

But she keeps her head down and goes right on stitching. Sean keeps looking over at the gap in the bushes that Veronica made when she pulled Dee through into the forest. He's getting impatient. I circle around to the front of the triangle, so I'm facing Sarah head-on. I put the barrel of my shotgun under her chin and tip her head up, so her blue eyes are looking into mine.

"Do it," I say.

She scrunches her face up at me, but then looks down at the gun, and back up at me. She closes her eyes, lays her gimp on the ground beside her, and puts her hands in the air.

Sean's face says he's both proud and jealous. My heart beats a bit faster. I knew the stick would come in handy.

Jake holsters his pistol—a piece of root like a Luger with a wonky barrel—and gently twists Sarah's arms behind her back. Following standard procedure, we walk her over to the fence, book her for robbery, and thread her cuffs around the metal post so she can't make a jail break.

"Keep an eye on the perp," says Sean, patting me on the shoulder. He turns to Jake.

"Let's roll."

"Ten-four," says Jake. They pull out their guns and sprint into the trees.

A plane flies over the house. A car with big tires rolls up the road, crunching gravel. A robin drops off a tree branch and cuts a worm in half with its beak.

Sarah sits on the ground, cross-legged, sweat making her hair stick to her face, which is red from the sun. She twisters her shoulders around, trying to get comfy, and stares at the picnic blanket with the gimp, looking glum.

Jake's parents keep the hose wrapped around a big metal spool with a crank handle. I haul enough of it loose to reach Sarah, then turn the water on so just a bit comes out the front end. Sarah sees me coming. Her eyes narrow.

"If you dare—" she says.

I tip my head and catch a mouthful of warm hose-water. I wait for the stream to get cold, then hold it out to Sarah, making sure nothing splashes on her dress. Slowly, watching me, she leans forward. She opens her mouth. I keep the hose steady till she's had enough, then turn it off and reel it back in. Little spurts of water jump out of the metal end as it clinks over rocks and dirt.

Sarah's post is right in the sun. The one next to it gets shade from the tree. Carefully, I pull the blanket over to the shady post, gimp and all. Then I pull the little lever that undoes Sarah's handcuffs, and sit her down on the blanket, locking her hands in front of her. By the time Sean and Jake reappear at the edge of the woods, she's finished her own stitch and is starting on Veronica's.

Jake carries Dee in a piggyback while she eats the SweeTarts he'd been keeping in his pocket. She drops every other candy in the dirt, and her big eyes keep drooping shut. Eventually she falls asleep on her brother's back, pudgy arms hanging over his shoulders.

Sean, looking full of himself, leads Veronica with one hand, squeezing her upper arm. She tosses herself back and forth, long hair whipping all over the place as she grunts and struggles to get free, without any luck. Which doesn't make much sense—she's about a head taller than Sean as of last year. Plus, I once saw her pick her brother off a moving bike and throw him on the sidewalk. She should be able to get loose any time she wants to, but she never does.

I wouldn't tell Sean, but Veronica freaks me out a bit. I do not understand that girl.

"What's this?" says Sean, gesturing at Sarah and her shady hangout.

She sticks her pink tongue out at him.

"Quick prisoner transfer," I say.

"We didn't talk about a transfer," he says. "And anyway, if her arms aren't behind her back, what's even the point—"

There's a swish—a flash of color—and suddenly Sean's hopping on one foot, gripping his calf. The sound comes again, and the skin on the outside of my right leg feels like it got an instant sunburn. I jump back to see Sarah, legs wide, feet planted, twirling a gimp chain as long as a belt. Six little plastic threads sprout off the end of it, a match for the red stripes growing on our legs. She swings again, and we duck back, out of range.

"You'll never take me alive!" she screams. Handcuffs still around her wrists, she turns and runs into the woods, gimp whip flying out behind her.

While Sean stares after her, Veronica slips behind him and shoves him forward with her shoulder so he trips over the blanket and falls on his face. Cackling like a witch, she takes off after her sister, arms still pinned behind her back.

Sean pushes himself to his feet, and smiles like a hungry wolf. Jake brings Dee inside to get her some lunch, and Sean and I run off into the dark forest, to catch the bad guys together.

Sean / Boston, MA / 2024

Back at the precinct, people start packing it in for the night. They shut down computers; shrug on coats; say goodnight on the way to the elevator. I take the grounds out of the freezer, and start brewing a fresh pot of coffee. The brown liquid farts out of the spigot as Carl walks up to me, jacket over his arm.

"Hey, bud," he says. "You doing okay?"

I try to say something, but I haven't talked all day and it comes out as a whistle. I clear my throat and go again. "Yeah. Why?"

"Oh, no reason," he says. He picks up a sugar packet. He puts it back down.

"You've just been working a lot lately, and you seem . . . tired."

I *am* tired. Shaky tired. Twitchy tired. The kind of tired where your insides vibrate, and you can make the connections that aren't obvious when you're well-rested. I'm purposefully tired. I need to be for the work I'm doing. Didn't realize I looked it, though.

"It's nothing," I say. "Just putting in a few extra hours."

He looks me over, and an eyebrow creeps up. Suddenly I feel the weight of the accumulated sweat under my arms, and on the inside of my pants.

"I'll go home soon," I say. "I promise."

It does the trick. Carl follows the rest of the team down to the garage, and for a precious evening I have some time to myself among the relative strangers of the night crew—people who don't really know who I am or care what I'm about.

Coffee's done. I pour a cup and take the rest of the pot into the conference room so I don't have to leave again. I put it down on the bundle of napkins I've been using as a coaster and take a swig from the mug. At the corners of my mouth, my five-o'clock shadow bristles against the rim.

The corkboard takes up most of the back wall. I bought it with my own money, back when I first transferred. At the moment, it includes: photographs of Simon Debs in various settings; a map of his usual daily route; photographs of the outside of his apartment; photographs of the inside; printouts of his previous ten blog posts, and six months of search history; a receipt salvaged from a trash can. I've got a good feeling about that one. It's from a visit to the CVS—Simon paid for lube and condoms with a card, then dropped the evidence right outside where I could pocket it without slowing down.

Between the search history and the blog posts, he's basically written his own confession. But everything helps. I've strung enough yarn across the board to make two sweaters.

In the hallway outside the conference room, the chief walks by the window on the way to her car. Seeing me inside, she pauses. She takes in the scene: the coffee, the corkboard, me looking like the "Before" photo in a detergent ad. Slowly, she smiles. She nods. Tipping my mug toward her, I nod back. She walks away.

Thanks to Simon, and his refusal to keep his mouth shut, I have a chance to prove myself. To make myself look like the most dedicated member on the new task force. A man obsessed with catching perverts. A man beyond suspicion. And I ought to be focusing on that. But I keep making the case personal.

The blog posts have titles like "Kink and the Sacred;" "The Truth About Monogamy;" "Polyamory as Temperance." On the board, mixed in with the photos of Simon picking up groceries or unlocking his front door, are pictures pulled from his Twitter account. Many show him standing with his arms around other people, smiling, all of them wearing outfits made of leather or latex and lit by the bright flash of a camera in a dark room. In others, he's up on a stage at the front of a conference hall, demonstrating a knot. In a few he kneels on the ground, holding another person close while wrapping rope tightly around them. One rare shot has him in the rope himself, hanging upside-down from a wooden frame. Yarn explodes out from the other figures in the photos, connecting to the mini-profiles I'm making in one corner of the corkboard. Facial recognition records put a handful of these people in and around Boston.

The profile and the photos are still up months after the Amendment was officially passed. It's like he doesn't care. Like he's not afraid. Even now he flaunts his life in front of the state. In front of me.

I need to think of him as a number. A case to be investigated, closed, and filed away. Anonymous. Just another opportunity to prove my innocence. Nothing more. If I get *too* involved, something might slip. Carl's worry, and the chief's pride, will turn to suspicion. They'll look more closely at me, instead of the patter. And I'll go where everyone goes when they get found out.

But when I go home at night and try to sleep, I think about Simon's friends, and the smiles on their faces, and the fact that the evidence is just *out there*, in the world, unhidden—where anyone can find it and know how he's been living. What he likes. What's going on inside his head, and his heart, because he's made it so readily available.

I think about these things—I can't stop thinking about them—and wonder what right he has to live like that, unafraid of what someone might do to him for being so free. I lie on my back, and stare up at the ceiling, and think about ways to make Simon afraid.

Pepper / Cambridge, MA / 2028

We go out five times, and he doesn't even bring it up. At the museum, in April, he puts a hand on my thigh and squeezes. Later that night, I pretend not to see him going in for a kiss on my front porch. I stop him by picking an imaginary crumb off his collar.

In May, we take a walk through Davis Square.

A White guy in a dirty woolen poncho picks out "Hey There Delilah" on a guitar covered in stickers. Families and couples with ice cream cones from the J.P. Licks sit on the walls and eat, or walk across the bricks on their way to the movies. Gary inhales his blackberry cone—he doesn't get brain freeze, he said. I take my time with a scoop of chocolate in a paper dish.

Gary hasn't said much since we got here. He stares at the ground and shuffles his feet on the sidewalk. He flicks a piece of ice-cream-cone paper off the bench.

"Is everything okay?" he says.

Across the way, one squirrel chases another up a tree. In that crazy way they do, where you think one's going to kill the other.

"Yeah," I say. "Why?"

"It's been three months," he says. "And we haven't. You know."

"Oh," I say.

Tiny nails skitter over bark. The lead squirrel screams as her pursuer chases her up a tree.

It's hot here, for May. An early taste of summer. My neck is in the sun, cooking like the spilled globs of ice cream that conceal on the low rock wall.

"I was hoping we could take things slow."

"I figured," says Gary, "and I don't want to pressure you. But there's slow . . . and then there's *slow*. Right?

"Listen," he says, "if you'd rather match with someone else, of course I'll be sad, but I'd understand—"

"No! No, it's not that—"

"Then what?"

I say nothing. The guy with the guitar moves on to "Dirty Water." Gary takes my hand, not roughly.

"What if we went back to my place tonight? Just see what happens?"

"Gary . . . I . . ."

He keeps the hold on my hand, but the grip changes. He looks away, at the ground, and the beginning of a pout pulls his face inward. It's not the full-on scowl of a child. It doesn't have to be. The hint is warning enough. It's a look that implies I owe him something. The look of a brewing shit-fit.

I don't like that look.

"My place is closer," I say.

Gary turns back to me. He beams. A fat acorn tumbles from the branches overhead and lands on the bricks with a *clack*.

A thumb can burst an eyeball like an overripe peach. A fist in the throat can collapse the trachea. An elbow in the right place can crack a rib. I hold these and a thousand other motions tight in the pit of my stomach and lie still.

With my clothes on, I was a mystery to him. Now I'm a puzzle to be solved. But it's taking too long, and I'm turning into a broken toy.

I know what he wants. Better than he does, even. For him it's subconscious—a longing he couldn't put into words if he tried. For me it's theory: Kinsey's surveys, and every book I've ever read on the subject, trying to figure out what it is that people get out of this.

I could give it to him, easily. I don't want to. I want him to stand there at the edge of my bed, my ankles in his hands, and keep jerking back and forth until he feels as dissociated as I do. I want to be as brave as all the people who've disappeared.

Instead, I take a breath, and moan.

Gary's eyebrows shoot up like he's found the Holy Grail in my pussy. Gritting his teeth and smiling, he rams the head of his cock into the section of vulva he happened to be brushing against when I moaned for the first time. I make more noises for him as he flips me over and clamps his sweaty hands onto my hips.

I do not reach between my legs and burst his testicles like ketchup packets. I give my face a rest, then put it back on and look over my shoulder, straight into the eyes of the man the computer picked out for me. Like the *Cosmo* article said to. He spasms like a fish in a pool of bloody water.

My sheets smell like him. I smell like him. He leans over, and his lips land on my shoulder.

"Was that okay for you?" he says.

"Yeah," I say. "It was great."

Lolita, Anita, & 'Ritas / "Ep. 267: Amendment A-schmendment: Casa Loca Habanero Tequila with Margaritaville Margarita Mix"

Lolita: See, my thing is—it's been a year. And we're still figuring out the etiquette.

Anita: Right.

Lolita: Like, Trevor and I. Is our anniversary the day we matched? The day we went on our first date?

Anita: I know, and it's like, either way, everyone's anniversary is in the spring because that's when PRTNR came out. And if yours isn't, everybody knows that—

Together: You fucked up the first time.

[Laughter. Sound of liquid being poured into glass.]

Anita: Remember how crazy it was that first summer?

Lolita: Oh my God, I don't even want to think about it. Those poor people—

Anita: That was messed up, right?

Lolita: So messed up. Violence—no, never. Even if you don't agree with what somebody's doing—

Anita: It's too much.

Lolita: It was just too much. Cheers.

Anita: Salud.

[sipping sounds]

Anita: Wow! That is better than I thought it would be.

Lolita: It's so good!

Anita: [laughter] Like, eighteen dollars for the liquor *and* the mixer, and somehow so good.

[sipping sounds]

Lolita: To get back to what you were saying. Obviously, you can't, like, justify what happened—

Anita: It was too much.

Lolita: Too much. But at the same time, I'm like—things were actually pretty bad, before the Amendment? And now they're better? I feel like I'm happier.

Anita: No, yeah, totally. People were hoarding, and now they're not. It's fair. [sipping] Did you hear about that study that came out, like a few weeks ago?

Lolita: Yes! They said that anxiety and depression are down for, like—

Together: Everybody!

Lolita: Just because everyone has a partner. It's crazy.

Anita: So crazy. I mean, for me, personally, I get it. I'm not, like, running around all the time, wondering whether I'm ever going to find someone, or whether the person I'm with is gonna leave—

Lolita: Where's the salt? I want more salt.

Anita: People are gonna think we started this podcast just so you can eat margarita salt.

Lolita: They can think whatever they want, just give it . . .

Letter from Marie Rosenthal to Ellen Willis / July 24, 2005

Dear Professor Willis,

    I never thought I'd miss the cold! D.C. is the stickiest place I've ever been. Seeing the sunrise through swamp mist is beautiful, but hardly worth it. I'd give it all up to share bagels and life stories in your office again.

I wish you'd write back to me.

You must think I'm some kind of puppet master, pulling all the strings in the darkness. I wish. I have panic attacks thinking about all the things I can't control. No one would travel if they knew.

Picture the security checkpoint at a mid-sized airport—not an LAX or an ATL, just a regional hotspot—in the days leading up to Thanksgiving. A few hundred tired parents, kids, and undergrads with their carry-on luggage. A long shuffling line of passengers, snaking back and forth around stanchion posts. A rectangle thirty people wide and twice as deep.

On that day—on any day—a team of men could exit a taxi at the terminal of their choice, unzip their suitcases, and pull out as many guns as they could carry. They wouldn't even have to aim.

I'm sorry I'm not the writer you were hoping I'd be. But maybe I can keep the next Hannah Arendt or Rachel Carson alive long enough to say what she needs to say. Because I like my job, Professor Willis. I like it a lot.

Do you know how many affairs I've discovered? The institutions I could destroy with a forwarded email? It's fun being the hunter for a change. You can appreciate that, right? And it's safe here, between the wires, watching the traffic go by. Quiet.

I've met someone. Another agent. He's witty. Pretends to be a nihilist, but he's really a softie. I think you'd like him.

Still Here,
Marie

Al / Boston, MA / 2030

"We caught four johns," says Schmidt. "Three financial analysts on lunch break, and a retired accountant."

"Never saw an old man run that fast," says Baptiste, frowning into a mug of coffee. "He was halfway out the window before I grabbed him. No pants, neither."

"We've got the men in custody, and CBP's taking care of the girls. Vietnamese, mostly. One from Thailand."

She hands over a crisp new file folder, stuffed no doubt with detailed reports on the Chinatown massage-parlor raid. I keep it closed.

"Excellent," I say. "And what's the connection to the Rosenthal case?"

They blink, and their eyebrows go up. They look at each other, then back at me.

"I mean, nothing direct," says Baptiste. "In terms of the broader systems of structural inequality at play, every hole we can patch makes the other ones easier to find—"

"I can appreciate that," I say, nodding, "but it's not what I asked about. What information did this raid, and the time that went into it, provide that will get us closer to finding Marie Rosenthal?"

"With all due respect, Mr. Bergman," says Schmidt, "other intimacy crimes don't stop because we've got one high-profile case to work on. Of course we're prioritizing work on the rope cell, but we can't just drop everything else to go after one person exclusively."

Schmidt has imposter syndrome. Which isn't saying much—everybody does—but it's especially strong in her. A young woman, with as many accomplishments as she has, in a police department not exactly famous for its gender-equity practices . . .

The doubt must eat her alive—when she's not too busy to forget it.

I let my shoulders sag. I keep my eyes fixed on Schmidt's while the corners of my mouth droop in a slight frown, and the rest of my aging face goes with them. No anger. That'd draw out the stubbornness that's gotten her this far in her career, which wouldn't serve any purpose. Disappointment is what's called for: to evoke in her the sense that I expected more and got less than what I was hoping for. I become her father; a handful of teachers; maybe a pastor somewhere back in time; and I project the question into the air between us, as if it slipped out by accident. As if she is uncovering, with her detective skills, what I truly think.

Why are you here?

I wait till she looks down at my shoes, then let out a small sigh.

"Well, thank you, anyway," I say, tossing the unopened file on the desk behind me. "Let me know if you do find anything."

They hurry out of the room, Baptiste following Schmidt. No need to work on him. He follows her lead, whether he recognizes it or not. Schmidt is the brains. He's just the muscle. Might even have a thing for her.

She'll be focused now. No more wasting time on bankers getting a handy on the way back from Sweetgreen. To prove me wrong, and to prove to herself that she has the right to do this job, she'll work extra hard to bring Marie to me.

I crack open a soda and look out at the bullpen through the window next to the door. Officers walk through, arms full of papers. One of the detectives takes a call. Sean, straight-backed in his chair, types something up.

I wish I didn't like him. I wish he were a prick with a bad attitude, someone I could use and forget about. But he's not.

For years, he's known what he likes. What he is. He knew, whenever he first heard about the Amendment, what it meant for his future. He knew, when it was passed, that a vote and a signature had turned him into an illegal human being. Someone unaccounted for, with no right to exist. And still he became a cop. One dedicated to hunting down his own kind. Why?

There are a few possibilities. He could be loyal, patriotic, to a pathological degree. I doubt it's that—he's too smart, and anyway people like that never seem to shut up about it. He could be cold, cynical, considering the odds and picking the bet with the greatest chance of ensuring his own survival. More likely, but I don't think that's the whole story, either.

I think Sean knows we don't have to accept our limitations. That, given enough effort, we can transcend anything—become something greater than what we are. Whether through crossed wires, upbringing, or some other unknowable factor, he got dealt a bad hand: He finds himself living at a point in history in which the goals of his society and government run contrary to his own deepest urges. Does he blame anyone or anything else for his brokenness? Does he make a stink and demand accommodation?

No. He gets to work on fixing himself, by cutting away those pieces of his experience that are not suitable. He makes himself better. And he does it all quietly, without complaint. Sean gets it. There's a purity about him. The grace people get from taking on impossible tasks.

And I'm taking that away.

I've given him permission to see what his life could have been like. What it could still be like, if he were willing to do some crazy things and risk it all in the process. I've tempted him with authenticity. My guess is he'll fall. And I have to be okay with that.

Carl / Wellesley, MA / 2027

Rob's grill could hold a large dog. Right now the three levels of wire grating are stacked with beef patties, sausages, steak tips, and wings. A fat red burger drips juice down onto the jets; fire leaps up and wraps the meat for a second, then fizzles back down. Rob closes the grill and takes a swig from the open beer can sweating on the porch railing. His seven-year-old daughter runs up the steps and pelts him with a foam football. Grinning, he roars, and chases her off the porch and into the crowd of friends and cop families standing around the backyard, laughing. As an afterthought, he grabs Sean's hand, and shoves the spatula into it.

"Keep an eye on the meat for me, will ya?" he says. He winks, and slaps Sean's upper arm before running off after the little troublemaker.

The way Sean grimaces at the spatula, you'd think Rob handed him a dead rat. The look of disgust is only there for a second—a flicker of the inside of his head, reflected on his face—but in that moment I know how much he hates Rob, and being here, and sharing food with him. I can't blame him.

Then the look is gone, and he's smiling again. It appears totally natural. I hold out my hand for the spatula.

"Grab me a beer?" I say.

By the time we got here there was no more room in the coolers—the Coronas I brought are in the fridge, through the sliding doors and across the kitchen. Sean takes the chance to be alone for a minute, and I lift up the hood to check on the meat. I'm plating when Rob comes up behind me.

"Looking good, champ," he says, giving my shoulders a hard squeeze. What sucks is that it feels good. Obviously it's weird—but we all carry tension up there, and the pressure itself is nice. I'm mad with myself for not being happier when he lets go to grab a platter of chicken thighs.

Rob whistles, and the crowd swarms the picnic table: slitting buns, squirting mustard, digging big spoons into cold metal bowls of potato salad. Slowly they fill up the yard again: Rob's buddies, with their arm tattoos and buzz cuts; off-duty cops in polos and jeans or cargo shorts; significant others; about a dozen kids, fooling around on the adult-sized obstacle course that extends from the back of Rob's lawn into the woods beyond. He has at least a few acres back there. Behind a nearby ridge, there's a shooting range.

Rob sways a bit, looking out at the crowd. He's been throwing back lager since before we got here (that's not a guess; he told us so when we walked in). He turns and notices me looking at him. He tips his head back toward the house.

"C'mon," he says. "I wanna show you something."

I check the grill to see if there's a hot dog I might have missed, a bit of pepper, anything. No such luck. I follow Rob through the screen door.

No sign of Sean; he'll be in the bathroom, reading something on his phone. Rob picks up what must be his daughter's doll from the kitchen floor and places her on a chair, back straight. Respectfully, he arranges her skirt, and gives her a once-over to make sure she looks presentable. His wife rushes by, arms full of salad dressing bottles. He gives her a peck, then pulls a set of keys from his pocket and undoes the three locks on a nearby door. He holds it open. Painted wooden stairs lead straight down.

"Monsieur," he says, and waves his free arm like a footman. I walk down the stairs.

No boxes of old clothes. No bikes. No washing machine, and no dryer. No windows. Instead, there are a few bare bulbs. A mop and rolling bucket in the far corner, next to a handful of folding chairs.

The floor is made of concrete. Embedded in the middle is an eye bolt. With a metal grate next to it. The room smells like bleach.

Rob closes the door behind him and clunks down the stairs. He waggles his eyebrows.

"Not bad, huh?"

He puts his hands out, and caresses the angular black panels covering the walls—and the inside of the door. "Give that a feel," he says.

The material is black and squishy. Like the foam you'd stuff around a window unit, but thicker.

"Soundproofing," I say.

Rob grins. "Check this out."

He takes a deep breath, and opens his mouth wide.

"HEEEEEELLP!!" he screams. He's red in the face. Spit and pieces of pork sausage fly out past his mustache. "HELP ME, PLEEEAAASEEE!!"

He stamps his feet up and down, crashing his boots against the grate. He slams into the black walls. He lets out one last yell. Then he bends over, hands on his knees, catching his breath.

"Hooo!" he says. He laughs. "Come on back upstairs."

Rob's daughter sits in the kitchen, braiding the hair of the doll. He kisses the top of her head and rubs a hand on her back.

"Sweetie," he says, "did you hear anything downstairs just now?"

"Uh-uh," she says, shaking her head no. Her eyes never leave the doll—she's focused on her task.

Rob looks up at me and winks.

Sean / Boston, MA / 2030

Mrs. Davis phones the hotline about once per week. This time it's urgent, she says: strange-looking visitors, coming in and out of her dilapidated Allston triple-decker at all hours, banging the front door on their way out. Highly suspicious, she says. They move too fast for her to get much of a look at them. But what she does see, she doesn't like.

Carl and I have no interest in following up on the call. But making people feel heard is part of the job. And with Smith's apartment empty, this nosy old woman is the best lead we've got on anything resembling a case.

I haven't told Carl about the rope night. I tell myself it's because of Al's instructions: to make sure anything Rosenthal-related goes through him, and him alone. But I've already violated the basic understanding beneath those directions. I met Marie Rosenthal. I know who she knows. And Al doesn't know that I know.

It'd be nice to talk to someone about it. Carl's a good guy. He'd have an idea about what to do. And he might understand.

After I come clean with him about the reasons I took this job in the first place. After he finds out that he doesn't really know the friend he's been hanging out with for thirty-five years.

We pull up to the curb outside Mrs. Davis's house at 10:35 p.m. . . . right behind a familiar gray Subaru Outback. When Carl's not looking, I snap a picture of the license plate.

"... and I don't mean to pry, you understand," says Mrs. Davis. She leads us up a creaking staircase. She flicks through a fistful of keys on a large ring, looking for the one that will open Unit 3. The hem of her lavender house dress trails on the dusty landings.

"But I have to think about what's best for the neighborhood."

We knock. Muffled country music plays inside the apartment. Otherwise, no response.

"We've got nothing," I say to Carl.

"Nothing!" says Mrs. Davis. "Not that I go poking about in other people's business, but the look of some of these—"

"We're sorry, ma'am," says Carl. "But we need reasonable suspicion to search someone's house without a warrant. And we don't have that here."

He's fudging the truth a little—the definition of "reasonable" has expanded a lot in the last few years. But I'm not about to call him on it.

"Thank you for your call," I say. "Let's go."

"I'm telling you," Mrs. Davis says to our descending backs, "there's something going on in—"

Over the twanging of guitars comes the unmistakable sound of a hand slapping bare skin, and a subsequent shriek.

Mrs. Davis would be rubbing her hands if they weren't busy unlocking the door.

We enter a single large room—kitchenette in one corner, couch and TV in the other. The music—and the regular thudding—come from behind a half-shut door, set in the back wall. I cross the room first, Carl and Mrs. Davis following close behind.

I will this moment to stretch out, forever. So that I never have to reach the source of those sounds.

The slaps are irregular. Long pauses—then two, three at a time. The floorboards creak. This building, like much of Boston, is old. The walls are mostly paint, the floor varnish. Decades ago, someone brushed over a penny, which is now embedded in the gloss. There are patterns in the ceiling stucco. The building settles into itself.

We reach the bedroom. I look back at Carl. *Too small for Mrs. Davis to see*, he shrugs. I push the door open, knocking it against a dresser.

A cool breeze blows in through the open window. In the far corner of the room, a suitcase lies open, clothes neatly folded inside. The rest of the floor space is taken up by a queen-sized bed.

Verity Smith sits on the edge, her arm frozen in mid-air. The pink outline of a hand radiates warmly from Pepper's left ass cheek. The small woman is tied up, and bent over Verity's knee.

They look at us. We look at them. Tim McGraw sings about church, and Mrs. Davis hisses.

"Hoookay," says Carl. His right hand extends, palm-down, in the universal cop gesture for *chill*—with the implied *or else*. The left reaches for his cuffs.

"Now, let's all just take it easy . . ."

He undoes the snap on the leather holster.

Pepper stares at him, shaking.

Verity watches me.

On the bed, next to a tidy pile of rope bundles, rests a curved metal tool—a blade, housed on the inside of a hairpin turn of molded plastic. An EMT's rescue hook. Designed to cut accident victims out of seat belts. Or bottoms out of rope.

"Knife!" I say.

I reach for my gun—making sure to elbow Carl in the solar plexus.

He groans like an old man sitting down in an easy chair and falls to his knees on the warped hardwood floor. Mrs. Davis screams and runs back out of the apartment, house dress billowing out behind her. Verity and Pepper stare at me.

Go! I mouth, tipping my head toward the open window. Verity nods. In a single motion, she rights Pepper, grabs the safety hook, and wrenches it down: ropes fall, severed, in a heap. By the time I haul Carl up to his feet, they're gone.

"Carl, I'm so sorry, I thought—"

"—fuck's sake—" says Carl, shaking his head and waving the apology away. He tries, and fails, to suck in some air. "—car!"

Pepper's taillights disappear around a corner as we clamber into the unmarked sedan. We pull away from the curb. The lights hidden in the grill throw flashes of blue onto the peeling paint and sagging porches. Carl steers with one hand, and shouts into the radio with the other.

"What part of 'naked women' is so hard to understand?!" he says.

Pepper is good—really good. In the two minutes we manage to keep on her, she demonstrates perfect evasive driving technique: she corners, serpentines, and skids so smoothly that the other drivers can hardly be aware any traffic laws are being broken.

We zip through red lights and swerve around cars, following the hatchback as far as Packard's Corner. We get stuck behind a passing Green Line trolley.

When we finally cross the intersection, she's gone.

Marie / Washington, D.C. / 2007

The van pulls up beside the woman as she walks down an abandoned street—the timestamp on the footage reads 1:35 a.m. The sliding door opens, and three men jump out onto the sidewalk. Silently, two of them grab an arm each, and start pulling her back toward the waiting van. In monochrome silence she screams, until the third man reaches around her face and clamps a gloved hand over her open mouth. She disappears; the door closes; the van drives off, out of frame.

Slowly, I close my work laptop while my heart flutters a bit in my chest.

It's fine, everything's fine—there was a witness off-camera who saw the whole thing and got the license plate. They arrested the men that same night, and the woman was back in her apartment before sunrise. So everything's cool. The way I'm reacting isn't weird.

My throat feels like it's full of superglue. I grab a can of seltzer from the break room fridge. It helps with the dry mouth . . . but not with the warm feeling spreading outward from my stomach till it reaches up to my nose and the tops of my cheeks. And down between my legs.

I'm agitated—that's it. This was a crime, and I'm in law enforcement. So I hate crime. Very, very much. I hate it so much that when I see something like this, I get flushed and light-headed and can count my pulse in my pelvis.

I only watch the video four more times before I delete it from my PC.

Al's trying so hard—pounding away like an otter with a clamshell. I do my best to be turned on.

I like him. I *love* him. He's handsome. I still obsess over his cheekbones. And those *eyes*—green like cut emeralds. For two years now those eyes, and that smile, and the way he somehow manages to hold open doors and slide out chairs without looking like a sap—these things, and my belief he could take on the world and win—they were enough. Enough to make me forget, for a while, what I am.

My cheap bed frame squeaks. Closing my eyes, I drift back to the office, and to the video I ought to be disgusted by. The one that should get me angry. The one that gets me excited, in a way I can't bring myself to talk about with the man currently inside of me.

Al's hand is on my chest, squeezing. I pick it up and bring it to my face. I brush his knuckles along my jaw. I kiss his palm. I turn his hand and hold it down over my mouth, pressing my lips shut and squeezing my cheeks around his hard fingers.

My head gets heavy and tight. I feel small, and used, and overwhelmed. I feel good. I arch up into him and he slips in deeper than I think we've ever gone—I'm wet like a bar of soap in a hot shower.

Al stops moving.

I open my eyes. Those green pupils are staring, looking down at me. The thing beneath him.

"Wh . . . what are you doing?" he asks.

We went on lockdown once because a man with a gun made it past the lobby and occupied the elevator bank for half an hour before being taken down. That was almost as scary as this.

"Nothing!" I say. I grab his wrist and kiss the back of his hand. "Keep going. Please."

Al smiles. He starts moving again.

The video comes back—I can't help it. Picturing myself on the floor of that van as it rolls quietly through the streets of Washington—imagining the sound of duct tape being ripped open, the smell of leather gloves—I finally manage to squeeze out an orgasm. Relieved, Al finishes inside me.

We lie next to each other, silently, for five endless minutes. I need to get rid of the silence—to say something that addresses the weird feeling between us. Anything. The first thing I can think of.

"Hey," I say to Al's chest. "Do you want to move in together?"

Sean / Boston, MA / 2008

I sit on the porch swing, reading *The Time Garden* again. I'm at the part in the story where the characters from the 1920s (Jane, Mark, Katherine, and Martha) run into their future children on a cannibal island. It's my favorite part of the book, and the series: the natives catch the kids from the '20s and tie them to gigantic spears stuck into the ground. The illustration of this moment gets a whole page to itself.

It's a really good drawing. The strands of rope are detailed. They wrap around the kids' bodies, squeezing them a bit against the poles. Where the rope crosses over clothes, the lines show how the fabric is stretched or bunched up. It must have taken a long time to do.

I'm not that good. We only learned about perspective in art class last year. I practice by drawing icicle monsters. Like giant turtles, but with rows of spikes on their backs.

I balance *The Time Garden* on my knees and, with the stub of a yellow pencil from last year's school supplies, draw pieces of gray duct tape over the characters' mouths. I've done this before—a few times—and erased it. There are smudges all around the kids' faces, and the paper is a bit thinner near their lips than on the rest of the page. I'm always afraid someone's going to go into my room, pull the book off my shelf, and see what I did. They'd be mad, and ask me why I drew something like that. I wouldn't even know what to tell them.

It makes me happy. It's exciting to draw people tied up, and to know that the drawings are in my room, hidden in the electronic piggy bank or under the waxy patterned paper at the bottom of the sock drawer. When I make these pictures, or look at them, some part of me stops feeling nervous for a minute. I feel safe. I did the same thing to Alice in my school copy of *Through the Looking Glass*.

Today I feel good about it. It's my book, and I can do what I want with it. And I do want this. Whenever I erase my drawings, I think about putting them back in the book. It feels better with them in.

I put the final touches on my work, and take a second to enjoy it. Then I put the book back in my room, in its white cardboard sleeve with the rest of the books in the series. I grab my bike out of the basement and take the hill down away from my house, coasting.

This is the hot, dead part of the summer. Most of the families in the neighborhood are away on vacation, and there are only a few cars on the street. The bike picks up speed on the slope, and I pretend I'm on a speeder, like Anakin in *Episode II*. I weave from curb to curb between manhole covers, blasting mailboxes and the crow that sags on the neighbor's fence post. Like a glob of the sandy black goo that holds electrical poles in the ground. He opens his wings to fly, then changes his mind and sinks back down.

It's nice to be alone. Sounds—an engine, a sprinkler, a tree in the wind—are cooler when I'm by myself because I'm not focused completely on the people around me. Making sure I know where they're standing, and keeping track of what they're saying, and whether it's bad. I don't have to pretend that I care about the Red Sox and what happens to them, or act like I'm something other than a Jedi flying through the Tatooine desert to kill a bunch of Tusken Raiders. I can do stuff that matters.

The air over the mini-mall parking lot is wavy. Heat moves up through the rubber soles of my shoes and into the bottoms of my feet. I clip my bike to the stand in front of the Blockbuster, and pull open the front door. Hot and cold air swirl around each other till the door shuts and the bell stops ringing. The teenagers standing behind the counter in blue polo shirts ignore me as I walk over to the magazine rack.

On the top of the rack is a row of magazines wrapped in dark plastic—the stuff kids aren't supposed to see. The thought of someone actually picking one of those up and carrying it over to the register to pay for it is crazy to me. The cashiers would know! They would know what you were buying and planning to look at.

You can't leave traces like that. Someone will find them. And then something bad will happen.

One magazine doesn't have any plastic wrap on it, even though it probably should: the *Sports Illustrated Swimsuit Edition*. Checking again to make sure the boy and the girl by the front desk aren't looking, I grab it off the top shelf—like I have every free afternoon this summer—and move over to the video games section, where it will be harder to see me if they look up.

The women are covered in paint. Some of them are done up to look like tigers, others like famous pieces of art. All except one. She's the centerfold: an Asian model, kneeling against a red background and holding a sheathed katana between her tits. Sort of elegant—lots of shadow. Classy.

If I could just bring the magazine home . . . The pages are glossy, which makes drawing harder, but Carl lent me his paint markers last week. I've gotten pretty good at ropes by tracing the illustrations in *The Time Garden*—I can imagine some wraps connecting her wrists to the handle of the sword . . . but I can only look at it here. They probably wouldn't even sell it to me. And even if they would, I could never take it up there and let them know I wanted to buy it.

Unless I didn't have to buy it.

There are cameras in all four corners of the store, and mirrors high up on the walls so that the people behind the counter can see down the aisles. Between the monitors and the mirrors, they have the whole floor covered. Except for one small area.

The Horror section faces the store's big display window, so all the VHS boxes are sun-bleached. The monsters—an evil snowman; an evil gingerbread man; an evil leprechaun—look even freakier with the color drained out of them. Like a bit of normal, everyday life thrown in makes the scare worse.

None of the people in the parking lot are looking this way. Lifting my shirt, I suck in my stomach so it makes a little cave, and tuck the magazine into my waistband.

The girl at the register is head-down in her phone, texting—tapping one key three times, another twice, the next one four times. I can leave right now, if I'm quiet about it. In and out, no worries. Instead, I walk toward the register.

The girl with braces looks down at the KitKat bar on the counter.

"No movies?" she says.

"No, not today," I say.

This is so stupid. I could have been gone! She takes so long picking up the candy, flipping it over, finding the bar code under the flap. Does she know? My stomach is getting sore. It starts to shake.

"One-twenty-five," she says.

I put the cash on the counter. She holds out my receipt. I reach for it without raising my shoulders and tuck it away in my Velcro wallet. Then I walk out the front door.

I ride straight off the curb, and my tailbone smacks into the seat. An old woman in a red car beeps at me. I pedal as fast as I can back to the house and lie on my bed till my body stops shaking. The markers are waiting on my desk.

Every line has to be perfect—the right thickness, the right shape. I leave the rope to dry and add in the tape, drawing the near edge so that it's a little wider than the one farther away. Feeling giddy with all of this, I go big and try adding a blindfold, which I've never done before.

It comes out perfectly. The picture is beautiful.

It's *Criminal Minds* night. This week's episode is about a boy named Nathan Harris. Sort of a twist on the usual story: Unlike the typical unsubs who have to be caught, Nathan reaches out to the team at Quantico himself.

Nathan's been feeling the urge to restrain people. To hurt them. He talks with Reed about the research he's done into "sexual sadism." There's a shot of his mom leafing through a magazine she found in his room, that has pictures of bruises and cuts pasted onto swimsuit models.

Nathan worries that, someday, his feelings will get the better of him, and he will kill somebody. At the end of the episode, he tries to kill himself to keep that from happening. He slits his own wrists, but Reed finds him in time to put pressure on the bleeding.

After they load Nathan in an ambulance, Reed wonders if he did the right thing. Maybe it would have been better to let Nathan die.

On the night of the spring dance, Carl steals a beer from his dad's basement mini-fridge. He and Jake split it behind the gymnasium. They're so sure they're wasted that they take out their dicks and piss on a pile of volleyball nets.

I don't have any beer. I never drink or smoke. I've seen the way older kids act when they're high. Loose. Like someone pulled all the fences down. If

I got that relaxed, I might say something. People would know what I was thinking. And anyway, you can't work for the CIA if you test positive for pot, and we learned in health class that it stays in your hair follicles for ten years.

Tracy Milligan rubs her tiny ass against Jake's crotch while the DJ plays "Promiscuous" by Nelly Furtado. Jake stands on the three-point line, hands in the air, protected from the chaperones by a group of kids that crowd around the two of them. Girls like Jake. He can afford to be drunk, and loud, and funny. He's got nothing to hide.

The library copy of the DSM is no help. It's just lists of symptoms. No explanation that makes sense. No good reason why I react to the wrong things: the pretty technicians at the orthodontist's office, with their huge eyes above tight masks that hide half their faces; Veronica, sitting in front of me in Latin class, who takes off her sandals during PowerPoints about Cicero or the Carthaginians, showing off the soles of her feet; a doctor's hand in a latex glove. The fucking cartoon about the spies running around in bright-colored rubber catsuits.

Veronica's down there, right now, writing down a song for the DJ, and instead of planning how to ask her to dance, all I can think about is lacing her into an armbinder, pulling her hair, and shoving a ball gag in her mouth. In my head, I do the same or worse to the girl from Chemistry class, and the girl who plays the timpani drum in the band, and the boy from the soccer team with the freckles. I'm in love with half the goddamn school.

I'm disgusting.

All the dancing and bright lights were harshing Carl's buzz, so he sits on the bleachers with me, watching the people we know move back and forth in sneakers, with their hands on each others' waists. During one of the slow songs, he leans his head on my shoulder and goes to sleep. I wonder if he blacked out.

His cheek is soft. He hasn't grown any hair yet, and he's self-conscious about it. He shouldn't be. His lips are open, a little bit. I can imagine them opening wider, and I wonder what they would feel like on my—

I slip out from under him, lay his head on the bench, run down the bleachers to the bathroom.

Cold water on my face doesn't help. Nothing ever helps. I'm wrong; I've always been wrong, and nothing is ever going to fix it.

The boy in the mirror stares back at me, water dripping from his nose and chin. There's nobody else by the sinks. I check under the stall doors. No shoes.

I wait a second to make sure no one else is coming in. Then I punch myself in the stomach, chest, and jaw, again and again, until I'm not horny anymore.

After the dance, I say goodnight to mom and dad, and go up to my room. I put on my pajamas and lie on my side.

It was really noble, what Nathan did. He was brave to tell the FBI what was going on, and to try the other thing when that didn't work.

It's just a TV show. I've never hurt anyone. I don't want to hurt anyone. Yet.

I wait until my parents are asleep. Then I get out of bed, and quietly pull the magazine out from underneath the dresser. Using the light from the streetlamp outside, I cut my work into tiny pieces. I mix the pieces up, divide the pile in two, and flush each half in one of the toilets, upstairs and downstairs. Then I take out an eraser and rub out my drawings from *The Time Garden*.

Sean / Boston, MA / 2030

"That's two of us you've put out on the street."

Pepper punches my arm. But she's grinning. Her hair has been trimmed down to the skull.

"Thanks," she says.

"Any time."

I'm back in the condo for the second time in as many weeks. Again, I met the crew at the theater. Again, I accepted the blindfold over my eyes, and got in the car. Again, we drove through a chunk of the night to arrive here, at Kevin and Daphne's. Mostly everything's the same. The couch, love seat, and coffee table are flush with the walls, as before. Rope kits lie on the floor, packed neatly or sloppily depending on who put them together.

Kevin mixing a pitcher of instant pink lemonade with his shirt off is new. As is the second metal tripod, which Jack is putting together with a wrench. The biggest change is in the tone of the room.

They're all different around me tonight. Still wary, but not on high alert like before. There are smiles and nods. When the lemonade is done, Kevin secures an upline to the first tripod, then claps me on the back with a meaty hand.

"You're welcome in this casa," he says.

From their point of view, a fundamental shift has occurred, signaling some change in me they can trust. I hit Carl—one of my own tribe—so that two members of theirs could make an escape. That's a commitment on my part. If I get caught hanging out with them now, they imagine, it'll be worse for me than it would have been before.

They're not wrong. I have skin in it now, and that makes them feel a bit safer than they did the last time I was here. Turning them in would mean turning myself in, too. It's a shaky kind of trust.

I'll take it.

Daphne, hanging upside down by her bent leg, says I'm a "nice young man." It's silly—she and Kevin aren't even ten years older than me. We laugh. Even Verity, though it's more subdued. She applies oil to a length of hemp, and keeps her head turned.

I hold my hand up to Pepper's head-stubble, and she lets me rub it.

"Sorry about the apartment," I say.

Pepper shrugs. "Be sorry about the car; I'll have to get rid of it now. We're lucky Kevin and Daphne are letting us crash. There are other places we could go, but . . . I want to stick it out with Marie."

"I thought the other groups were . . ."

"Gone?" says Pepper.

I clear my throat.

"They are," she says. "But we have friends. Vanilla poly people. Lots of queers. Even a few straights. The underground is big."

She jolts like her morning alarm just went off.

"Not that I need to be telling you any of that . . ."

She sips from her glass of water. I pull my lip.

"I will miss my rope kit," she says. "Had it since I was eighteen. . . . Do you remember Hubba Hubba? Up near Central?"

"I passed it a few times."

"That's where I bought it. They were good people."

Pepper turns to leave, then pauses. She gives me a quick hug, then goes to help Verity at the other end of the room.

Jack looks down from his perch on a kitchen stool. He's finished putting the bolts in, and now he hangs a suspension ring from the point of the tripod.

"You surprised us, detective," he says.

"I surprised myself."

He removes a set of three heavy nylon straps from a cardboard box, and lines them up on the ground beneath the tripod. They meet in the middle, where a steel ring holds them together. Each of the outer ends gets attached to one of the tripod's feet. Then Jack ratchets down the straps till they're good and tight, pulling the legs in toward the center. Seems like overkill—the metal looks pretty sturdy by itself.

"Do you really need those?" I ask.

"You have no idea," says Jack, shaking his head. "There was this one convention where the organizers didn't put them on. One of the presenters saw, and rightly raised hell about it, and then the organizers started attacking *her* online . . . just trust me, you always put the straps on."

He's meticulous—checking over all the bolts one last time to make sure it's sound—guaranteeing that his friends will be safe when they go up there. When he stretches up to test the connections at the top, the hem of his shirt lifts a bit, past the top of his pants. The skin there is smooth.

Marie appears next to us.

"You know, Jack didn't want to bring you here," she says.

"I just thought it was a little rash," he says.

"I believe your exact words were 'batshit lunacy.'"

Jack blushes—red on white—and goes back to rigging.

"Well," he says. "He's here now."

Folks settle into the evening. The pink lemonade is passed around. Kevin and Daphne regale me with tales of their seafaring adventures in the Caribbean.

"I looked over the edge, Sean, and I'm telling you, I could see right down to the bottom," says Daphne. "The water down there is like glass when you're up close to it, or bright blue if you're sitting on the beach. You can see crabs walking along on the sand..."

"We'll have to take you out to the Harbor sometime," says Kevin. "Sure, you've been on the ferry, but sailing it... that's a whole different beast."

About an hour in, people gather around the original tripod: Verity's going to take Pepper through a complicated suspension sequence, and Pepper wants an audience. As she starts to go up, Marie beckons me to the side with a finger.

"I've got something for you."

Pepper whimpers as Verity applies even more tension to some shin rope. Marie and I leave the group and make our way toward the window, where the curtains are still drawn shut, like last time. Her bag sits on the floor. She bends down and starts rummaging through it.

As an afterthought, she pulls the curtains aside.

At first the scene makes no sense: a confusion of colors, depths, and intensities. But after a few moments the various shapes and their relationships to one another snap into place, and it's almost a physical thing, like being shoved backward from the glass.

Far below me is a street packed end to end with cars; farther away is a stretch of bright green grass, with brown dirt forming a diamond at one end of it. White lines radiate outward from one corner of that diamond to meet the towering wall that surrounds the field, all of it illuminated by three-story stadium lights. A milling crowd of thousands swarms over the streets, all funneling there, to this glowing heart at the center of a few city blocks.

We're across the street from Fenway Park. A ten-minute walk from the movie theater garage.

Marie pokes me. She's holding out a hank of rope.

"Hemp," she says.

"What?"

"This rope," she says, enunciating, "is made of hemp. Easier to work with than that . . . stuff you've got now."

"Oh . . . thank you."

I know this block. I know this exact building. From a west-facing unit on this floor I could probably see the Pond. My house.

". . . a whole *hour*," I say. "We went on the highway . . ."

Marie smirks.

"We know you a little better now," she says. "Welcome home."

Across the room, Jack shows Luke how to put on a "gunslinger" harness. Ilana stands between them, hands on her hips, lending a leg to each man. Verity and Pepper finish bundling rope, and Pepper lies down with her head in Verity's lap. Verity runs lazy fingertips over the girl's stubbly scalp. Together, Marie and I watch the group of them, playing with each other, being who they are. The rope in my hands is heavy.

"Why did you bring me here?" I say.

"Well," says Marie—again with that fucking grin—"somebody had to teach you how to tie a proper harness."

"Seriously," I say. "I need to make sense of this. You're all criminals. I'm a *cop*. So how do you justify—"

She holds up a hand. Finally, the smile is gone.

"Spare me," she says. "I've had the whole argument with each of them a few times over."

Daphne's curled up in a ball in Kevin's lap. She dozes, and the hairs on Kevin's chest move back and forth with her soft breathing.

"Call it a hunch," she says. "But something tells me that a guy who would go through all that effort just to find some videos—even though watching them could cost him his job, or worse—might be someone who knows how important all of this is. He might be more than *just* a cop."

For a few moments, the only sounds in the apartment are the creak of the rig, the buzz of one strand of rope running under another, and lo-fi beats on the surround-sound speakers.

"There was a nightclub around here," says Marie, "called Machine. Dark inside, no windows. A gay bar on most nights. But once a month, on the third Saturday, they'd open up the downstairs level for a themed night—a fetish night—called SinOMatic.

"The music was just okay: industrial, goth, that sort of thing. And there were always at least a few straights slumming it with the weirdos."

"Doesn't sound like much fun," I say.

"It could be. And it was what we had. Sometimes it'd be raining, or snowing. We'd stand out front, anyway, waiting in fetish gear to get inside. Or it'd be a game night, and all these Sox fans with mustard stains on their cargo shorts would walk by and stare. . . ."

She shakes her head. She's smiling.

"You didn't feel . . . weird?" I say.

"We *were* weird," she says. "We're still weird—the ones who are left. But we were weird *together*. Not just the people in Boston's cozy little scene, where you had to network for months just to get your foot in the door. But all of us. The New Yorkers, who'd pull crazy suspension stunts in the middle of Central Park and post the pictures anywhere. The ones from Chicago, Austin, LA—even the small towns had little groups that kept to themselves.

"A web of us, Sean, all around the country. All around the world. All the weirdos—non-monogamists; the rope freaks; the hypnotists, impact tops, and needle players—sharing space with the goths and the circus people, slipping in and out of the normal world to hold down jobs that could pay for airfare and convention tickets. Only becoming real at night."

She pauses, watching the others play.

"We were a tribe," she says. "You could find your people anywhere, if you knew where to look. A whole hidden world . . . I don't know how many of us are left."

I do. At least, I know how many people are still on the IAB's wanted list. The number is small. I helped reduce it.

I'm responsible for that strained note in Marie's voice, well-hidden but just barely disturbing the smooth flow of her talk. Thinking about that makes me uneasy.

"What happened to the club?" I say.

Marie takes in a small breath, and lets it out. She raps the wall behind her.

"It's condos now."

Carl / Boston, MA / 2030

Sean is in Al's office for an hour and ten minutes. Door closed. When he finally comes back out, he doesn't even sit down—just grabs the coat off the back of his chair, heads for the door.

"Good talk?" I say.

"Yeah, just stuff for the Smith case," he says. He turns around. Partly. But he doesn't slow down.

"You mean *our* case?" I say to his back.

But he's already gone.

Al sits at his desk with the door propped open, head down over some paperwork. I knock.

"Mr. Berg—Al?"

"That's my name," he says, not looking up. "What's up?"

"I was just thinking," I say, "I know Sean's been talking with you about the Smith case."

Now he leaves the paperwork alone. He raises an eyebrow.

"Hmm?"

"Verity Smith?" I say. "Local rope person?"

"Ah, right, sure," says Al, nodding.

"Anyway, Sean and I have put in a lot of time on that one together, so I know the details. If you ever need some extra help—"

Al puts up a hand. He smiles. "I appreciate the offer, detective," he says, "but Sean and I are all set for now."

"But sir—"

Still smiling. Wide. Lots of teeth. "I said we got it, Carl."

I back out of the office. "Cool," I say. "Cool."

I should leave it alone. Al's a Bureau guy. This is clearly Bureau business. If it were good for me to get involved, I'd be involved. In whatever it is.

Sean's been ducking me for weeks, but it feels different from the way he normally avoids socializing. Normally there's the sense that he's actively trying not to see people on a given night. He'll have excuses ready to go, like he thought them out ahead of time. They always check out: NOVA really *is* airing a special on black holes for one night only; he really *does* have a doctor's appointment.

Lately he can't even be bothered. When I ask if he wants to hang out, he mumbles about "doing something for Al," then fades back into whatever he's working on. Like I'm not even there.

If they'd just tell me what's going on, instead of pulling all this need-to-know, in-too-deep bullshit, I could help. The more resources you can put into a case, the more likely it is to be solved. The secrecy doesn't make any sense.

Unless there's a reason they're boxing me out.

That's paranoid. Sean barely talks, anyway—this is just a more annoying version of the same thing. And maybe Al wants to minimize the number of people on the case to prevent leaks. Marie Rosenthal has gotten away from the Bureau before. It'd be an embarrassment to him if the same thing happened again when they've got her cornered like this.

She's definitely the priority. He made *that* clear the day he walked in. Every time it seems like someone's working on anything else, he redirects them back to Rosenthal. Schmidt's going to give herself an aneurysm, the way she hunts this woman while still trying to hold down the usual caseload of exhibitionists and subway masturbators. Always, always back to the one undying topic: Bring me this leader from the local rope community.

But there are other ways in. More developed leads, that might even get us to his ultimate target. Why the obsession over one woman ... and why does everything have to go directly through him?

And Sean allows it to be this way. He's happy with the new arrangement.

Al locks his door when he heads out at five. A few hours later, the night shift starts to trickle in. Then Oscar, the man from the cleaning service, arrives.

Oscar always goes clockwise when he's cleaning, moving from office to office around the floor. When he's done emptying the trash cans and vacuuming the rugs, he comes out here to the bullpen, and sweeps the laminate floor with a big push-broom before giving it a once-over with a decaying gray mop.

Al's office is third in line. After a few minutes, Oscar reaches his door, unlocks it with the big ball of keys on his belt, and pulls his cart inside. While he hums along to something on his headphones, I walk past him and into the bathroom. It's empty.

The toilet in the far stall is still broken. We've been told that the wrong kind of pressure could cause serious damage. We aren't to touch it under any circumstances. I check the stalls, one by one. All empty. And no footsteps in the hallway.

I open the door, aim, and kick the pipe connecting the toilet to the wall.

I'm lucky. No one sees me run to the locker room to swap out my wet shirt for a dry one. No one notices my shoes squeaking slightly as I walk back to my desk. I let Oscar vacuum for a few minutes. Then I wave at him.

"You smell something, bud?" I ask.

Oscar puts up a finger, turns off the vacuum, and pulls off his headphones. He leans in the doorframe.

"Sorry, what'd you—oh, *shit*!"

Oscar stares, wide-eyed, at the puddle that's spreading quickly from beneath the door of the men's room. From his cart, he grabs a plunger and a tool belt, then sprints down the hallway toward the flowing water. He shoulders the door open. A small wave of water laps over his boots, and he dives into battle.

"*Pinche baño*—!" he says, before the sound of hissing water cuts him off.

The detectives around the bullpen holler and whistle. The officers run their hands over their faces and groan.

While they're all focused on Oscar, I slip through the open door into Al's office.

On the desk is a business card: contact info for a high-ranking member of the IAB. I put it in my pocket. There's also a fuzzy manila folder, with a tab that says *Rosenthal, Marie*. I open it.

Marie Rosenthal: Boston Latin School, class of 1990. Bachelor's from New York University; doctorate in computer science from MIT. Never married. Before spending several quiet years as a corporate cybersecurity consultant, she made a name for herself in the aughts and early '10s as an expert in the tracking of online behavior.

She spent the first chunk of her career gathering intelligence for the NSA ... where she worked closely with one Alan Bergman.

Al / Boston, MA / 2006

Marie's the first person who's never made an explicit comment about the way my leg bounces when I'm sitting. Even at the dinner table, when the water in the glasses shakes. She just goes on eating like it's no big deal for the floorboards to creak that way.

I haven't tried to thank her for this. It means more than I can figure out how to put into words—the *not* doing anything about it. Just letting it be. I can get control sooner when no one else brings it up.

The leg is going full speed now as we make our descent into Logan. Like an oil derrick on overdrive, sucking crude up out of the ground. All of my concentration will stop it from moving, but the second my mind wanders to my hair, my breath, or the state of my clothes, it cuts loose, hammering away at the cabin floor and rocking the tray tables in their skinny plastic arms. The old White lady in the aisle seat levels me with a stink eye, which I can fully appreciate.

The *Fasten Seatbelt* light flashes on. Marie puts a hand on the inside of my thigh, leans over, and kisses me on the cheek.

"If my parents don't like you," she says, "I'll disown them."

The pumping slows down a little.

Marie's father greets us at the front door of the condo, reading glasses hanging from a chain around his neck. Forgetting about them, he wraps his arms around Marie and squeezes her tight to his sweatered chest.

"There's my little mouse," he says. Then he puts her down, and holds out a hand with big, round knuckles.

"You must be Alan," he says.

"Call me Al," I say.

His grip is surprisingly warm, and strong. He wrestles Marie's bag away from her and leads us into the living room. Then he steals my bag as well, and tips his head toward an open doorway, through which wafts the smell of roasting vegetables.

"Mom's in the kitchen," he says to Marie. Turning to me, he adds: "Don't worry, she doesn't bite. Often."

Then he winks, and disappears down a hallway. Marie closes her eyes and folds her hands in front of her face. Now is exactly the wrong time to poke.

"'*Mouse*'?" I say.

She folds an arm over her chest, and with the other hand pinches the bridge of her nose. "Because I 'like computers' so much," she says.

"I think it's cute."

"You will never bring it up again."

In the kitchen, Marie's mom wrangles a cut of meat the size of my thigh into an ancient Dutch oven. Hands dripping with blood and brine, she gives Marie a side-hug around the shoulders, pulling her fingers back to keep them out of her daughter's hair. A piece of gristle clings to the underside of one manicured nail. I get air-kisses, one on each cheek. Mrs. Rosenthal's dangly earrings tinkle as she swings her head from one side of my face to the other. The kisses snap in my ears like chewing gum.

"Anything we can do to help?"

"Oh, God no," says Mrs. Rosenthal. "I'm on a tight schedule, and I don't need you kids crawling around underfoot—"

On the counter, a digital alarm goes off.

"Jesus Christ, the potatoes," she says. "Out! Out! Everybody out!"

Shooed back into the living room, I close my eyes and sink into an overstuffed armchair. A wooden serving spoon raps against a porcelain dish; a sheet is thrown up into the air and drawn, gently, down onto a bed; the old radiator knocks and gurgles in the corner. Then there's a hand on my wrist—a counterweight pulling me up, tearing me away from the cushions' fluffy embrace.

"Let's go," says Marie.

"I haven't even taken my jacket off."

She puts her shoulder in the small of my back, and pushes.

"Mom will be in a killing mood till the cooking's done," she says. "I always go out and do something fun till it's time for dinner. So move."

Across the street from the condo is a trolley stop, with a green streetcar moving fast toward it. We sprint through the freezing air and hop aboard just as the driver is shutting the doors. Bell clanging, we roll east, toward downtown Boston.

At the Museum of Fine Arts ticket counter, Marie pulls out her old MIT student ID and gets a small discount on general admission. I have to pay full price.

"That's technically fraud," I say while we wait for the coat check guy to come back with our little plastic tags.

"Oh, yeah, I'm a big white-collar criminal now," she says, shaking her fist in front of her crotch.

A silver call bell sits on the counter. I run my finger slowly around the little button till Marie sees what I'm doing. She blushes, and glares at me. I ring the bell.

"All right, all right," says the harassed man in the branded polo. "Got 'em right here. You know there's a tip jar, too, if ya wanna get my attention."

We emerge into a high, marble rotunda. Four murals arch over us, featuring prominent figures from Greek mythology: Athena; Pan; Apollo and the Muses. While my neck is craned, Marie socks me on the arm.

"John Singer Sargent," she says.

An archway opens onto a bright dining area, where patrons can sip a glass of wine while talking about art. A door at the far end leads to the galleries.

We pass through rooms and centuries together. Adam and Eve are tossed out of a lush, green Eden through a hole in a rock wall, made to wander naked into a black land of twisted trees. A fashionably dressed lady leans one elbow on the railing of a box seat, taking in a show through a pair of opera glasses. A grinning South-American funerary mask looks on while we make out in front of it.

In the European section is a large painting focused on two figures. One, a girl in fine clothes, lies curled up against a fence, seemingly napping. The other, a dark-haired boy with a rake and a beat-up hat, leans on the fence from the other side, gazing down at her. It's *Haymaker and the Sleeping Girl* by Thomas Gainsborough. I pull Marie over to look at it with me.

Her exact words: "That painting sucks."

"It's my favorite!" I say.

She laughs. "Seriously? He's just *staring* at her. While she's *asleep*."

She's wrong, or only part right. She's describing, barely, what's happening on the surface of this painting. And even there I'd argue she isn't being fair. Beautiful as it is, the basic content in the frame isn't what matters here.

There is a fence between the haymaker and the girl. She glows in the afternoon sunlight; he is shaded by a nearby tree. They are effectively in two different worlds, which just so happen to run up against each other at this frozen instant in time. The boy is so close, he could reach out and drag his fingers through her curly hair.

But he won't. He can't. And that's what the painting is about. The flimsy link between their two worlds—want so strong it hurts. It's no coincidence that the boy folds his arm over his heart.

This is life on canvas. Knowing what you want, having it within arm's reach, and being too afraid to take it. The boy should hop over the fence. Or better yet, break it, and shove that yappy dog out of the way with his rake if he needs to. He should tell the girl what he's thinking, and how he feels. He should say exactly what she does to him, and what they ought to do about it.

He's a coward—hiding behind that fence like an archer afraid to lean around the wall and take the shot. Back there he's safe in his silence, and his worker's clothes, and the shade. Back there, he doesn't have to put himself on the line. He can torture himself thinking about what could be—without having to find out what *is*. He's stuck, in the place where we all get stuck—inches from the thing we've always wanted. Not content to stay where we are, but terrified to move any closer and watch it wake up and run away.

Thank God she's asleep, the boy thinks to himself. *Thank God she's not fully here, after all. That's the only reason I'm allowed to get so close. If she woke up, and saw what I am, she'd laugh in my face.*

"I just think it's well-done," I say.

"It's creepy, is what it is," she says.

On the way out, we each drop a dollar bill in the coat guy's jar. We go around back, past a pair of chubby eight-foot-tall baby heads planted on the MFA lawn, and cross the street to reach a grassy area crisscrossed with tiny creeks.

"Call it 'the Fens,'" she says, "or you'll sound like a tourist."

The wind is sharp, pinching my cheeks and the tips of my ears. Trees, black in the night, sway back and forth, their bare branches clacking. The light of the moon shines down through the spaces on a carpet of dead leaves, frosted grass, and water like wet ink. It gurgles around sheets of ice full of captured bubbles—they rock side to side in the current. We step lightly along the footpaths, passing in and out of shadows before taking a pause on a wrought-iron footbridge, where we rest our elbows on the railing.

"Now *this*," says Marie, spreading her hands to take in the trees, the leaves, and the deathly cold water, "is beauty."

Her face is pale except for her cheeks and the tip of her nose, where the wind has pulled rosy red to the surface of her skin. Her eyes glitter like the icicles that hang from branches all around us. They're just as sharp. I tuck a loose bit of her hair back under her knit cap.

"It really is," I say.

Looking down, at the reflections of the stars, she smiles.

A gust of wind booms toward us over the Fens, tilting the trees to one side and rippling the water in its path. It finds its way into my collar and up my pant legs, stealing the warmth from my very asshole before I have the chance to shiver. My nuts feel like they got stepped on.

"Even so," I say, "this state and its weather are crimes against nature. Snow in March . . . I can't wait to take you home."

She chuckles and opens her jacket. Holding me close, she guides my numb hands under her shirt, gasping when my frozen skin meets her warm belly. I slide my fingers around to the small of her back, pull her close, and kiss her mouth while the bridge creaks.

We board the Green Line and ride it back to the Rosenthals' place as tiny, dry flakes of snow whirl in the light of the streetlamps. Marie leans on my shoulder and dozes. I play with her hair, pulling the black ringlets until they spring back up to her scalp.

Seder food, it turns out, is delicious. And Mrs. Rosenthal is a far better cook than her daughter.

In the hours since we left, the population of the condo has swelled. Rosenthals ancient and young bump elbows as they reach for steaming plates of tzimmes and stuffed cabbage. They stand in the corners and the doorways. No one's *trying* to shout. But minute by minute the volume creeps up as everyone, trying to be heard, puts just a little more breath behind their stories of the past year's victories and losses: who graduated; who got married; who died. I am appraised on all sides by glances and questions. Marie's half-deaf grandmother pinches my stomach, shakes her head, and hands me three rugelach wrapped in a napkin. I eat them in front of her, and she pats my cheek.

Marie's little cousins sprint around the place, looking for the afikomen; they make way for Elijah, and pester the tipsy aunts and uncles to watch where they put their feet. The prophet wears sandals, they explain. They don't want anyone stepping on his toes.

Marie, flushed red after a few glasses of Manischewitz, calls her parents to task for converting her childhood bedroom to a guest suite.

"I wasn't in Virginia two days," she says over kugel and brisket, "before Dad started picking out curtains."

"You go in there tonight," Marie's father says, pointing at me with his fork, "and you tell me they aren't a perfect match for the coverlet."

In the middle of the table sit a salt and pepper shaker—a white ghost and a black ghost, hugging each other. Later in the evening, I see Mr. Rosenthal pass these quietly to Marie, who holds them tightly in her hands before giving her father a hard hug.

Eventually the last glasses of wine are drunk, and the coats peel off our bed in twos and bunches as couples and families say their goodbyes. The four of us stand at the door, waving at a minivan on its way back to Newton. Then we shut the door against the cold.

The dining room table is a blasted wasteland of egg noodles and raisins. I go hunting in the kitchen drawers for tinfoil till Marie's mom flicks my hands away.

"Go to bed," she says. Then she gives me an exhausted smile and squeezes my arms. "Happy Passover, Al."

Putting on her pajama pants, Marie stumbles, badly. I catch her before her head crashes into the nightstand, feeling something in my back click. She ruffles my hair and gives me a kiss on the cheek.

"Told you. They love you lots," she says, dropping onto the bed like a wet rag. "Jus' like I do."

I untangle the covers from her limbs and climb in beside her.

"Y'all have good taste," I say. "... mouse."

She goes for a smack but falls asleep before it's halfway done. Her arm lands across me. I leave it there.

Lying next to Marie—beneath that tasteful coverlet, head spinning from sweet wine—I think about the angel of death, hovering over the firstborn, and about the nature of lamb's blood.

Jack / Boston, MA / 2023

Sunlight like lemonade pours through the open window and onto the bed, splashing over our arms and the corner of Verity's face. Her fingers wrap softly around mine. I am filled with warm, wet sand. I could lie here for a week, sinking into the mattress and breathing in the back of her neck. But I have to piss.

I reach behind me to nudge Simon away, but my hand swings through empty air. He must've gotten up already. I kiss Verity on the temple. Eyes closed, she smiles.

Simon's hallway seems much longer than usual. He's in the kitchen, whisking eggs while bacon fries in a pan, filling the house with the smell of maple and pork fat. I lock the bathroom door, flick the plastic lid upright, and let go. It's like I'm coming again.

The bottom of the tub is wet. So was Simon's hair—and he's completely dressed, and breakfast is half-done. He's been up for a while.

In the kitchen, Verity sits at the counter in her bare feet and one of Simon's band t-shirts, chopping a cantaloupe. He stands by the stove, working a pan of scrambled eggs, a pitcher of pancake batter, and a hot griddle like a Baroque organist handling knobs, pedals, and keys. I squeeze his hip, and reach around him to grab a bag of coffee beans from the shelf. He smacks my hand, shakes his head, and points at a different roast. While the pot brews, Verity and I set out the plates.

One of the benefits of dating a chef: morning-after food that makes the walk of shame feel like a walk of acclaim. The pancakes are so airy they float in my mouth. The eggs are as yellow and fluffy as the baby chicks that might have been. The coffee is bitter, like dark chocolate. I've got to admit—it pairs perfectly with the buttered-up pancakes, drizzled with the syrup from the unlabeled glass bottles Simon gets from his "guy in Vermont." The bacon crackles like autumn leaves.

Verity sips her coffee with both hands. Her eyes peek out over the rim of her blue mug.

"So that was fun," she says.

I nudge her knee under the table, and she pushes back, smirking.

It still feels so fresh. The two of them; the three of us. Three years we've been doing this thing, and we still flirt like teenagers and laugh like little kids. Some new dimension reveals itself every time we get together: in him, or in her—or, best of all, in me. Sometimes in all three of us at once. As fast as I try to figure them out, they grow from their contact with me and with each other. Suddenly, they are no longer the thing I was studying. *We* are always a minute ahead of *me*, becoming something new I can never catch or pin down, as hard as I try.

Three *I*s, one *we*. And what passes between us like a baseball from hand to mitt again and again on a warm summer afternoon is free, and infinite, binding the whole world together and making us live.

Simon smiles when Verity squeezes his shoulder on her way back to the bedroom, but it's tired. He stares at his perfectly seasoned eggs, stirring them around his plate with a long fork.

Verity has to get to the lab early this morning, so I kiss her goodbye before I hop in the shower. When I get back out, Simon's lying on the couch, staring up at the ceiling. I lie down on top of him, folding my arms over his chest and resting my chin on my wrists.

"You're failing to enjoy your day off," I say. There's a pancake crumb on his collar. I pick it off and eat it. Simon doesn't move.

"The Amendment's going to pass," he says.

"No it's not," I say. "They're just a bunch of kooks who want to get laid. No one who wants to keep their job is going to vote for it. There's no way."

"We've said that before."

I scooch forward and kiss the underside of his jaw, still smooth from a morning shave, and make my way up toward his neck, where the tattoo of an abstracted circuit board merges into the bristle of his hair. He doesn't pull away, but neither does he lean into it. He doesn't turn his head down to meet mine or shift around to make room by his side on the couch. I move my hand down between us, until it's resting on his crotch, and give a gentle squeeze. He lies there like a dead body.

I hate this. This is the thing I hate, more than anything else. Simon's hurting. He's worried about silly things, impossible things—so in his head, he can't even appreciate what's in front of him.

It's his own fault. Him and his overextended sense of self. Soaking in the news all day, taking every bad headline like a sucker punch. He likes pain enough to go out and borrow it from others when he can't find enough of his own.

He's trapped in his own mind, in some ridiculous doomsday scenario he built all for himself—and he won't let me help. I'm here, another person, wanting him to feel better, and happy to do what it takes to make that happen, and he ignores me. Not even the dignity of a *no* from him. Just that cold, troubled face staring up at the underside of a coffin lid.

I push myself up, get dressed, and go to work, leaving Simon to himself.

Pepper / Cambridge, MA–Boston, MA / 2028

Rob's arm lies across my stomach like a wet seal. At three in the morning, I slide out from underneath it, and he rolls over onto his other side, never waking up. I take my laptop into the living room and sit before it, cross-legged, on the floor. It's an old machine. The fan hums. I start searching.

People tied up leads to a local traffic report. *People in rope* automatically corrects to *people* AND *rope*, which leads to sponsored content from national hardware store chains. *Hojojutsu* and *shibari* redirect to a Japanese-English dictionary that refuses to define those particular terms. *Pretty rope* offers up macrame.

It's like the whole web was wiped clean. Before I ever got the chance to explore it.

There's a notification from my email inbox. I open it and read the new message that just arrived.

I took the liberty of clearing out your search history at the source, it says. *You should be more careful what you look for.*

My name's Marie. We should talk.

She sends me to a condo off Newbury Street. Ritzy. Ivy climbs up the walls of the building. A copper awning, green with age, grows out over the entryway like a broad leaf. The knob is in the middle of the door.

This side street isn't crowded, but it isn't empty, either. It's the first warm night in a while, and the shops stay open late. Couples in tailored shirts and blouses stroll by on their way to Copley, or the Garden. I stand out in jeans and a t-shirt. I'd be easy to remember.

I ring the bell.

No one talks about the seconds between when you ring the bell and when the person comes down to meet you. That long stretch of time between a decision and the first of its consequences. I've done it—there's no returning to a world in which I did not press that button, and instead just turned around and walked off the steps. Back to my apartment, and my ongoing search for pilot jobs that don't exist anymore. Back to my approved partner. Back to anonymity and safety, maybe. Every part of that universe has been obliterated by a finger touching a white circle. And until the person I've come to see makes it down her steps and opens her front door, there is nothing there to replace it. I hang out over the void, and wait.

The funny knob turns. The black door swings open.

"Glad you came," says Marie.

There's carpet on the stairs. Beautiful carpet. Beautiful stairs. They wind up and up in a big, art deco spiral. A chandelier hangs from the middle of the ceiling, dripping with glass. There's wood paneling. Books on recessed shelves. A freaking globe in a bronze stand. Next she'll show me a stuffed gazelle head, and tell me about coming back from safari.

"Nice place," I say.

"Glad you like it," she says. "I'll let the owner know. He's a friend of mine."

I get the feeling I'm being laughed at. But by someone who wants good things for me. It's just a little bit terrible.

She brews a pot of tea over a stainless steel stove that has to be worth more than my life. She pours it into matching glazed mugs, and we sit across the counter from one another, steam rising up between us.

"So, Pepper," she says. "What can I do for you?"

"... You brought me here."

"I let you know where I was staying," she says. "You left your house, got on the train, walked up the steps, and rang the bell. So: What do you want?"

She's left the big windows open. Conversations float up from the street. I stare at a bowl full of exotic fruit.

"I..."

"Do you want to learn more about us?" she says. "Who we are, and what we do? Do you want to know how to hide? Or find out who you are?"

"Uh..."

She's looking me right in the eye, this whole time.

"Do you want to tie?"

"Oh! What? Me? No, I—No. Don't get me wrong; that's very kind of you to offer, and I'm flattered, but it's not really my ... what I mean is, I don't..."

She sits there, sipping her tea, listening to my word vomit. I could stammer for a week, and she'd just be sitting there. I focus on my breath for a moment, like they taught us in combatives.

"I don't ... do ... sex," I say.

She raises and drops one shoulder, and smiles. "Okay," she says.

Other than that, exactly nothing has changed. I still feel like she's waiting for something. I still feel awkward.

"So ... I'm sort of out of the running, as it were. Rope-wise."

"I disagree," says Marie. "Sure, for most people, there's an element of sex to it. But I've known many asexual folks who did rope, for many various reasons. For some it was a purely artistic thing. Others liked that it offers a way of being intimate without sex, if that's what everyone involved agrees to. Rope means different things to different people.

"Frankly, I'm surprised you haven't figured that out by now. You spent enough time reading up on *hojo* at the Academy."

I must look like I swallowed my own tongue because Marie goes on:

"I don't reach out to anybody unless I've done a very thorough background check. There are only so many of us left. We can't be too careful." She puts her mug down on what I think is an ivory coaster. "The fact that we're having this conversation right now means I have a good feeling about you."

An honest-to-God grandfather clock chimes the hour in the hallway. The woman from a world I know nothing about leans forward on the counter, hugging her elbows.

"Look, Pepper," she says. "Don't ask to tie if you don't want to. That'd be silly. But if you do want to, don't say 'no' when you mean 'I'm afraid.'"

The last weak little wisps of steam curl up out of my mug and disappear into the air. I take a breath, and swallow.

"I am afraid," I say. "And I do want to tie."

In her rope, I fly.

It's tighter than I expected—she says that's for safety, once we go up. But nothing pinches or gets uncomfortable in a bad way. In fact, it feels so good, it's hard to think. She works like a surgeon, each perfect motion opening me up, cutting away something that weighs me down. Knot by knot she takes away my hands, my feet, even my mouth. By the time she's ready to hoist me up off the ground, I can't move anywhere except where she puts me.

And I've never felt freer.

My body hangs from a beam in the living room, turning slowly in the air. My mind floats, somewhere. A place I've never been while awake. This person is literally a stranger I met online, and because of choices I've made tonight I can do nothing while she brushes her fingernails along my neck, my back, the arch of my foot. And that's good, because right now I don't want to do anything except look my own strange desire in the face—to examine this thing I've been hiding from for years—that a soldier isn't supposed to want— that no one is supposed to want— this loss of control and power, this unbearable closeness—I want to stare right at it and open my heart and say yes, and yes, and yes.

I sink into the bands, and fibers pull at my skin. It hurts. I'm moved, and I turn. I sweat into the twisted ropes. Her hands go everywhere we agreed, and nowhere we didn't. It's intimate, and because I'm not used to that, I become a mess.

Marie brings me down to earth. On the ground, in her arms, I cry.

Jack / Boston, MA / 2030

The old Korean man who likes to bike around the neighborhood collecting cans squeaks by my building, twin jumbo trash bags swinging from the broomstick on his shoulder. In the vacant lot down the street, a crowd of kids lights off a pile of firecrackers, and their gunshot popping ricochets off brick facades up and down the block. I sit in the window, sipping a gin and tonic while the sun sets behind the minaret on Malcolm X Boulevard.

It's good to relax. The evening is hot, and muggy. Slow. The glass in my hand drips, and I rub it against my forehead so the water trickles down into my eyes. The old box fan from the dollar store down the street drones in the corner.

My last place was cold. Freezing, even in the summer. Central AC and UV-filtering windows insulated everything. Quiet as a tomb, and on the thirteenth floor, overlooking Chinatown. A gym on the ground floor, with accompanying smoothie bar, and a swimming pool on the roof. I hosted dinner parties there. Fancy get-togethers, with white wine and fish. We'd talk about the latest political embarrassment, shake our heads, and feel powerless and drunk. Then Steven would bring up Proust, and that'd be the rest of the evening right there.

And in between, when I couldn't find an excuse to stay at the office past seven, there'd be those long weeknights by myself. Alone in an apartment designed with one bedroom, but with space enough for three.

When I broke the lease after six months, they kept my deposit. The owners of my current building were the first landlords I met who would talk to me about any date other than September first.

The toxic couple from the housing development walks past, husband and wife screaming at each other on their way to the grocery store. One car nearly clips another by jumping out of a side street without stopping. The offended party lays on the horn, the pitch getting lower as he speeds away. On a stoop across the street, two women, one old and one young, play with a shirtless baby. The kid reaches up and grabs a fistful of his mother's hair, making her yelp. The grandmother laughs.

Surrounded by people, steaming like a dumpling in my damp t-shirt, I lean my head against the window frame, and relax.

The knocking is desperate, shaking my flimsy door on its hinges so the bolt jumps around in the lock. I dump the ice out the window. Thinking about all the movies where a darkened peephole leads to a bullet in the eye, I look through the little glass tube anyway, having no better alternative.

Luke and Ilana stand on my landing, panting and covered in sweat. Their eyes are locked on the staircase at the end of the hall. I open the door, pull them in by their collars, and lock it behind me.

"Two of them," says Luke, fighting to pull in enough of the hot, heavy air. "Plain clothes . . . bag . . . caught on the turnstile, tore open . . . they saw . . ."

He clutches the torn remains of a backpack to his chest. Through the rip, the ends of six hanks of rope stick out to the side, plainly visible. And he carried it all the way here. . . .

"Leave it," I say. The fire escape is through my bedroom window—past my art, my bookshelf, and the closet with my clothes. I haul open the old wooden frame as footsteps pound up the stairs.

"Come on."

We squeeze out onto the metal grille and sneak down to the alley. Working together, we lower the ladder as quietly as we can, and hop down to the pavement just as an enormous Black man rounds the corner, badge on his waist, gun in his hand.

Luke and Ilana shrink back, and the man's eyes narrow. Thanks to the arrangement of the buildings, he and I stand only inches apart. The top of my head is about level with his nose.

My fingers are wet, and the alley smells like gin. I look down. I'm still holding the tumbler. The cop notices it, and then looks at my face. He raises a finger, as if to say *Now, hold on a minute*.

Appalled with myself, I pivot in my loafers, and smash the glass into his ear.

We're halfway up the block when the second detective bursts through the front door of my building. She shouts, and sprints after us, running straight beneath my open window—where she slips on the ice cubes melting into a puddle on the sidewalk.

While Starsky and Hutch pick themselves up, we turn a corner toward Jamaica Plain, and put another block between them and us. Suddenly there's a chance.

The inside of my throat sticks to itself. I can't just go back home and get a drink of water from the tap. That apartment will be watched now. It isn't home anymore. No place is.

I can't even buy a Gatorade from a corner store. I left my wallet on the nightstand. But not my phone. Which has been on this whole time.

Marie's good—she might even be good enough to keep them from tracking us, if she knew. Which she doesn't. And I can't risk connecting her phone to mine by calling, now that they might be listening.

We pause on the overpass spanning the Orange Line and Commuter Rail tracks. From Ruggles, a line of purple train cars barrels toward us, heading for Forest Hills and points south. I hold out my hand.

"Phones," I say.

They hesitate. I do, too. I close my eyes as I drop the little rectangles over the railing and onto the tracks. The train thunders by before disappearing underground.

"Now what?" says Ilana.

Miraculously, I remember the address Marie mentioned the first time she brought Sean up to the group. With no better idea, I start walking in the direction of the Pond. Toward our detective's apartment.

Marie / Washington, D.C. / 2010

It's just an overnight bag. Just to give us both time. So we can calm down.

I pack: three comfy pairs of underwear; some t-shirts; an extra pair of jeans; the pajama bottoms I haven't worn since I stole Al's sweatpants; a comb; and a toothbrush and toothpaste.

Just a little time. Some space. We've said a lot to each other over the last few months. Just what any couple goes through, moving in together. Normal stuff. Nothing we can't fix.

A few days—a week, at most—and one of us will call the other. We'll meet at the TGI Fridays where we go for trivia once a month, and we'll split an order of spinach and artichoke dip and drink sugary margaritas and say we're sorry. Al will drive me and my roller board full of rumpled clothes back here, back to our house, and we'll nestle into each other on the couch. I'll kiss his face, and he'll run his fingers through my hair, and we'll go to sleep in our king-size bed and promise to work it out in the morning.

It'll make up for the times when I feel like I'm drowning in my own life.

It wasn't a lie. I could never lie to him. I told him I could change—that I could choose him, and him alone, over "that stuff," and over every other person I'd meet for the rest of my life. That I could feel alive without pain, without giving and receiving restraint. I said it, and I wanted to mean it, and our relationship—the deepest, most important thing I've ever been a part of—is contingent on it. So it must be true.

It has to be true.

Walking out through the kitchen, I notice the salt and pepper shakers. They're from my house, growing up—a black ghost and a white ghost, molded to hug each other. I dump out the condiments, unzip my tiny suitcase, and pull out a pair of socks. I wrap one around each glass shaker and tuck them in next to the hairdryer.

I reach out to close the bag. I stop.

My suitcase is open on the kitchen table. In it are toiletries, undergarments, and some basic outerwear. A bathing suit. My laptop and charger in one of the pockets. Everything I need for a few days at a hotel. That, plus my family's novelty salt and pepper shakers.

Every item in the bag is something you might pack for a business trip. Utilitarian things. Nothing with sentimental value. All except for those two little ghosts. They have no purpose on the trip I've told myself I'm about to take. The hotel will have salt and pepper. The shakers are a reminder of home, and a gift from my father—a symbol of his wish that Al and I might be happy together. His weird form of blessing. They're supposed to go wherever I make my home.

So why would I pack them if I'm only going to be gone for a few days?

I wipe my eyes, unwrap the pepper shaker, and leave it on the table, next to my ring. Then I think better of it, and wrap the shaker back up. I go to the hallway closet and pull out the big suitcase.

Sean / Boston, MA / 2030

I'm clipping my nails when Jack rings the doorbell.

He shoves past me into the apartment, dragging Ilana and Luke behind him. He almost slams the door, then seems to think better of it. He closes it softly and throws the deadbolt.

"We were in the neighborhood," Jack says. He's breathing heavily. They all are. Luke holds Ilana close to him. She bunches the back of his shirt in her fist.

"Thought we could all . . ." Jack takes in my room, and the lack of furniture in it. ". . . sit and chat."

He darts to the windows and draws the curtains. Gently, he pulls the couple toward my mats.

"Shoes off," I say.

Jack looks at me.

"Please."

They sit in the middle. They whisper.

"*. . . can't stay here . . . find us . . . what if he . . .*"

I pull back the curtain a fraction of an inch. Schmidt and Baptiste are arguing on the corner down below.

"Wait here," I say.

The light in the hallway is out again. I keep my hand on the railing. My shoes creak on the sidewalk.

". . . I told you they went *right*!" says Schmidt, sticking her finger in Baptiste's puffed-up chest.

"Well, maybe if you'd run a bit faster—"

"Your fat fucking feet slamming on the sidewalk are what tipped them off!"

"Trouble in paradise?" I say.

They turn, notice me, and relax. Baptiste smiles.

"Come on, man," he says. "I don't need any more grief tonight."

"Three of them," says Schmidt. "Two from that apartment you and Nguyen were watching."

"You're lucky," I say. "While you two were bickering, a cop was doing some actual detective work."

I pull my phone from my pocket, and show them the picture of Pepper's old license plate. The one I took the night we chased her and Verity through the streets.

"They hopped in on the corner," I say, lying to my friends' faces. "Then they turned left on the Parkway."

Baptiste writes the number down in his notebook. The two of them head back toward Centre Street and their parked car—off to run down what, by now, should be an unremarkable cube of rubber, glass, and steel, rusting in a Chelsea junkyard.

When they're gone, I glance up at my apartment. The corner of the curtain falls back.

Jack already has his loafers on.

"Thanks, bud," he says. He's walking out the door—I grab him by the collar.

"Aren't you forgetting something?" I say.

Luke and Ilana sit in the corner, arms around each other, looking up at us.

"Come on," says Jack. "I need to make arrangements. I'm faster alone. Just a few hours."

They're breathing like they just ran a marathon together. Luke leans against the wall and wraps his arms around Ilana, who curls in a ball and presses her face to Luke's shirt. The door clicks behind me.

Jack is already halfway down the stairwell. He blows a kiss at me.

"You're the best," he says, then disappears through the front door. His feet tap down the porch steps and up the street.

Ilana and Luke look at me like lost puppies.

"So," I say.

Upstairs, a clock ticks.

Something gurgles. Ilana lifts her head off Luke's stomach and puts her hand on it, rubbing. I move to the kitchenette and start setting out pans.

I pile onions, broccoli, dry noodles, and beef on the counter. I grab the soy sauce from the fridge door, and fetch down rice wine from the cabinet. When I turn back around, they're standing side by side where the tile meets the hardwood.

"We can chop," says Ilana.

I heat the oil and boil water for noodles while the two of them process the mound of vegetables and meat. They wear bands around their left ring fingers—identical wooden circles.

"We wanted them to be biodegradable," says Luke.

"How long have you been married?"

"Two years last week," says Ilana.

The app put them together in college when Ilana was a freshman and Luke a junior. They came out to each other after less than a month. They used Luke's neckties whenever one of their dorms was free. They're a legit, sanctioned couple.

We dump everything into the sizzling-hot wok. I stir quickly, to keep anything from getting singed. Luke and Ilana get plates out of the cabinet. The designs on theirs are crisper than mine—I use and wash the same plate at most meals. It lives in the drying rack.

Ilana eats with chopsticks, but Luke can't get the noodles to his mouth. I grab him a fork, and play some jazz through my laptop's tinny speakers. We sit in a circle on the floor, slurping.

"When things go back to normal," says Luke, "we're gonna buy land up in New Hampshire, and build a cabin."

"A rope resort," says Ilana, beaming. "Hard points everywhere. We'll have our friends up for long weekends. We'd been saving..."

She trails off.

They don't have to be here. Ilana sells high-end glasses frames in the Prudential Center. Luke's a data analyst. They have an apartment in Somerville. They're on file with the IAB. They could have kept to themselves—played alone—and nobody would have known. They could have stayed safe.

Instead they chose this. They chose us.

Luke keeps a pack of cards in his coat pocket. We play poker for ripped-up pieces of napkin, and Ilana cleans out me and Luke. The two of them fall asleep watching *Frasier* reruns on my laptop, limbs tangled. I cover them with my weighted blanket and lie back on the floor, tracing the lines in the ceiling, while Niles tortures himself over whether to confess his love for Daphne.

My phone vibrates. It's a push notification from PRTNR—a reminder to fill out my profile before the upcoming deadline.

At 1:00 a.m., the old doorbell buzzes. I bring Jack upstairs, and nudge Luke and Ilana awake. The two of them rub their eyes and tie their shoes. Luke shakes my hand.

There's a minivan parked on the corner. Luke and Ilana meet the driver, then climb into the backseat. The sliding door rolls shut behind them, and they pull away, heading toward the Jamaicaway. Jack and I stand in front of the shuttered coffee shop, watching them drive off.

Marie / Boston, MA–Chicago, IL / 2011

The fat kid with the buzz cut yawns, scratches a soft, pimply cheek, and x-rays the contents of my duffel bag. Nothing in there violates TSA regulations. I should know—I helped come up with them. But even so, I'm stiff with fear.

Coiled bundles of brand-new hemp rope pass beneath the scanner. Lips hanging open, the boy blinks. Behind him, men in black fatigues and baseball hats lean their heads together and whisper. One holds a German Shepherd on a leash. The other rests his hand on the butt of his gun.

It's all a show. We literally call it "security theater." A big to-do to make people feel safer. That's all.

So why am I shaking?

My bag comes bumping down the chute. A filthy rubber glove waves me on. Shoeless, I carry my bins past the agent with the tissue on a stick, to the benches by the big window where we all reassemble ourselves: belt, phone, keys. The ingredients for a person.

The bracelet Al got me sits in the bottom of the bin. It's heavy. The links carry a metal charm for each of our biggest moments. The day we met near the Pentagon. The ice cream shop in Myrtle Beach. A house.

The whole thing lands neatly in the garbage can next to the Cinnabon, sliding down a wrapper into a puddle of frosting.

The line for Dunkin' Donuts is short. I buy my stale donut and sit with the other safe people, taking little licks of the Boston cream filling. The sugar makes me jitter. Every minute and a half, a hitch in the belt on the moving walkway makes the whole thing go *ba-bomp*.

The terminal is one of the last sacred places. We sit quietly and listen for our destinations to be called out.

A big lady getting off the flight from Dallas calls her husband a *moron* in front of their two daughters. The girls giggle. The man grins, eyes on the ground, and shuffles off after them, hauling the bags. Flight 9842 to Chicago is up.

The gate agent scans my boarding pass, and I wait with the other members of Group C in the metal hallway. By the time I get to my seat, the overhead bin looks full. But rope is flexible—the bag just squashes in between two roller boards. A man in a sharp business suit is already snoozing in the middle seat. Hands on the headrests, I pick my feet up and over him, and slide down into the window seat.

They play the safety video. We take off.

We hit rough air over the woods of Pennsylvania. At first, it isn't much. A mild bump every minute or two. Just enough to jiggle our sodas. People cocooned in the thin red airline blankets sleep through the motion. Then it gets a little worse—buffets that shake the body of the plane. Our flotation-device cushions shudder beneath our ass-cheeks. People exchange nervous laughter with the strangers next to them.

Then comes the bump that lifts us all off our chairs.

For a split second we all remember where we are—thirty-five thousand feet in the air, with nothing between us and the hard ground but clouds. Then we thump back down onto our tailbones.

In the back, by the bathrooms, a baby cries. The businessman takes a rosary out of his pocket and starts murmuring while the beads flick through his fingertips. The plane rolls, and our wings turn nearly perpendicular to the ground. Through the rain-streaked porthole, the surface of a deep, blue lake is thrashed to gray in the wind. A green forest heaves around the water.

The other passengers scream. I laugh.

The hotel room is empty.

I drop off my bag, take the elevator back to the lobby, and stop before the black curtain that divides the convention area from the rest of the hotel. A fat man with a walkie-talkie clipped to his leather kilt nods as I walk past him toward the registration tables.

A middle-aged woman with pink hair takes my driver's license. On a laptop, she checks the information against what I provided online. She nods, hands over a bag filled with condoms and sponsors' business cards and gives me my badge.

MorganLeHey. The screen name I made up for the website that led me here. It's spelled out in black letters on a white rectangle, which will hang around my neck for the rest of the weekend.

There's a map in the bag. One of the ballrooms is labelled "Vendor Area."

I enter a pervert's bazaar. Around the edge of the ballroom, shopkeepers sit with their wares arrayed before them on plastic folding tables. Metal suspension rings hang from a rack. One's shaped like a heart. Another has the anarchy "A" welded through the middle. Whips, paddles, and gags are lined up on a long table by the back wall. A White woman—it's mostly White people—sells hand-woven kimonos. More than anything, there's rope, tables and tables of it, in untreated beige but also in black, red, purple, yellow, pink, green—with and without conductive metal threads. In the corner, a young woman drools over a cattle prod.

All this in the same room where, not a week ago, a group of regional sales managers might have met to discuss last quarter's earnings. The chairs stacked by the retractable wall are the same kind I've sat in while listening to conference keynotes. The carpet is the same ornate pattern, thinly spread out over concrete, the only interruption a large rectangle of laminated plywood, smack in the middle of the room—a dance floor, bearing the scuff marks of a thousand bar mitzvahs, weddings, and first communion after-parties.

Looking at any one thing for too long—acknowledging it—makes me feel like I'm in danger. Which is silly. If I'm safe anywhere, I'm safe here, with the woman who can spin a pair of colorful leather floggers like nunchucks, and the grown man wearing cat ears without a trace of irony. I came here specifically to be weird. To try things without being judged. I paid good money to isolate myself from the world for a weekend.

But the world has a funny way of following you. Wherever I go, I'm still the person who can't go into a physical sex shop without having a panic attack; who couldn't talk about her real turn-ons with her partner until it was too late, and clammed up at the first whiff of a negative reaction from him; who is ashamed, somehow, of both the things I want and of my inability to go after them. I've flown across time zones, but I haven't gotten away from the person who crushed her own feelings, lied about it, and committed to half a mortgage for a man I mistakenly thought could make up the difference.

I leave without buying anything.

"Now, you never want to *push* your rope—see how it comes untwisted? That will hurt your rope over time, and that will make you sad! And we don't want anyone to be sad—unless you've negotiated it first."

The fat man in cargo shorts pauses for laughter. His tying partner rolls her eyes.

"Instead, you want to hook your finger—yes, just like that—stick it beneath the bands, and *pull* the rope through. . . ."

I sit on the edge of the conference room with my notebook and pen. Couples and small groups kneel on blankets and yoga mats, watching the presenter run through basic rope-handling techniques.

". . . so try to minimize friction, and for goodness' sake, watch out for your running ends. Those knots can take out an eye if you're not careful, so take your time. . . ."

There's a girl at the front of the room—at least, I think she's a girl. She's lying by the stage in a tangle of young people of unclear genders. They wear their hair in neon hues, cropped close or shaved on one side. Their chests are mostly flat, and a few of them have hairy legs—but they're all wearing makeup. And they're prettier than boys that age tend to be.

Or not. Maybe I don't know anything anymore.

"As much as possible," says the presenter, tugging on the rope so it goes taut, "you want to keep *tension* on the rope as you're tying. . . ."

The one I'm looking at has lavender hair, falling down from just the top of her head in big, bouncy curls. The rest is shaved. There's a star tattooed on the near side of her skull.

She picks her head up from the people pile. She catches me staring. She half-smiles.

I snap my head down. The page in front of me is covered in my aborted attempts to translate what I'm seeing into notes: Lists of terms I've never heard before butt up against lumpy drawings of torsos with arrows zinging in every direction. Half of them have been crossed out, and replaced with other, more emphatic sketches. The presenter is saying something important about jute vs. hemp rope when the tip of my pencil breaks off. I get up to go to the front desk and ask if they have a sharpener, and whether I can use it. Like a third-grader.

The person with the pretty hair watches me as I slip out.

An older woman teaches her class how to turn a standard length of rope into a flogger and demonstrates its effectiveness on her collared husband.

The hotel restaurant is full of old people in leather clothes. Alone at the bar, I eat a grilled chicken sandwich. The enzymes in my stomach tear the protein to shreds while dopamine lights up my brain like a Christmas tree. I forgot to eat today.

An obese woman takes off her clothes in front of a conference room full of strangers, and endures half an hour of slapping, tight bondage, and calculated insults about her weight. All of it pre-negotiated—requested—by her. She cries. So do we. There is applause.

Too quickly—but at the same time, after what feels like ten years—it's time for the play party.

I try to look cool.

People hang from wooden A-frames and metal tripods: mostly women, but a few men, too. The DJ plays Dope's 1999 cover of "You Spin Me Round."

I've gathered that rope people like nu metal.

The dungeon opened at eight. It's now twelve-fifteen in the morning, and I haven't tied with anyone. Because I haven't approached anyone. Because I haven't spoken to anyone since I got here. If there were a punch bowl, I'd be standing next to it, fingering my latex dress while the other kids slow-danced.

In the photo lounge, a white-bearded old guy in a Hawaiian shirt snaps pictures of a fit young woman, who hangs upside-down by a single folded leg. She wears pointed ears, fairy wings, and a gauzy little dress that slips up around her hips. The man takes a break to rearrange the folds. They laugh about something, then she goes back to posing, her mouth slightly open—as if completely overwhelmed by eroticism. The backdrop looks like an old-growth forest.

I've seen his work online. He doesn't look at all the way I thought he would.

I'm surrounded by people having fun—people who are definitively into the same things I am—and I'm miserable. Only *I* could blow a grand on a plane ticket, hotel room, and registration fees, invent a cover story, fly a thousand miles from home, and still be too chickenshit to find a willing partner at a dedicated rope bondage convention. I left my fiancé to squeeze into a rubber cocktail dress and be lonely in a crowd of strangers. My left wrist, where the charm bracelet used to sit, feels too light. Exposed. My right hand drifts over to cover the nakedness.

I want something with chocolate and peanuts.

I leave the convention area and make my way to the nook by the front desk where they keep the snacks. Pods in his ears, the janitor pushes his mop across the tile floor. The nighttime concierge looks up from his magazine, and beams.

"Evening," he says. "Can I help you find anything?"

I shake my head and clop my way into the store on the stupid heels I bought for this weekend. The staff are looking at me and hating me. They must be. And why not? I'm one of *them*—one of the pervs taking over the hotel. The concierge, the maids, and the janitor are here, getting underpaid to fold our towels and throw out our trash, when they could be home with their normal families. They *must* hate us. I'd hate me. I grab a packet of Reese's Cups off the shelf and turn around, setting my face.

No one is looking at me. The janitor whistles along to "Mambo No. 5," and the sleepy concierge doesn't even look up till I put the candy on the desk. He rings me up, smiles again, and hands it back to me. Like the dress is nothing. Like this whole situation is just another night at the Sheraton. Maybe it is. I go outside to eat the chocolate and breathe.

Pretty Hair sits on a smoking bench, wrapped in a leather jacket, watching cars go by on the freeway.

I whip around to run back into the lobby—then I stop. I walk back out to the front. Then back in. When the doors whoosh open a third time, she turns toward me, eyebrows raised.

I swallow. I grit my teeth. I walk over to her.

She sits with her knees tucked up into her chest, arms wrapped around her shins. The cigarette in her fingertips is stained purple with lipstick.

"Having fun?" she says.

"I like to pretend I'm a Jedi," I say. "Move things around with the Force." I wave my hand in front of her face, and do my best Alec Guinness:

"*You do not think I'm weird.*"

She smirks. She sticks out her hand, and her nametag slips out of the jacket. The pronoun sticker on the bottom reads "they/them." I commit to remembering that.

"Susan," they say.

"Really?" I say. "I would've thought, like, 'Akira' or something. Maybe 'Jet.'"

"Nope. Just Susan. Like the spinny thing where they put the condiments."

We sit for a little while, watching the cars speed by along the highway. Massive halogen lights towering above the median suck the light from the stars, turning the sky into a void and reducing the world to a few uncanny set pieces: the hotel, the road, and the KFC on the other side of it. It occurs to me that I've found the heart of America—a lonely person, awake in the middle of the night, trying to make some meaning out of her life within spitting distance of a box of fried chicken.

"First con?" says Susan.

"How'd you know?"

"You seem hella nervous," they say, "and you take notes like you've got an exam coming up."

"Lifelong student," I say. "You know I'm a doctor, technically."

"No fooling?"

"Yep. I'm hella smart."

The smoke from Susan's cigarette wafts up into the air between us and the streetlamps, turning into a silver cloud. Across the highway, from on top of a metal pole taller than most of the buildings in Cambridge, a glowing Colonel Sanders grins down at the two of us.

"Are you hungry?" I ask.

"So you got 'bored' of the high-protocol leather house?"

"Yeah. Too stuffy. No sense of humor."

They flip another piece of popcorn chicken into their mouth.

"These are fucking amazing," they say.

Besides the kids frying up chicken in the back, we're the only people in the restaurant. A dirty-looking guy came sauntering our way when we first walked in, but then Susan looked at him like he was an insect, and did something with their back muscles that made their jacket squeak. The man left.

"I can't believe you've never been to KFC."

"I can't believe you've never been to a rope convention. It's pretty obvious you've been needing it. I'm amazed you held out this long."

"Yeah, well. I had other goals."

"Actually, I take it back," they say. "I can totally believe it. It takes a while to find your people."

The trash cans are full to overflowing with greasy parchment paper and balled-up napkins. We smoosh the hump down with our manicured hands, then head back out to the road. The highway is mostly empty, but I can see headlights off in the distance. I'm turning to walk toward the far-away intersection when Susan grabs my wrist. They grin. Then they pull me off the sidewalk and onto the road.

We sprint across the lanes as fast as my wobbly, patent-leather shoes allow. Susan boosts me over the divider, then hops over. I scream as we make one last dash. We clear the opposite curb just as a pickup truck zooms by, honking at the two idiots in fetish gear. We hold each other and laugh. I grab the backs of Susan's arms and squeeze.

They must do a lot of push-ups.

Back in the convention area, the lights are up and the music's gone. Volunteers haul frames around the floor, lining them up for the waiting truck.

"The party's over," I say, falling into myself like a broken soufflé.

"Yeah," says Susan. They look at me sideways. "Guess we'll have to go to your room."

I choke on my own spit, cough for a minute, then clear my throat and straighten out a fold in my dress.

"I guess so," I say.

On my bed, I open my bag, unwrap my pristine bundles of rope, and proceed to do every single thing wrong.

The armbinder I learned this afternoon is supposed to draw the bottom's arms tight together behind their back. Mine sags like a sock with a busted elastic. I'm supposed to keep tension on the rope. Instead, it hangs from my hands like wet spaghetti.

I *do* hit Susan, square in the eye, with the flying knotted end of the rope I was repeatedly told to watch out for. It takes me seven long minutes to secure a Somerville bowline over their ankle.

None of it matters. We're laughing too much to care. Their skin—the first new skin I've felt in six years—is soft, covered with invisible down that tickles my fingertips. With awkward, lunging movements, I somehow pin their arms over their head, and secure their wrists to the headboard. From on top of a crumpled top sheet, they look up at me through messy strands of that lavender hair, mouth open, chest moving up and down.

Clumsy as I am, I'm still the one in charge. I scratch them, squeeze them, choke them, until they make noises I've never heard before. An electrical current courses through their body and into mine, lighting up a world that suddenly feels worth living in. I stick my fingers in the socket, then my tongue. We fry each other's circuits till we pass out.

The next morning, I leave Susan sleeping in my bed and take the elevator down to the convention area to see about coffee and a scone. The weekend is evaporating. Roadies haul wooden beams and hardware into the back of a waiting semi. Half of the vendor tables are empty, and the remaining sellers have started to pack up their wares.

A wide leather wristband catches my eye as it goes into a cardboard box. I buttonhole the owner before he seals the top, pay for the strange, heavy thing in cash, and snap it onto my left wrist.

Verity / Boston, MA / 2023

"I just don't see why you have to put your name on it."

Simon types while I talk.

"Legitimacy," he says, mouth hanging open over a tricky clause. "The fact that I'm putting myself behind the blog makes it more meaningful."

He's like a fucking puppy. Or a first-grader learning about civics. He believes everything he's saying.

"A pseudonym would be safer."

I drop my book on Simon's couch and go into his kitchen. The tap water feels cold on my face.

There's no line between him and the rest of the world. He's bi and poly—therefore, everyone else must be, too, under their straight disguises. He's generally disposed to be kind toward people, and to mind his own business—so surely every other person is the same way. If we all just got over our inhibitions and had more sex, he thinks, all society's problems would be solved.

He thinks being kinky is the same thing as being gay. He wants parades, clubs—public ones. Our own TV shows. Our version of *Will & Grace*, or *Queer as Folk*. Eventually a reality program. Our *Queer Eye*.

This is a fantasy. And he writes about that fantasy, publicly, while self-proclaimed incels demand "sexual justice" from the steps of the Lincoln Memorial, and senators nod their heads.

He's so shocked that it's happening with a normal, boring Democrat in the White House.

Simon comes into the kitchen behind me and squeezes my shoulders. He pushes my curls to one side and kisses the back of my neck.

"I'm sorry," he says.

He's never been poor, or hungry, or stepped on. He's never hated anyone; he doesn't understand why anyone would hate him. None of them do. Not really. Flaunting their leathers, their collars—cramming a hundred pins on a backpack, each more damning than the last. Simon can't comprehend the idea of people who don't want to hear what he has to say. People who hate complications like us. People who will do more than argue about it.

I don't want a party. I don't want to be liked. All I want is a heavy door with a good lock. I inhale, deeply, through my nose.

"You'll take your name off?"

"Verity . . ."

I shrug him off, grab my coat, and walk out the door.

"Your funeral," I say.

Jack / Boston, MA / 2030

We stand on the sidewalk with our hands in our pockets, like dads sending their kids off to school. The car holding Luke and Ilana turns the corner and disappears up the Parkway, and I sag against the wall behind me, sliding down till my ass touches warm pavement. Sean leans on a fire hydrant. It can't be comfortable, but to look at his face you'd never know either way.

"How are you getting to Kevin and Daphne's?" he says.

It's a good question. I hadn't gotten that far. Even this late, there'll be another 39 bus or two heading toward Longwood—but my CharlieCard is in my wallet.

Which is in my apartment.

Which I can never go back to.

The walk would take about an hour, with plenty of trees to duck behind along the Riverway. I rock forward to get to my feet . . . and slowly fall back. My legs are on strike.

"Just put me on a log," I say, "and stick me in the river. I'll float there by morning."

Sean grabs my hand, and hauls me upright.

"Come on," he says. "I'll drive you."

The passenger seat cradles me in vinyl fabric and high-density foam as we wind along the Parkway, following the path Ilana and Luke left on minutes ago. Sean takes the curves slowly, deliberately. The car rocks from side to side in the dark. It's hard to stay awake.

"That was nice of you," I say. "Helping them out."

He shrugs. The white, chalky light of each streetlamp sweeps his face like the line on a radar display. No blips to speak of. It's like driving with a gargoyle.

He only does this around me. With Pepper, he laughs and tells jokes. With Marie, he smiles when he learns a new skill. He's nervous around Verity—I see the slight hunch in the shoulders, the tightness in the jaw. But I get nothing at all. No emotion.

"What's your deal, anyway?"

It's a foolish thing to ask. Dangerous territory, with anyone—let alone this weird, quiet cop. I shouldn't go poking around in his head, trying to get more than what's offered. But there's so little offered to me, in particular, and I want to know why. I'm not supposed to scratch mosquito bites, either, but I always do.

He keeps his eyes on the road while he talks. "My deal?"

"You know. A cop, hanging with perverted outlaws after dark. That's a *decision*. Can't be easy."

"I dunno. I guess I'm in it for the same reason you all are."

"And you think that is . . . ?"

"Looking for people like me."

Basic. I've heard the same thing at every munch I ever attended. The guy's a fencer. Everything's a parry.

We climb the overpass above Huntington Ave. Down on the other side, a raccoon looks up from the remains of a hot dog, eyes glowing.

"There's got to be more to it than that," I say. "You don't just turn on your job and join up with a group of criminals because you're looking for new friends."

I lean over the cup holders and waggle my eyebrows. "Maybe you're putting together a secret dossier on all of us?"

"Heh," he says, smiling. It's all teeth, and it comes too quickly. Like he had it ready to go. The next turn, around the creepy baby head statues at the MFA, is jerky, rough. I feel the urge to do something nice for him.

"You know, Sean, if you ever wanted to talk about anything, I'd be open to that."

"Thank you," he says.

"I mean, if you're ever having a tough time. Or if something's bothering you. Maybe I could help—"

He brakes hard at a red light, and I'm thrown forward against my seatbelt. The car lunges forward with the momentum, then springs back. Sean's nostrils flare, and his upper lip is starting to curl. Like a cornered dog's.

"... No," he says. "Thanks."

The light changes. We cross the intersection, and Sean pulls into the undeveloped lot on the corner. I pull myself out and watch him head back the way we came.

Well fuck him, anyway.

People pour out of the bars on Boylston, hanging off each other, shouting, puking in the gutter. Exhausted rideshare drivers fight for space along the curb, waiting with blinking lights to pick up their drunk White passengers. My brain's been run through with a curling iron. Shutting my eyes as much as possible, I stumble through the crowd till I get to Kevin and Daphne's building. I almost decide not to check whether I'm being followed. Then I haul myself the extra twenty yards to the gas station, so I can look back over my shoulder at the sidewalk behind me.

Aside from the bouncers, nobody is standing upright. I plod around to the back. Kevin waits by the door, holding it open with his foot and smoking a cigarette. He sees me staring.

"I hid a pack back here for rough nights," he says. "Don't tell Daphne."

He holds out the cardboard box. I put up a palm and shake my head. He takes one last drag, then drops the butt straight to the ground, rather than flicking it away. He crushes the glowing paper under the toe of a house slipper, and holds the door open for me.

My skin tightens in the cold air. There's a towel waiting for me on the sink, folded up into a fluffy white rectangle. Under an endless flow of water, sidewalk grit washes off my hands. The sweat on my face and in my hair rinses down the drain.

The others waited up for me. They crowd around, ask me if I'm okay, if I need anything. I wave them off to bed and change into a pair of Kevin's flowing plaid pajama pants. Daphne set up an air mattress while I showered. I climb into it, and pull a crisp, clean sheet up to my armpits. Pepper sleeps curled up in a ball, her whole body fitting on a single love seat cushion. She rests her head on a folded elbow, and twitches. Verity lies straight up and down on the couch, her hands folded on top of her like a mummy.

I'm so tired it hurts, but sleep takes its time coming. I lie on my back, staring up at the ceiling and listening to the air moving in the ducts. I wonder how Sean's doing without air conditioning.

Carl / Boston, MA / 2030

Three of them. The two kids from Smith's apartment, and the red-headed guy who was standing in front of the station that night Sean and I got back with the photos. They turn the corner at a run. The ginger guy drags them up the steps to Sean's building. He leans on the buzzer—the door opens.

Sean lets them inside.

At the end of the block, I scrunch down in the front seat of an unmarked car. Not the one Sean and I ride around in. A different one. Nobody notices.

They get inside just before Schmidt and Baptiste appear on the corner. The two of them argue, the way they do, until Sean comes out wearing flip-flops. I wait for him to wave them upstairs, to hand over the three suspects hiding in his apartment.

Instead he sends them the wrong way. Sean shows our squad mates something on his phone, and points up the road, and the two of them run off after nothing. He goes back up to his apartment. A minute later the other guy bangs through the front door and down the porch steps. He jogs past my open window.

I could open the door—he'd crash into it. I could reach out a hand and catch him by the sleeve—he'd stumble and fall.

I let him go. I wait.

The sun goes down. Streetlights come on. A young couple walks by pushing a stroller with two kids in it. A tiny schnitzel lunges at a dopey retriever, who shies away behind his owner and whines. Pots bang and oil sizzles up at Sean's place. Wooden chopsticks *tink* against cheap ceramic plates.

I turn on the radio—commercials on every station at once. I turn it off.

Three hours in, a minivan pulls up to the curb. The redheaded guy hops out, and rings the doorbell. The kids climb into the back seat, and he slides the door shut behind them. It closes with a *whumph.* They drive away. Sean and the redhead talk for a while. Then they get into his car together and drive off along the Jamaicaway.

This is Sean, who stopped working out with me, and hasn't bothered to tell me why. Sean, who just lied to two detectives. Sean, who doesn't tell me anything about what's going on here, about what he and Al have been doing together these last few weeks.

Sean, who keeps me out of it.

Not so much traffic in this residential area at this time of night. I can stand here in the middle of the street, halfway between my car and Sean's front door, and stare up at his dark windows as long as I want to. Turning my back on his building, I pull my phone out of my pocket and dial the number they had us all memorize.

Rob picks up on the first ring.

"I've got one," I tell him. I share my location and text him the plate number.

I catch up with the minivan farther down the Parkway. I follow it through Longwood; up Boylston, past Fenway Park; down Storrow Drive toward the Museum of Science. We get on the Tobin, and Rob's white van falls in behind me.

No lights. No sirens. Just a nice, quiet ride.

Spotlights shine on the Bunker Hill Monument—a big white splinter. Sean once called it an *obelisk*. He would.

We go up over Somerville, running parallel to the Mystic River, then due north from Medford. This drive is pretty at sunset—big trees on either side of the highway, and long shadows cutting across the lanes. Now, after midnight, it's all black. Just us and the road.

These are the people Sean's been hanging out with. The ones who have his head all twisted around so he doesn't tell his partner where he is, or what he's doing. Three of them—a driver, and the kids from the Smith case. I-93 will take them as far north as Mt. Washington. From there they could make the switch to I-91, or head east and cross into Canada somewhere along the Maine border.

They won't get that far.

Traffic thins out past Woburn, Stoneham, Reading. By Tewksbury, we're the only three cars on a long stretch of road. The van pulls up next to me. Rob sits in the passenger seat. He looks at me. I nod. The van falls back, into the dark.

I step down on the accelerator—slowly. Carefully. I match the minivan's speed, and turn on my left blinker, as if I'm about to pass. Instead I drift over to the right. Ribbed asphalt shakes the chassis as I inch the front corner of my car closer and closer to their rear bumper.

We're not really supposed to do this at more than thirty-five miles per hour. It's exciting. I turn to the left.

The minivan spins out onto the shoulder as I shoot past in the left-hand lane. In the rearview mirror, the top-heavy car hits a bump and takes a bad hop, rolling over on the grass before crashing into a tree trunk.

I pull over, breathing hard. Then I reverse back along the shoulder, flipping on my blue lights as I go.

Rob and his guys are already at work. No point grabbing the driver—a hunk of windshield the size of a pizza slice sticks out of his neck. They leave him hanging upside-down, and pull the unconscious passengers out of the back seat. Rob puts zip ties around their wrists and ankles, and the others carry them gently back to the van.

A handful of cars drive by. I wave them on.

Rob's team piles back into the van. My phone buzzes while I wait for them to pull out onto the highway. It's Levi.

Hey! Everything okay?

Yep! Sorry, working late tonight. Eye-roll emoji.

Aw, well be careful hero. A kissy face. *Love you.*

Rob and the others are idling, waiting for me. I tap back out:

Love you too

Rob points a thumb down the stairs.

"You coming?" he says.

I shake my head.

He shrugs. "Make yourself comfy. There're some sodas in the fridge, and the remote's on the coffee table."

The door's almost shut when he pops his head back into the kitchen.

"Just keep the volume low," he says. "It's way past Christine's bedtime, and I think Eleanor's sleeping, too."

His head disappears, and the latch clicks behind him.

I open the fridge, and air rushes in through the broken seal. The light inside clicks on. On the shelves are: a pint of apple juice; a gallon of one-percent milk; two dozen eggs; and a few bags of greens, all organic. Assorted vegetables. A brisket thaws out on the bottom shelf, thick brown fat on one side. I turn away from it and examine the sodas in the door. Also organic—sweetened with Stevia. I pick up a cola and put it back. Then a root beer. Then an orange-flavored one. I let the door swing shut—I can't tell whether I'm thirsty or not.

The door moves too fast on its hinges—it slams, rattling cans and glassware. I stand with one hand uselessly extended toward the handle. I breathe through my mouth.

The fridge's motor hums. The clock above the microwave ticks. That's it. I swallow and move into the living room.

The top of the coffee table is made of clear glass. Rob and his wife have stacked a few board games on the shelf below: Clue; Twister; The Game of Life. The corners of the boxes are dented, some torn. They must play a lot. I leave the remote where it is and get up off the couch. Behind me, there's a tiny sniff.

Rob's little girl, Christine, sits on the staircase, looking at me through the slats.

She's taller than she was a year ago. She wears a pink t-shirt and purple pajama pants. She holds the same doll she had the day of the barbecue.

"The cherry ones are mine," she says. She's missing a few baby teeth.

"What?"

"The cherry ones," she says. "The last time Dad brought police over, they drank all of the sodas except for the orange ones, which are gross. That was rude. So now I have to tell everyone that the cherry ones are mine."

"I actually didn't have any," I say. "I didn't feel like it."

"You can have any of the other ones," she says, "just not the cherry."

"Okay," I say.

"Okay."

Christine's been fiddling with the doll's hair. There's just enough moonlight to make out a French braid.

"Do you think Dad'll be up soon?" she says.

I have absolutely no idea. I've never actually been here for it before—usually we just call, give Rob the details, and find out how it went in the morning. As much as we need to.

I really don't know if Dad'll be up soon. I hope not.

"I don't think so, sweetie," I say.

Christine wrinkles her nose, and frowns. "Don't call me that," she says. "I'm nine."

"Sorry."

"Usually it takes a few hours," she says. "Dad and his friends think I'm asleep, but sometimes I'm awake. I look through the window, and watch them carry people in." She tips her head to one side. "What do you think they're doing down there?"

My gums are stuck to my cheeks. I swallow and try to work everything loose. "I think," I say, "you should go to bed."

I'm ready for sass, or some kind of fit. But no. Christine gathers the doll to her chest, stands up, and climbs the steps to the landing. She stands there, pale against the dark hallway behind her.

"Good night," she says. Then she steps through, into the shadow, and is gone.

"Good night."

I check my phone. 3:00 a.m. No texts. No voicemails. No emails. The rest of the world is asleep.

The house is quiet.

It's chilly on Rob's back porch. His deck chairs are the big wooden ones that look like they're made of fence pickets. Seat grazing the ground, back tilted at forty-five degrees. I sit and shiver, feet propped on the edge of Rob's fire pit. The sky is all clouds tonight.

I roasted a marshmallow here, at the last barbecue. Too close—the skin caught fire, bubbled, and blackened, while the insides turned to liquid. The blob fell down, landed splat on a log, and cooked till there was nothing left but a shiny black stain. . . .

The glass door slides open. Rob stands there, hands on his hips, breathing hard. He's sweating—and grinning. His hands and the front of his white t-shirt are stained red.

"Sorry about the wait," he says.

He reaches into the back pocket of his jeans and pulls out a folded scrap of paper. There are scribbles on one side. It's sticky.

"Want to hang out?" says Rob. "We'll be at it a while longer. There's whiskey."

"I should get home," I say, hauling myself up from the low chair.

Funny—Rob isn't much taller than me. Especially in just his socks.

"Do you need me to call the coroner?" I say.

Rob shakes his head. "Teddy's got a boat," he says. "We'll drop them somewhere tomorrow night."

In the car, I turn on the overhead light, and take in the story recorded on the paper. Names, dates, factoids. A circled address near the bottom of the page. I know what Sean's been up to. I focus on breathing.

Rob's driveway is long and twisting. I back up it, turn on my high beams, and drive into the city. The sky is just beginning to brighten when I pull up to the building on Boylston.

I take Al's boss's business card out of my wallet. I call the number and leave my message. Leaning on the passenger-side door, I look up at the apartment where Sean's new friends are sleeping.

Verity / Boston, MA / 2024

I'm supposed to update the venue for the POC munch, but the stupid site isn't loading. I shouldn't be surprised. The site is old. It's the only social network explicitly for us—a monopoly. The black and red interface hasn't changed in more than a decade, and the event-planning tool runs like a bicycle with a rusted chain. But it's ours.

After the fifth time, I check Instagram to see if anyone else is having trouble. My photos sit in neat rows of three: a collection of meals, sunsets, and dogs I've met out walking.

My friends' accounts have been suspended.

It could all be a coincidence. The site breaks down all the time, and random users are always flagging shibari photos. It could just be a bad week, and everything will be back up and running in a few days. Back to normal.

I message Simon through the encrypted app I forced him to download.

Pull down the blog, I write, *erase your hard drive, and come to my place. Something's happening.*

Five minutes go by. Ten. No response. Not even any dots. I leave the lab, check out a bike from the rack, and pedal.

People paddleboard on the Charles or sun themselves on the docks by the Esplanade, like nothing's wrong. They buy chocolate-dipped ice cream cones from the truck by the Hatch Shell and kick at the geese that swarm their feet for cone crumbs. They talk, or laugh, or jog with ponytails bouncing.

It could all be coincidence. Just a lot of things going wrong all at once. Everything could be fine tomorrow morning.

I pedal harder.

Over the footbridge that crosses Storrow Drive, down the handicap ramp and through the alleyways connecting the back ends of Beacon Street condos to the neighborhood proper. Three blocks away. Two. I try to swallow. I can't.

The flashing red and blue lights are reflected in passing windshields. Uniformed officers walk in and out of Simon's building. One plainclothes detective stands off to the side, taking in the scene with his hands in his pockets. He grins like a kid who just crushed a bug.

I don't stop. I don't even turn my head. Knowing they can see me—that they'll notice anything suspicious—I ride straight through the intersection, pulling the corners of my mouth into a distracted smile.

Sean / Boston, MA / 2030

The way to Kevin and Daphne's place takes me past the movie theater. Jack stands on the corner, looking at the posters.

"You should be inside," I say.

"Pepper microwaved a leftover buffalo chicken sub, with the blue cheese dressing still on it," he says. "I had to get out for a while."

He turns and starts walking. We hang a right on Kilmarnock and fall into step as we turn left up Boylston. It's awkward. We haven't spoken since the car ride.

He was asking how I was. He was offering to help.

He's made my life very complicated. They all have. It was easy, when the question was *Will you do the right thing?* That was simple. There was a Law that could be obeyed. But now these people, these strangers, have come into my life and mucked it all up. They've posed a new question.

What is *the right thing?*

The first time I read Orwell, back in high school, I thought I would make a good Boxer. Say what you will about Napoleon—Boxer had a purpose. His morality was a single ray, starting from a point—work—and stretching to infinity—work harder. The pigs might have had control of the farm, but it was the horse who had the key to fulfilment, to happiness. Every day, another stone on the windmill. A hard bed to collapse on each night. Orders to follow, and the will to carry them out. Freedom.

We're glue before we get here, and we'll be glue again.

That was so comforting. Glue doesn't fuck up at being sticky. Glue stays where it's put and holds what is given to it. Glue does its job. I wanted that. But it's the one thing I'll never get to have. I'm not glue. And I'm not a horse. I don't know what to do, and there is no correct answer to the other, deeper question.

Now what?

What I'm about to do feels dangerous. It feels like disobeying.

"I'm sorry," I say, "about the other night. It was . . . rude."

"Okay," says Jack.

They've planted trees, out in front of the Target. Jack catches his foot on a root and falls forward. I grab him before he hits the ground.

We hang out like that, for a second—him in my arms, off-balance. His hair smells like salt. Then we untangle ourselves and stand on either side of the crack in the sidewalk. We clear our throats. Jack picks up the pace.

He walks with his spine straight, eyes forward, but not stiff. Like he's proud and self-assured. No money, no apartment, no legal right to be alive—and he walks like that.

I like him. I'm afraid of him.

I elbow him lightly in the side. A few steps later, he bumps me back, a little harder. I shove him. He shoves me.

We're behind the apartment building, laughing and throwing fake punches at each other's stomachs, when Pepper opens the back door to let us in. An iced coffee dangles from her fingertips.

"Y'all are weird," she says.

"Come on," says Daphne, "tighter!"

I'm practicing a Guatemalan on her lower leg. Rough jute rope digs into the thin layer of skin over her shin and squeezes her calf so tight it looks like a challah roll. She has a high tolerance for pain.

When she's finally had enough, I unravel the rope and check the clock. It's about the time when we usually pack up and go. I'm getting my kit together when Jack puts his hand on my arm.

"Hang out a minute," he says.

We find our own corner. We talk. He asks what he must think are simple, direct questions about what I want. Answering is like trying to ride a panicking horse in a straight line.

More than anything, I *want* to keep the awkward words out of my mouth. To ride off perpendicular to this conversation, if it's already too late to go back the way we came. I *want* to keep pretending. To lie.

But what I *need* is different from what I want. And I need to tell the truth.

Pulling and jerking myself back in the right direction every time I try to change topics, we get there. Jack smiles. I touch that pile of soft, red hair. Then he unbundles a length of hemp and, mouth dry, I hold my hands behind my back.

I've built this moment up in my head as something transformational—one of those inflection points that divides everything into *before* and *after*. There was always an assumption that I'd never get here, and that if I somehow did, doing what we're doing now—saying what I've said, allowing what I'm allowing, making it happen—would resolve everything else, all the other contradictions and worries. If I could only confess to the right person, in the right context, something would change in me. And all the rest would just fall into place.

If that change is happening now, I'm not aware of it. All I can think about is my stomach. My gross stomach. Not bulging, but never quite perfect, either, no matter how many miles I run; how heavy the weights I lift; how many minutes spent pummeling a heavy bag while imagining the face of someone I envy. Does my gut stick out tonight? Is it bothering him, the way it bothers me?

Pepper's front is hard, and hairless. The jealousy is more pressing than the ropes winding around me, pulling me into myself. Jack finnicks with a knot, pauses. Decides where he should go next.

What does he think of me? When he makes a mistake, is he as frustrated with himself as I would be? Does he yell at himself, inside his head? Does he hate me for being here to see it?

He doesn't move like he's thinking those things. He's relaxed. He's smiling.

The floor is harder than I would have liked, and chilly. Jack's so thin, so pale, I always assumed he'd be cold, too. But he's warm.

His hands, his lips, are warm.

Verity / Boston, MA / 2030

We could do anything to Sean right now.

He kneels there, eyes closed, while Jack winds rope around his bare chest, his chin on Sean's shoulder as he works. The set of Sean's face is familiar. The wide nostrils; the line of the mouth; the twitch of muscles struggling to relax; the flush in his cheekbones. Sean's afraid.

He should be. We could take photos, and email them to his bosses. We could take him hostage and start making demands. We could kill him.

The cop kneels, and takes deep breaths, until my friend wraps his arms around him, and puts a hand on the back of his head and guides him gently to the floor.

Together—all of us, hiding here in this place—we sink. In the quiet, we pull each other down, down, down, into warm earth that closes over our faces like water.

We move, and are moved. Bound one to the other in a net of fibers . . . a constellation of roots.

Breath in the darkness. Humming. The thrum of tectonic plates in motion: a lullaby.

Letter from Marie Rosenthal to Ellen Willis / Boston, MA / 2030

Dear Professor Willis,

    Been a while, hasn't it?

I suppose it's gauche to send a string of letters without getting a reply back first, but I need to write to someone today, and you're very much on my mind of late.

The day I read your obituary was the worst of my life up till that point. For the longest time I figured I'd understand, in time, why you stopped writing me back. I thought it would somehow all become clear when I reached the age where you stopped responding to my letters; or maybe when I got as old as you were when you died. Well, here I am, staring into oblivion myself... and I don't get it, Ellen.

I can call you that now, finally. I'm not so starry-eyed anymore, and we're both in our sixties. You'll be sixty-four forever, I guess, and we'll see how long I have.

How could you stop writing to me? Did you have so many former students trying to get your attention that I got lost in the mix? Or was it, as I've always suspected, that you really were *that* disappointed in me for going my own way, and working with people you considered the enemy? Maybe it was a bit of both.

Were you so blessed with human contact, Ellen, that you could pick and choose who you would shine your brilliance on, and who you would leave alone to stumble through the dark? Were you so rich in friends that you could afford to cut someone out of your life over a disagreement?

Must've been nice.

Most of my friends are dead, like you. I'm getting very familiar with this apartment, though. On average, it takes a raindrop twenty seconds to travel from the top of Kevin and Daphne's windows to the bottom. Less if it catches other drops along the way. Kevin drinks these nasty, bitter IPAs that no one else will touch. When he and Daphne were at work the other day, I threw one on the kitchen floor, just to have something to do. It was beautiful. Brown shards of glass flying up into the air; foamy suds bubbling over as the brew ran into the cracks between the tiles . . . when the others rushed in to see what had happened, I told them I'd dropped the bottle by mistake.

I have to keep it together, Ellen. For them. You and I both know who I am: the same nervous girl who showed up late to your seminar that cold fall day in Manhattan. Maybe not as easily impressed now as I was then.

But *they* don't know that girl. To them I'm a leader—Pepper, I swear, thinks of me as some kind of guerrilla general. Ho Chi Minh of the queers. Che of the kinksters, biding my time, waiting for the moment when we'll strike and put the world right again. . . . But you know the world was never right to begin with.

I have no plan. And I shouldn't be in charge of anything. I'm just the one who survived the longest. I have no idea what to do, beyond keeping as many of us alive as I can.

But Marie, you say, tearing out your ghostly hair, *you brought a cop into your group. A fucking COP!*

And I have to shrug because I have no counterargument. And he's a *vice* cop, on top of everything else. A man paid to sniff out and exterminate the uncontrollable, vibrant parts of the human experience. Does it drive you insane?

It did me. I tried not to reach out. I've skipped over potential contacts in the past. Some people are unsafe to bring in, through no fault of their own. No matter how badly they need us. No matter how they're hurting in isolation. I only move in when I'm completely certain. Yet here I am, hosting a cop at my rope nights when I'm not even sure which side he's on. I don't think he's sure, either. And maybe that's what made it impossible to pass on him.

Think about it. If I could free one of *them* . . . a brother freak so confused and scared he's taken to hunting his own kin as a cover . . . what a *prize*! What a blow against the little demons who drafted the Amendment and the cowards who let it pass! What a thorn in the side of every fat fire-and-brimstone preacher who tells children they'll burn in Hell for loving the way they want! I'm getting all hot and bothered just thinking about it, Ellen. . . .

But that's Ahab talk. Craziness. The real reason is small, and sad.

It feels like something is coming to an end, here in Boston. It's been a long run of years, and I'm tired. We all are. There's a vibration in the air when I wake up in the morning, in my friends' guest bedroom, that makes me think this may be the last summer when rope is unraveled and bottoms hang giddy from ceilings.

I haven't told anyone this, but: Since I went on the run, I've always been able to see the next step. The right bus to ride; the next city to check in on; what bridge to sleep under while the searchlights flashed by overhead. This apartment, this year, is as far as I've seen. Whatever angel guided me this far has left me on my own.

Which is to say: Having an idea of what's to come, maybe I wanted to let a confused rope boy in on our secret for a month or two. We might be his last chance to play.

Well, I sound downright certifiable. If you're anywhere, I know you're reading this. Thank you for that. And I'm sorry I accused you of not caring. You just broke my heart, is all. But then I know I broke yours, too.

Enjoy Heaven, or whatever. See you soon.

Love,
Marie

Pepper / Boston, MA / 2030

As the one initiating the breakup, Gary has to fill in our "Reason for Separation." I hand him the tablet so he can select "lack of enthusiasm" from the list of options. He clears his throat and shifts in his chair.

The PRTNR rep at his little desk wears a sympathetic frown. He nods along, eyes half-closed as Gary and I enter our Social Security Numbers, rate each other on various factors on a scale from one to ten and select how long we'd like to mourn the passing of our relationship before being put back in the matching pool. The longest chunk of time available is six months. I take it.

On the last page, Gary enters his account password. I enter mine. The machine pings, and a pair of vector-art scissors cuts a string connecting our avatars. The two of them put their stubby hands to their heads as big cartoon tears roll down their cheeks. An 8-bit cover of Boyz II Men's "End of the Road" swells in the background.

"I'm sorry it didn't work out," says the clerk, taking the tablet back. "But don't you worry; we'll be working extra hard to find both of you the right fit."

On the sidewalk, I check my phone to see how long it will take to get home.

"Pepper," says Gary. I turn to look at him.

His lower lip is shaking. Jesus Christ—his eyes are wet.

"Is that it?" he says.

"Gary," I say, "you broke up with *me*, remember?"

"Yeah, but it wasn't easy!" He stares at the phone still in my hand. "We went through a lot together. We dated for almost two years! And now we're not going to see each other anymore."

Somebody plays on a set of paint buckets over in the Quincy Market. A teen with a big pair of headphones over his ears walks between us.

"Aren't you gonna cry, or anything?"

He really means it.

"I'm sorry, Gary," I say, "but no."

He disappears, sniffling, down into Haymarket station. Dazed, I walk away with nobody scrabbling at my hand.

Seagulls wheel over the North End. In a second-story apartment, a man yells at his wife. Different scents on every block: fish, red pepper, and tomato sauce from the restaurants; sugar and ricotta from the bakeries; lemon from the gelaterias.

Across the water, planes scuttle back and forth over the Logan tarmac. It's dark now, and the bodies are hard to see. They move like shadows between the lit-up edges of runways. In the air, three passenger jets are queued up for descent. The lights on their wingtips form a diagonal line from the harbor to outer space. On another vector a plane takes off, rising up over the water before disappearing into the clouds. I turn away and walk back into the neighborhood.

Streetlights come on. In the little residential area off Hanover Street, a brick archway leads to an alley, lit by a single, old-fashioned lamppost. A white egg on a black stick. I lean on it, and feel the sidewalk under my feet, breathe in the salty air.

Sean / Boston, MA / 2030

Late afternoon. Verity and I are the first two awake.

Straps hang from a beam; unwashed glasses crowd the sink; a forgotten sweatshirt is wedged between the couch cushions.

We sip hot tea by the window. North, past Fenway and Kenmore, the clouds ripple on the face of the Charles.

The patterns on my wrists, chest, and ankles have darkened from red to purple—lines of symmetrical dots. I trace them around my torso. They don't hurt at all.

"You had fun last night," says Verity.

"I think we all did," I say.

"Yeah."

Traffic crawls by on the Pike. Verity runs her thumb around the edge of the mug, scraping at a stain with her nail.

"That took a lot of trust. Bottoming, I mean. And I'm assuming for the first time."

"It was. And it got easier. I mean . . . you all make it easier."

Verity smiles at me.

"Well, I'm glad we trusted you," she says.

She leans over and gives me a hug. On her skin is the scent of bergamot and orange.

She takes my mug to top it off with more hot water, but I barely notice.

Instead, I'm sitting at my desk, reviewing a case file. I'm in the apartment where we took the photos. I'm staring at the face of a man I hunted and caught. I'm picking a forgotten dress up off the floor.

The sun is shining. The leaves glow green on the trees, and the sky behind them is the crayon blue you only get a few times each spring....

They give me the SWAT guys, like Simon was a rogue arms dealer, and not just some guy putting the wrong content online under his own legal name. The vans look weird, in Back Bay. They're boxy, black, and metal, blocking off a section of street dominated by brick townhouses with ivy-covered walls. Incongruous.

Been a minute since they hustled up the stairs. They'll be back down soon, and then it'll be over. Months of work—really the first time we've done this here in Boston. We're behind the other cities.

No more late nights out here with a zoom lens. No more tailing him to and from work. What'll I do with myself?

I wore a tie today. My only tie. Maroon. Seemed like the thing to do.

I should be happy. I put together a solid case. I got my man. But I'm like an empty tub of ice cream. Nothing left but damp, waxy paper. I got what I wanted.

There are boots on the stairs. The front door opens, and Simon steps out blinking into the afternoon, hair a mess, hands behind his back. On the other side of the street a young Black woman pedals a bike through the nearest intersection, smiling at some inner thought. I stand to one side, hands in my pockets, as the agents lead my suspect to a black van.

It's exactly how I've pictured it. It's all there, in his eyes. Now Simon gets it. Now he's afraid....

Verity comes back in and sees my face. She sits down beside me.

"What's wrong?" she says.

The lies are stacked and ready to go like cold bullets in a magazine. I'm so good at lying. Practiced. And now's the best time for it—I've won her trust.

She'll believe anything I tell her. All I have to do is pick the right words, and we'll both get to live in a better world. A world where I'm not a monster.

Instead, I say:

"You knew Simon Debs."

Our experience of the moment is always a fraction of a second delayed. The words need time to leave my mouth, and travel through the space between us as sound waves vibrating on the air. The information is transformed again into electrical impulses, which are sorted and interpreted quickly but not immediately. So there's an interval of time, however small, between the moment of my confession and the realization that pulls Verity's eyes slowly open. A last little while where everything's okay.

"It was you, wasn't it," she says. "The day they took him away. You were there. You were watching."

The lies are there, even now, ready to salvage something of what's been lost. Eager to get out.

"I was directing," I say, instead. "He was my case."

Her face has gone flat. Cold.

"What happened to him?" she says.

"I don't know," I say. "It was a high-profile case—the Bureau took over after a while. Verity, I . . ."

She's still like a cave is still. Like the bottom of the ocean.

"I'm sorry."

Without looking at me, she says: "Get out."

And I do.

"An Answer to the Problem" / Posted to r/SexualEconomy by cnghm89 / 2020

The incel views the world through his own need and desire for sex, his lack of it, and the injustice of a perceived inequity in its distribution. The incel, in other words, is a kind of political economist, deeply concerned with questions of who gets access to what, in what quantities, etc. That members of the incel community draw sex, intimacy, and love into the realm of factories and supply chains and speak of these intangible things as if they were so many shipments of cement, wheat, or tires has earned them no small amount of criticism and ridicule. But they are not the only voices arguing that sex is fair game for economics—in fact, depending on when you date the origins of the incel community, they might not even be the first.

In her 2010 article "Erotic Capital," sociologist Catherine Hakim argues for the existence of an additional form of capital, to be considered alongside those identified by sociologist Pierre Bourdieu (economic, cultural, and social). "Erotic capital," Hakim claims, is "a combination of aesthetic, visual, physical, social, and sexual attractiveness to other members of your society, and especially members of the opposite sex, in all social contexts." To put it bluntly: the degree to which others want to fuck you.

The incel sees himself as the victim of a laissez-faire sexual economy, which allows some to inherit or accumulate inordinate amounts of erotic capital and exchange it for sex, while others are forced to do without, even to the point of sex-starvation (a condition Hakim would refer to in subsequent work as the "male sex deficit").

Outside of the incel community and certain anti-feminist circles, the very existence of sex-based capital is hotly contested. The arguments and counterarguments have been presented elsewhere. Given that the theory exists, and that some do believe in it, and are acting on it, the most pressing issue isn't whether or not it's true.

The real question is—what do we do about it?

The Real Problem

We have focused our examination, so far, on the incel. The one who articulates his own singledom as an undeserved punishment. The one who pulls the trigger. We have articulated his interpretation of his existence—as a free-floating cell, excised from a nourishing body for no other reason than spite. We have spoken of his behaviors—his murders—as the problem that needs to be solved.

But that's not quite right, is it?

Something is wrong. Something's been wrong for a while, and it's getting wronger. You feel it when you stand in front of the fridge at three in the morning in your underpants, staring at a red and white carton of fried rice and a half-empty liter of almond milk. You hear it in jam-packed subway cars in which no one says a word, and the slurred curses of a drunk are cause not for laughter but fear. You touch it, once a week, in the self-checkout line at the grocery store.

If the incel does indeed exist in relation to a social body—as we all do—then he is not the disease which truly afflicts it. He is merely a symptom—a pustule bursting over our collective skin. The real problem is marrow-deep.

Our social body is disintegrating.

We are single, or together out of fear of being alone. More and more we eat by ourselves, think by ourselves, go to sleep and wake up by ourselves. The relationships we do have are with other individuals, and even then we drift away from each other constantly like stars in an expanding universe. Organizational affiliation is a joke. Who, lately, has been honestly proud to be an American? Who has meant every word of the Nicene Creed? Who hasn't stood in the middle of the family Christmas party, and wondered whether he was the only real thing in the room?

We yell at the incel for articulating the pain of social and sexual isolation. But insisting on the reality of these feelings isn't his real mistake. The incel goes wrong by embracing solipsism, assuming that his experience is somehow unique. The truth—which we hate, which we do not want to look at—is that we know the pain these young men feel all too well. The killer lives in all of us.

There are ways of fixing this. A sudden radical disruption of mental health stigma could pave the way for greater investment in therapies and treatments, and greater willingness to use them; widespread adoption of certain feminist theory in homes and schools could result in a generation of young people who view sex as a creative act between enthusiastic adults, an art to be refined rather than a resource to be collected; greater civic and religious involvement could reconnect us with our neighborhoods, countries, and souls. With time, and care, the social body could be healed.

Now we must ask ourselves: How likely is that to happen?

At the time of this writing, there are eight billion humans on the planet. How many therapists, working for how many hours, and at what cost, do we need to heal ten thousand years of their accumulated trauma? How many professors, teaching how many courses, would it take to open up the minds of an entire species? Who's going to make everyone do the hard work of change?

There is another way. Less attractive, but quicker, and more effective.

Intimacy Allocation

Assuming Bentham's "greatest amount of good for the greatest number" is something worth striving for—and recognizing that physical and emotional intimacy are highly efficient means of promoting the "good" in the form of pleasure—a therapeutic intervention for the social body and its individual members begins to take shape.

In describing how the deployment of sexuality works, Foucault also identified and articulated the concept of *biopower*, and explained what distinguishes it from an earlier form of power based on killing in defense of the sovereign: "It is no longer a matter of bringing death into play in the field of sovereignty, but of distributing the living in the domain of value and utility [...] A normalizing society is the historical outcome of a technology of power centered on life." His ultimate goal in pointing these things out, of course, was to facilitate resistance—in *The History of Sexuality*, he hoped to create a diagram of the mechanisms of biopower, which would allow subsequent thinkers to dismantle the whole structure.

With apologies to Foucault, we must abandon this project. The thing to do with biopower is not to resist it or eliminate it. We must use it, consciously, to promote "the greatest amount of good for the greatest number."

In the context of this essay, this means that we can no longer remain victims of the deployment of sexuality. Knowing what we now know, we cannot feign ignorance of what sexuality is, the influence it holds in our society. We must take responsibility for the power that surrounds us; we must become fully aware strategists and tacticians in the "field of force relations" which Foucault describes. We must consciously deploy sexuality ourselves.

In the context of our current situation, the most obvious deployment would be a rapid, sweeping redistribution of erotic capital, facilitated by technology and protected by law. A shift, in other words, from a system in which no one claims responsibility for biopower, and each is left to his own devices in a sexual "war of all against all," to a controlled sexual economy guaranteeing some amount of intimacy to every individual. A fair portioning out of the limited resource of love.

Most likely this would take the form of a compulsory serial monogamy, in which suitable partners are identified and matched with the aid of questionnaires and algorithms. To prevent the concentration of erotic capital in the hands of a few, such a shift would also call for the explicit prohibition of those lifestyles and forms of social organization that contribute to intimacy inequality, along with any practice which does not align with sexuality's ultimate *telos* as a form of stress relief and—most importantly—harm reduction on a societal level.

Such an arrangement would obviously proscribe app-enabled "hookup culture" and every variety of non-monogamy. It would also discourage or outright ban kink, fetishism, and other tangential erotic practices—i.e., not intercourse—as wastes of fundamentally limited erotic capital. It would outlaw the gratuitous use of pleasure as an end in itself, rather than as a means to the end of preventing violence.

This project, after all, must be a "normalizing" one—a deliberate use of technologies of power to efficiently direct every iota of erotic feeling available to us into that expression of sexuality that will do the most to quiet our rage and relieve our loneliness. In other words, to finally, deliberately deploy sexuality in a way that promotes life over death.

Because those are the stakes. Death is what we are fighting here—death, in its most obvious form, in the murders that snatch up a few dozen young lives every year and leave the rest of us hollowed out; death of any sense of social consciousness; death of the heart. In our time, in our society, sex is the quick and dirty way to start patching up these wounds—enough of it to go around to soothe those feelings that otherwise erupt into violence against others but also against ourselves. Remove the conditions that create the perception of oppression, and we cut through the logic of the martyr.

This is distasteful. It violates a liberal mode of individuality to which we've clung for centuries. It feels like giving in. So be it. It was Hobbes who pointed out that "peace is good, and therefore also the way or means of peace are good."

If we have a chance at peace—at healing—we ought to take it.

Sean / Boston, MA / 2030

Gulls cry and hover in circles over the station, their wings like sails. An empty bottle of Sam's clatters along the sidewalk. It comes to rest against a sewer grate.

In the break room, somebody's brewed a fresh pot of coffee. I pour myself a mug. It's hot and strong. In the bullpen, phones ring and pens scratch; the ceiling fan ripples papers on faraway desks.

A few hours, at least. I need to give Verity time to tell the others, to pile them into Kevin's car and drive somewhere far away from here. Where I can't find them. In a few hours I'll pretend to have some big insight. A whole production: running back and forth between my desk and the corkboard as I connect the dots. Then I'll hammer down Al's door, and tell him I've got them, so we can all drive over to the abandoned condo near Fenway.

Then I guess we come back here. And I never see any of them ever again. And I settle in for fifty more years. Of this.

Carl is talking into his phone, referencing information from a bunch of handwritten notes stacked next to him. He sees me looking at him and turns away.

"I'll meet you down there in five," he says.

There's something weird about the way he clutches the papers to his chest. He didn't say hi when I came in. He hasn't tried to get my attention at all today. I've had plenty of space to stew in my depression. Only now does it occur to me that something's off. I want to sink into my chair and begin the long process of dying—but some small part of me demands to see what's written on those pages.

Bracing, I walk straight into Carl just as he's standing up.

We crash into each other and fall to our tailbones. Somehow, I keep most of my coffee in the mug.

"Jesus—!" says Carl, dropping all his papers. He's breathing hard.

"Ha," says Baptiste from across the room. He smiles, winces, and grabs his gauze-covered ear.

Carl's things have gone all over the place. I put my coffee on my desk and bend over to pick them up.

"Aw, you don't have to do that," says Carl, scooping things up as fast as he can.

"It's fine," I say. "I don't mind."

"No, really," says Carl, "just go back to your . . ."

I'm holding up a single piece of notebook paper, scraggly fringe still attached to one side. It's covered in sticky brown fingerprints. In Rob's neat handwriting there's a list of names—my friends' names. Kevin and Daphne's address is circled at the bottom of the page.

Carl holds out a hand, palm down.

"Sean . . ." he says.

I stand up. I take a step backward. The rest of the bullpen has stopped typing, filing, and chatting. Everyone's staring at us. Al, holding a can of soda, pokes his head out of his borrowed office.

"Jeez," he says. "Who died?"

"Don't," says Carl, looking at me. "Please."

I drop the paper. I turn. Shoving past Al, I sprint to the garage.

Al / Boston, MA / 2030

Sean's partner slips on the debris around his desk. Catching himself, he swears, and tries to run off toward the garage. I grab his arm.

"What's going on here?" I say.

He bares his teeth at me, trying to pull away. After a moment, he relaxes. He gives me a hard little smile.

"Two-fourteen Garber Place," he says. "Washington, D.C."

My hand drops to my side.

"Nice little love nest for you and Marie," he says. "Sorry it's empty."

"How..."

He shoves past me.

"I don't have time," he says. "We'll deal with you later."

And then he's gone, through the door to the garage.

The floor's a mess: printouts, surveillance photos, floor plans, a dirty piece of notebook paper with an address written on it... and a business card. My boss's business card. The one I lost the other night. His number is circled in black pen. On a bit of blank space, in Carl's round handwriting: "8:00 p.m."

It's 7:45 now.

While everyone else tries to figure out what just happened, I slip away through the front door.

Sean / Boston, MA / 2030

I've emptied my pockets. I stand next to my car with my wallet, phone, and pocket knife on the hood, scrambling around for my keys.

I don't have them.

There's a rumble on a lower floor. Two cars come around the corner: Carl, followed by a black IAB van.

He stops next to me and leans out the window. My keys are in his cup holder. When we bumped into each other... when I was staring at the note...

Carl searches my face.

"Why didn't you tell me?" he says. "About you. About all of it. I can help."

I sigh. I run my hands through my hair and open my mouth to tell him. Then I shove his jaw into the headrest and lunge for my keys.

Growling, Carl gets hold of my wrists and pulls. Hard. My head smacks off the steering wheel, and I fall back on my ass on the damp garage floor.

Carl stares down at me, squeezing his mouth shut. He wipes his eyes. Then he sniffs, spits in my face, and roars away up the ramp. The black van follows quietly.

There, on the floor, half my ass in a patch of old engine grease, I sit for a full minute, frozen.

They found me. They've seen me, and they're coming, and there's no escape. And it's all my fault. I deserve it. I disobeyed.

Stupid to think they weren't watching. That they didn't know. Someone's always watching. Someone always knows. I can run forever and their eyes will always be over my shoulder; in the guts of my computer; inside my head.

My heart thuds, slow but hard, like a hammer driving a nail through flesh and into wood. Final. I'm slipping away to that safe, numb place where the world becomes a projection on a movie screen, and sounds arrive wrapped in cotton. Here, the fact that I'm about to die is just another piece of information. Nothing to get upset about—something to look forward to, even. I think ahead to what's going to happen to me, and it's like skipping forward to the last few chapters of a book I've already read. All very predictable and tidy. The mess that is me finally wiped away. I think about my future and feel nothing.

Then I think about the same things happening to my new friends. To the only people I've ever really touched.

I get up.

At the top of the ramp, a brown sedan brakes hard, stopping a foot away from my shins. I shove my badge in the driver's face.

"I'm commandeering this vehicle," I say.

"Bullshit," says the man. "That ain't real."

"*Posse comitatus*," I say.

Then I reach through the window, open the door, and toss the man out by his collar.

"And wear your fucking seat belt."

I call Kevin. No answer.

IAB field agents can clear out an apartment in minutes. Usually the neighbors don't know anything happened.

Pepper's number leads to voicemail. I'm dialing Jack when the phone buzzes in my hand—a push notification from PRTNR, letting me know that I have till midnight to update my profile and fill out the matching survey.

I throw my phone out the window.

Red lights—honking horns. No time to turn off the radio.

"*Top of the eleventh, here at Fenway,*" says the announcer. "*Red Sox down by two, with runners on first and second ... and here's the pitch ... swing, and it's a big hit! Up and into the right field stands ... and it's all over. The Red Sox bring it home at the end of a long night.*"

A block away from Kevin and Daphne's place, a Star Market semi pulls into the intersection, and begins a three-point turn.

The van is already in front of Kevin and Daphne's building. Men in bulletproof vests are shutting the doors. They're pulling away. I don't know what to do—

Then Al's gray Buick rockets up Ipswich, cuts around the trailer, and plows into the front bumper of the van, sending it spinning into the pumps at the Sunoco station.

I jump out of my stolen car, leaving the door open. I've got seconds.

Gasoline sprays out of the broken pumps like water from a lawn sprinkler. The agents in the front of the van are passed out. I take the keys and open the back door. Kevin and Daphne slide out first, shaking. Jack, Verity, and Pepper follow. They all hold out their zip-tied hands, and help Marie hop down from the bumper.

Al limps out of the Buick, rubbing his neck.

"Sean," he says, nodding. "Marie."

Marie's mouth hangs open.

"C'mon," I say, slitting plastic cuffs with my knife. "We've gotta go." Jack and I have just got Al's arms hooked over our shoulders when Carl appears from behind his car. He's pointing his gun at Al's back.

"You're not going anywhere," he says.

"Carl—" I say.

There's a lot of metal between us and him. I haul Al away from the wreck, toward the public gardens near Park Drive.

"Sean!" says Carl. "Get back here . . . goddammit, Sean, come back!"

He fires twice and misses. The third time he hits one of the bleeding rubber hoses—and the dirty little gas station, older than both of us, turns into a fireball that knocks everyone to the ground—and sends the growing crowd of baseball fans around Fenway Park into a panic.

Al shakes me. My skin is cooking. There are sirens now, getting closer.

"On your feet, pal," he says. Favoring one leg, he hauls me up. "Let's go."

I look back. Carl is sitting in the middle of the street, dazed, waiting to see what I'll do next. Leaving the fire behind—leaving him behind—I grab the others, blend into the crowd, and slip through the darkening Fens.

The dock needs to be re-stained. The wood is already gray with sun-bleaching; soon it will be ashy, with dry splinters poking up from the boards along fault lines. White and yellow seagull shits dry and crust over on the planks. They'll leave stains.

Kevin and Daphne dart back and forth over their sailboat, whispering orders to Jack, Verity, and Pepper. In the dark, they hook metal clips through brackets in the jib and mainsail; an electric winch hoists the canvas. It squeaks. We flinch.

Kevin says he can get us out of sight from the shoreline before sunrise. If we make it past Deer Island, it's a straight shot to Nova Scotia. Daphne has friends in Yarmouth. An easy three-day cruise, Kevin says. They've done it half a dozen times.

They had food and fresh water those times.

The hull is hollow, plastic. Waves thump against it. In another marina—a busier, fancier one north of here—I used to walk up and down the dock with a shovel, scraping mussel beds from the side of the dock. I pushed them into the open water and watched them sink.

A flag kicks against its pole, and the grommets ring. It's cold. Kevin's promised there will be no storm.

Al and I have clear shots up the gangplank, if we need them.

He holds down a belch, winces, thuds a fist into his chest.

"You've got to stop drinking those sodas," I say.

"Don't tell an old man what to do," he says, and hocks a loogie into the Harbor. He stands there, hands in those big pockets, and looks me up and down, head on one side. His eyebrows scrunch together.

"What?" I say.

He turns to Marie.

"You were there, weren't you," he says, "that night at the beginning of the summer, when they first brought Sean over."

She sits on a fiberglass footlocker, watching the crew work. She keeps her head pointed away from Al, but nods.

Al chuckles. He turns to me. "I'm not surprised Carl went behind my back, Sean, but you... you're a good liar."

The sails are up. The boat looks about ready to go.

"At least," says Pepper, tying off a line with the knot Daphne showed her, "it'll be nice seeing Luke and Ilana again."

She catches my face. One at a time, they all do, and stop working. They wait. I shake my head. Verity wipes a tear away with her palm, dragging it across her face.

After a moment, Kevin stands up in the stern. "We're ready," he says.

"Good," says Al. "Sean, it's been a pleasure working with you. The rest of you I don't know, but good luck out there. Let's go, Marie."

He starts limping toward the gangplank.

The others straighten up. They tense.

"I'm sorry. What?" Pepper looks back and forth between the two of them. "I don't know where you're going, pal, and I don't really care. But Marie's coming with us."

"Marie," says Al. "Come on."

Verity climbs out of the boat. She puts a protective hand on Marie's shoulder.

"Marie," she says. "What's going on?

Marie sighs. It's huge. She stares at the water. "Al and I used to know each other."

"That's one way of putting it," says Al. "We were engaged."

The boat rocks in the swell. Kevin coughs.

"Look, Al," says Marie, "you saved all of us. And I'm grateful for that. But—"

"I've got a career's worth of favors to call in," says Al. "I can keep you safer than they can. No offense."

"None taken," says Jack, frowning. He and the rest have all left the boat, and now stand in a tight knot behind Marie.

"Al," she says, "it's not about—"

"I kept the house, Marie," says Al. He grabs Marie's hand.

"It's funny . . . I was able to get rid of everything else that reminded me of you. The pictures, the knickknacks, the clothes. I even saw other people. But I still own that empty little house in Palisades."

"Al," says Marie, gently, "I'm not going with you."

There's a beat while this processes.

"I'll come with you, then," says Al. "Whatever kind of life you want, that's fine. Whoever you want to see, whatever you want to do, that's fine. I'm fine with it. Just as long as I can be where you—"

"That won't work, Al," says Marie. "We don't work. You know that."

Al's suit billows around him in a salty gust of wind off the Harbor. He drops Marie's hand, and her fingertips float up to touch her mouth.

"I'm sorry," she says.

Al stands. Turns his back to us. He takes a few steps away and puts his hands in his pockets. Mouth open, he shakes his head.

"Jesus, Al," says Marie. "After twenty years . . . after the way it ended . . . what did you think was going to happen?"

Al chuckles—a single breath, out. "Not this," he says.

Then he turns and points his gun at Marie's chest.

You can't wait till you see the hit coming—you have to move. So I do, instead of shooting. I'm there, suddenly, in front of Marie, with the barrel of Al's gun pressed into my heart.

Nothing moves but the dock under our feet. Then something clamps down, hard, on my upper arm. A hand. Verity's hand. Frozen in the act of pulling me out of the way. For half a second, I take my eyes off Al to glance at her. From the look on her face, her hand might've jumped off her wrist and grabbed me of its own accord.

Al's eyebrows go up. "You know it'll just pass through you and probably hit her, anyway, right?"

A bead of sweat rolls down my lower back and is absorbed by my waistband.

"You'd get in my way—again," Al says, "for someone you only met two months ago?" He presses in, a fraction of an inch. Fabric and hair crinkle around the metal tube. "You'd die for her?"

I blink. I look Al in the eye. "I guess so," I say. And I'm more surprised than anyone.

Al lowers the gun. "I don't blame you," he says. He turns around and leans on the railing of the gangplank. "Go."

Verity / Boston, MA / 2030

We keep still, waiting for the man to change his mind. He stays where he is, looking up at the buildings above our heads. The boat rocks as we step off the dock one by one.

Sean's the last in line. When he moves to join us, I step between him and the boat. He searches my face for any give. Then he looks down at the dock.

"What's the holdup?" says Kevin, the last of the jolly finally gone from his voice. "We need to go."

"Sean's not coming with us," I say.

"Verity, get over it," says Jack. "He saved our lives; I think he's earned the right to—"

"I killed Simon," says Sean.

Jack's mouth hangs open. Kevin's hand goes slack on the bowline, and Daphne grabs the rope to keep us from floating away. We all stare at Sean. We wait.

"I worked his case," he says, "with everything I had. I found him, and I turned him over to the IAB. I knew what that meant for him."

"I'm sorry."

Jack looks around at the boat, the water, and the man next to me on the dock, blinking a lot, as if none of it seems quite real to him. He turns away from Sean and takes a seat near the front of the boat, forearms on his knees. He closes his eyes.

"This is a mistake," says Marie, standing up. "He didn't know what he was doing. We can't—"

I turn and lock my eyes onto hers. And the woman who put us all at risk because she wanted to be someone's savior feels the decision being taken away from her. She sits back down.

"Verity's right," says Sean, standing up straight again. "I can't go with you. I'll stay and figure out a way to help from here."

"But what'll you do?" says Pepper.

Sean takes a long breath in. Then he lets it all out. "Something," he says.

Sean joins Al as we shove off. The boat's little motor takes us away from the dock till it's safe to hoist the sails. They fill with wind, and we glide away from the two men who stand side by side on the dock, watching us go.

Al / Boston, MA / 2030

They rock back and forth like a metronome, full sails getting smaller every moment. I watch them go, crossing between me and the lights on the other side of the bay. I wave.

It's important to take stock when things come to an end. Did I do what I set out to do? Did the goal get my full, honest effort? Did I get what I wanted?

Not entirely. I wanted Marie to myself. Barring that, I at least wanted to be back in her life. And now she's on a boat, sailing away into the night—and even if I had a boat of my own, I couldn't follow her. Because she doesn't want me.

Her life has been a response to what we went through together. I held her back from what she wanted—and in response, she dove into her wants the moment we were through. I took the opposite approach. My life continued on as it would have had I never met Marie. I made sure of that.

I had my own impulses: I thought of becoming a reactionary, of hating anything that reminded me of her. But I decided against it. I didn't want everything to be some twisted reflection of where I'd been.

That doesn't make sense. God, I'm tired. It's been a long night.

Why didn't I just kill Sean? Kill all of them. I've killed before. And I don't let things stand between me and what I want.

Yet that's what Sean did. He put himself in between me and Marie. Now she is gone and I am alone, when I would have had it otherwise. Because I did not kill him.

Sean stands next to me, watching the boat disappear.

"You okay?" he says.

I think it over. "No," I say. "But that's all right. Me being okay was never the point."

Somewhere in the dark, a buoy clangs. A big, choppy wave sucks the dock downward before slapping against the side, sending up a plume of salt water and wetting the tips of our shoes. I look down, to keep my balance. By the time the dock settles, the silhouette of the boat is lost, impossible to pick out from a horizon bleached of stars by the glowing light of Boston.

Sean, suddenly tense, turns toward me. "Now what?" he says.

I hold in a laugh. What he means is, *What should I do next?* Five minutes from now; tomorrow; the rest of the year.

He's still young. He hasn't learned yet that the minutes pile up on top of each other, one decade into the next, and that your to-do list gets shorter and shorter until, one day, you find yourself crossing off the last reason you had for sticking around and giving a damn. That the list runs out before the minutes do. And the thought of filling them all up with nothing makes your body turn cold.

"*You* get a head start," I say. "I stay here and make up a story about what happened tonight."

Sean puts his hands in his pockets then, and his shoulders sag just a bit. From the look of it, he's coming to grips with the loneliness that is the inevitable result of sticking to principles—which is something different from the loneliness he's known up till now.

"Then, tomorrow," I say, "you start your life as a nobody."

He goes, quietly, up the gangplank, to make his way unseen out of a town where every cop knows his face. I sink down onto a pile of broken, moldy stanchions, and sit with my elbows on my knees while the damp wind gets under my collar and behind my ears.

The center-console fishing boat tied off to the right of me has its keys dangling from the ignition, a bright orange floaty key chain hanging from the ring. I'm no pilot, but I could improvise well enough to make a desperate beeline for the Atlantic Ocean. I could zigzag my way northward up the coast in big searching arcs till I either found the sailboat or ran out of gas in the middle of nowhere. Assuming I found her again, I could keep talking, keep arguing, until I found the right combination of words that would get her to come back with me and make the last quarter of my life something other than the solitary wait it's shaping up to be. That's worth the risk of failing again. Worth getting lost on the water and crashing into a rock, or just dying of exposure off the eastern shore of Maine. I could do it right now. Try to get what I want, one more time.

Knees crackling, I stand up. The fishing boat rocks gently up and down in the swell, and the ocean and possibility open up in front of me. I turn away from both, and walk back the way I came, stepping over little gobs of seagull shit as the sky starts to change from black to pink.

One Year Later

Verity / Québec, QC / 2031

"Okay, I'm sorry, I've got this... um, *où est la sauce de dinde?* Is that right?"

The Québécois rolls his eyes, but points to the other side of the store. "*Allée cinq*," he says.

Beneath his green apron, he wears only a t-shirt. Like he doesn't notice it's already down in the fifties. No—the tens. They use Celsius here. A rainbow flag tattoo sits on the inside of his right arm, near the bend of the elbow. Anyone can see it.

Key areas of the shop have been plundered. A few bags of instant stuffing lie on their sides on an otherwise empty shelf; errant green beans (*haricots verts*) are ground into the black rubber mats in the produce section; a dented can of sweet potatoes rolls by my foot. The cardboard box I need is wedged at the back of one of the shelves, behind untouched rows of tomato sauce. Lone survivor of the purge.

"*Le dernier!*" I say.

The clerk takes the gravy from my hand without looking up from his book. "Most people buy their ingredients before the actual day," he says, dropping box and receipt into a plastic bag.

I flush and nod. I pick up the bag and turn to leave.

"Hey," he says, as I'm walking out. "*Joyeux action de graces.*" He offers up the most smile he can manage, and the ring in his lower lip sticks out a little. I smile back.

"Happy Thanksgiving," I say.

The snow people—Canadians—wander around in cargo shorts. Red and orange leaves swirl about their calves. I am not looking forward to November.

It makes sense that they celebrate on the second Monday in October. There won't be much to be grateful for once the average temperature drops below forty—nope, it's four. *Quatre degrés Celsius.*

A luxury, to walk down the street with a plastic bag dangling from my fingertips and squint into the afternoon sun. To feel uneven pavement beneath my feet. To look people in the eye as they go about their own business.

Wind—cold wind—numbs my nose and my cheeks. My hips and lower back are sore. A man with a big mustache dumps powdered sugar onto a circle of fried dough—an excess of sugar, far too much of it. Granules float above the sidewalk, glinting a moment before the treasure falls to the ground.

My key sticks in the door again. The only way to get it free is to let go and breathe for a moment, after which it will slide out as if greased. I struggle with it just for the pleasure of being annoyed with something.

A black SUV pulls up to the curb.

I could drop the gravy and be over the railing in two seconds. I've run on a rolled ankle before.

The door of the house on the right opens, and two little girls in cleats and jerseys sprint off the porch, lacrosse sticks in hand. Their mom follows, shouting, carrying two helmets under her arm. She passes these through the driver's-side window and chats with the woman in the front seat, whose own daughter is making fart noises with her hands.

The first mom waves as the car pulls away, then drags her hands across her face as if she could wipe away ten years of fatigue. The woman sees me looking at her and nods. I lift a hand. We go inside at the same time.

The stairs help. I take a few deep breaths before entering the apartment. I force the air out through pursed lips. I open our front door.

Pepper jumps up from the couch and snatches the gravy.

"You're lucky we didn't starve to death," she says. She pecks me on the cheek and scurries into the kitchen. A pan bangs on the stove; a muffled "*Shit*" rolls down the hallway, along with steam, and the aroma of butter and cloves.

Jack gets up to follow, snorting as he bumps into the door frame. He and Pepper have been sipping mugs of what he calls his "world-famous mulled cider," spiked with Crown Royal.

On our little TV, men in lederhosen spin dirndl-clad women in circles, as scores of Bavarians promenade down a main street, cheered on from the sidewalks—Canada's answer to the Macy's Parade. A drummer in Mountie red breaks formation to help an inebriated radio host off a manhole cover.

"Looks like fun," says Marie.

Her voice is flat. She holds her arms crossed in front of her, and picks at a loose thread on the neck of her sweater.

Rare, to have us all in one place at the same time. The manager of the coffee shop gave Pepper the day off. And normally Jack and I would still be sleeping off our shifts at the bar this early in the afternoon.

Marie makes her rent—and then some—teaching at the Montreal rope studios. Plural. With an s. I've seen her smile a few times in front of the classroom. Never outside of that.

I was so mad at her, for so many months. In a quieter way, I still am. But even so, to see her like this. . . thinking about her mistakes every minute of every day . . . it makes me sad.

The doorbell rings. Kevin and Daphne bustle in with arms full of bags, talking about the traffic. Daphne takes the gravy from me and the two of them push their way into the kitchen, adding their voices to the clamor of pots and pans.

Marie stands in the middle of the floor, staring at the TV. I put a hand on her shoulder.

"I wasn't sure you'd come," I say. "I'm glad you did."

She turns her face toward mine, and the corners of her mouth lift up just a little. I see the smallest crinkle at the edges of those eyes that used to sparkle.

We walk, together, into the warmth of the kitchen.

Rosa / Nashville, TN / 2031

They're everywhere.

Stupid—stupid—stupid—left the shade open, they saw the rope—

Run. Don't think, just run.

Sirens. Boots banging on the sidewalk. Shouts, behind me but getting closer. Amplified banjos twang from inside a dozen neon-lit honky-tonks as I shove my way through the drunken nighttime crowds on Broadway. I make it to the end of the block, put the corner between us, but—

Oh, fuck. This is it. My legs weigh a ton and my chest is on fire and I can't do it anymore.

They're going to get me

oh, shit

oh my god, I can't—

A hand darts out of the alleyway—grabs the front of my shirt—hauls me off the street and into the shadow behind a dumpster. A rough palm claps over my mouth. I bite at it—try to pull the arm away—but an expert sweep takes my legs out from under me, and suddenly I'm facedown on the pavement, a stranger's weight pressing into my back.

"Be quiet," a voice whispers. "Keep still."

I lie there, cheek pressed into pavement that smells like beery piss. I want nothing more than to suck in a big, noisy breath of air. Instead I hold it, as the footsteps round the corner.

Ten feet away. Five.

Zero.

In the gap between the asphalt and the bottom of the dumpster, I see four pairs of boots hustle up the street—past our hiding place. The weight disappears. Slowly, I get up.

The man is halfway down the alley, wrestling a manhole cover off its base. His hair and beard are filthy. Looks like he's been out in the sun for a year. He wears a weathered green poncho over a camping backpack. On his wrist is a paracord bracelet.

"Who are you?" I say.

He finishes hauling the cover aside, and lays it down next to the opening. Breathing hard, he gives me what I think is his attempt at a smile.

"My name's Sean," he says. "I'm here to help."

Get Your Free Prequel Today

Mark Cunningham can't stop obsessing over Sam Healey. The pretty undergraduate lights up his classes with her intelligent questions. She reminds him why he became a philosopher in the first place.

The more Mark talks to Sam, the more alive he feels—and the closer he moves to a decision that could destroy his career. With the semester drawing to a close, Mark must make an impossible choice.

But acting out of love couldn't be wrong...right?

Setting up the dystopian world of *Knots*, this gripping prequel short story introduces the man whose work inspired the 29th Amendment to the Constitution—which guarantees every U.S. citizen one monogamous romantic and sexual partner.

Download your copy of "Wrong" today to find out how Mark Cunningham came to empathize with incels everywhere—and how this lonely philosopher felt about his own work in the end. . . .

Get your free copy at
BookFunnel.MylesMcDonough.com

Made in the USA
Middletown, DE
29 October 2023